Three sisters, daughters of a lately deceased vicar, leave their country village and come to London to find work and, to make lives for themselves.

They dream of love, riches and prestige.

How each of them succeeds in obtaining her heart's desire is told in this sensitive and moving novel by Barbara Cartland.

THE DREAM WITHIN

Barbara Cartland

"There is a dream within us all
Secret, deep hidden in a shrine apart.
I search the sky, the moon, the stars
For that which lies adreaming in my heart."

PYRAMID BOOKS ▲ NEW YORK

THE DREAM WITHIN

A PYRAMID BOOK

First published by Hutchinson & Co. (*Publishers*) Ltd. 1947

Arrow edition 1969

Pyramid edition published April 1974
Second printing, May 1976

ISBN: 0-515-04118-1

Printed in the United States of America

Pyramid Books are published by Pyramid Publications (Harcourt Brace Jovanovich). Its trademarks, consisting of the word "Pyramid" and the portrayal of a pyramid, are registered in the United States Patent Office.

PYRAMID PUBLICATIONS
(Harcourt Brace Jovanovich)
757 Third Avenue, New York, New York 10017

THE DREAM
WITHIN

One

"What are we going to do?"

The question was a cry of despair. It was Sally who answered, turning round from her perch on the wide window-seat where she had been looking out over the mist-covered sea.

"We shall have to find work."

She spoke seriously and calmly while her two sisters stared at her wide-eyed.

Marigold spoke first.

"Work? But what sort of work?"

There was a moment's silence and then Anne added in her sweet voice:

"Sally's right of course! She always is! We shall have to work, but goodness knows at what!"

Sally got up from the window-seat and walked across to stand on the shabby hearth-rug in front of the fire.

"I have been thinking about it for some time," she said, and it seems to me that the best thing we can do is to leave here altogether."

"We have got to leave the house, we know that," Anne said. "As soon as the new man is appointed, he will want to live here."

"I wasn't referring to the house," Sally answered.

Her two sisters stared at her again.

'You mean leave St. Chytas?"

Sally nodded.

"But where would we go?" Marigold asked.

"Somewhere where we could find work," Sally replied.

"You mean just anywhere?"

Again Sally nodded her head. Anne and Marigold turned from the contemplation of their younger sister to look at each other. There was a long pause broken only by the crackling of the fire and the scream of the sea-gulls outside the window.

"She is right," Anne said soberly at length.

"Then we'll go to London!" Marigold ejaculated. "London! Why didn't we think of it before? But of course, it's the obvious solution!"

Sally, watching them from the fireplace, gave a little sigh.

She had known before she made her suggestion that the idea of London would thrill both Anne and Marigold and she knew how she hated the idea of going away, of leaving.

It was not only the house which had been her home ever since she was born, but also the countryside, the soft, glowing beauty of the Cornish coast with its dark cliffs and golden sands and the great vistas of sea and sky which she had loved ever since she could remember.

She hated to leave, but she knew that there was nothing else for them to do.

Sometimes it seemed to Sally as if for years she had anticipated this wrench, this bitter parting. Always she had felt as if she could not look long enough at the views she loved, could not enjoy too fully the wind-swept land or the temperamental sea.

Always it seemed to her that her instinct was prompting her to live fully every hour of her life because all too soon such happiness might be taken from her; and now the moment had come—her father had died.

Vicar of St. Chytas for twenty-five years, Arthur Granville had been content to pastor a very small flock. He had had no ambitions, no desires for larger or more important livings.

A Cornish man, he had been born and brought up

only twenty miles away from where he had finally settled.

Sometimes his daughters used to tease him and suggest that not only the fisherfolk and the few country people who lived round St. Chytas were his parishioners, but also the birds and animals, the heather-covered hills, the rugged cliffs and the giants and fairies, pixies and mermaids which still live and have their being in the imagination of Cornish men and women.

It was true indeed that Arthur Granville knew and loved them all and it was Sally, his youngest daughter, who shared his pride in his heritage and his passion for the history and legends of his forebears.

Anne had been born first, only three years after Arthur Granville had come to St. Chytas.

She had been a beautiful baby, golden-haired and blue-eyed, and she had increased in loveliness year by year until her father would often wonder how he, any ordinary man where looks were concerned, could have produced anything quite so exquisite. But Anne soon had a rival in her sister Marigold.

Very different in temperament from her elder sister, Marigold was aptly named, for her hair was red-gold, dancing in tiny curls over her head, and she was vivacious, quick-tempered, and hungry for laughter and gaiety.

She seemed to dance through life as if she were a sunbeam.

If Arthur Granville was disappointed when his third child turned out to be another girl, he never said so; but perhaps his devotion to Sally was originally begun because he was afraid that she might feel unwanted.

Her mother, it was true, had prayed for a son, but Arthur Granville had seemed quite content with yet another daughter and Sally resembled him far more both in features and in character than the other two.

"I am not only the Cinderella but the Ugly Duckling of the family!" Sally used to complain laughingly.

She certainly had not been blessed with the glowing, sensational beauty of either of her sisters.

She was small with a little pointed face which seldom had much colour in it and her hair had neither the fairness of Anne's nor the gold of Marigold's, but was a soft dusky brown as if she had tried to imitate the gentle mist which so often hung over her beloved land.

The fairies who had come to the christenings of the three girls had certainly doled out their gifts fairly.

Anne had beauty, Marigold charm, and Sally wisdom. It was always Sally who was consulted in the family when there was a decision to be made; it was always Sally who came to the rescue if life got difficult or out of hand; it was always Sally who could be relied on in any emergency, however tremendous.

It was difficult for the others to remember that she was not yet eighteen; Anne at twenty-two and Marigold at twenty-one seemed far younger; but then years do not always make one wise.

It was typical of the relationship between all three of the girls that Sally should decide their future. They accepted it without argument.

"How I have always longed to live in London!" Anne exclaimed. "Do you know, I haven't been there for four years—then I was only passing through to stay with Aunt Mary."

"It is a pity she is dead," Marigold said reflectively; "we might have asked her to find us somewhere to live."

"I thought of that too," Sally interjected. "We shall have very little money of course. We shall have to find somewhere to live that is very cheap; but whatever happens, I think we shall all want to stick together."

"But of course!" the other two cried in unison.

"What do you think we could do?" Marigold asked.

"Well, Anne can type," Sally suggested.

"Not terribly well," Anne replied.

"Well, you had enough lessons!"

"Yes, I know," Anne said, "but they were so boring. I suppose now I could practice every day and get a bit quicker."

"What about me?" Marigold asked. "You know there is nothing I can do."

"We will think of something," Sally promised.

Marigold got up and started to dance round the room.

"I might get a job on the stage or in a shop, or I could be a mannequin. Why not? My figure is good enough even though it is I who says it!"

Sally said nothing, but Anne got up and standing on tiptoe stared in the mirror which hung over the mantelpiece.

"Perhaps we shall take London by storm!" she said. "I was reading about the two Miss Gunnings only last night. Do you think people will stand on chairs in the park to see us walk by?"

"The best thing we can do," Marigold laughed, "is to be a tremendous success and get married."

"As a matter of fact," Anne answered, "it is about the only thing we are any of us capable of doing; running a house, making a man comfortable and being charming!"

"Men don't propose because one is a good housekeeper," Marigold said.

"That's true," Anne agreed. "Oh dear, how exciting it all is! I feel as though we were just starting a chapter of a particularly exciting book and of course it must end in wedding-bells!"

"Of course!" Marigold said. "Let us wish what sort of man we want to marry."

Anne looked again at her reflection in the mirror.

"I should like to marry a duke!"

"A duke!" Marigold exclaimed. "Good gracious, why?"

"Because he would possess all the things that I like most," Anne said slowly. "Wonderful houses with great traditions behind them—beautiful furniture, pictures and silver—a family whose ancestors have done great deeds in history. That is what I should like—to marry a duke with a magnificent family place."

"Which will be crippled by taxes and without good sanitation!" Marigold teased. "Not for me, thank you! Dukes are out of date, Anne. I want to marry a millionaire. I want to go to the Riviera and Palm Beach, to have wonderful clothes and even more wonderful jewelry. That is my idea of a good future. I should never get that from a stuffy old duke!"

"All right then," Anne said, "I'll have my duke and you can have your millionaire. We certainly shan't interfere with each other!"

They both laughed and turned to Sally.

"Sally, you're very quiet; you haven't told us whom you wish to marry. What sort of man do you wish for?"

Sally smiled and it seemed as if there was a secret in the depth of her dark grey eyes.

"I want to marry a man I love."

Her words were spoken lightly, but somehow her sisters became serious.

"But we want that too!" they both cried.

"You didn't say so," Sally answered.

At that moment there was a distinct clanging of the bell.

"That's the front door!" Anne exclaimed. "I wonder who it can be."

I'll go and answer it," Sally said.

She sped away leaving the door of the sitting-room open and a moment later they heard a voice in the hall.

"It is David," Anne said, looking at Marigold.

Marigold made a gesture of impatience.

"What a nuisance he is! I suppose he will stay to tea. I wanted to make a list of all the things we shall want for London."

"We can make that anyway," Anne said. "David doesn't matter."

Sally heralded him into the room.

"Here is David," she said.

The man who followed her was young and attractive, broad-shouldered and tall; he seemed to fill the small, shabby sitting-room with his presence.

"Hullo, Anne," he said, then looked at Marigold almost apologetically. "Hullo, Marigold."

"Hullo."

"I wondered if you were doing anything or if you would care to come for a drive."

"I am much too busy."

"Too busy? You don't look it."

"Well, I am," Marigold answered. "If you want to know, we are making plans to go to London almost at once."

"To London?"

"Yes," said Marigold. "To London! We are going to seek our fortunes."

David Carey stood in the center of the room staring at Marigold and then at last he looked to Sally for an explanation.

"You are going to London?" he asked.

"Yes," Sally replied. "You see, we cannot go on living here, and there is no possibility of earning our living in this part of the world, so it is London for the three of us."

"But this is too wonderful to be true!" David exclaimed.

They all glanced up in surprise.

"The reason I came to see you today," David explained, "was because I have had the offer of a post as House Surgeon at one of the big London hospitals. It is

13

a splendid opportunity of course, but somehow I had hated the idea of leaving here—of going away from . . ." he hesitated for a moment, ". . . from you all."

He looked at Marigold as he spoke and it was quite obvious whom he really minded leaving.

David Carey was the son of a doctor in St. Ives, the nearest town to St. Chytas. The three girls had known him all their lives. They had played together as children, they had teased each other and David had come to be looked on as a kind of elder brother.

It had been a surprise to them when he had fallen in love with Marigold, but it was tragic for David, for Marigold's affection for him was entirely a sisterly one.

It was Sally who exclaimed with joy at his news.

"But, David, that's wonderful! You will be in London! We shall be in London! At least we shall have one old friend to look after us."

"Perhaps David will be too busy to worry about his country cousins," Marigold suggested.

"You know I won't," David said. "But what are you going to do, where are you going to live? Tell me all about it!"

He moved forward and sat down in an armchair by the fireplace.

"We do not know yet," Marigold said. "Don't be so tiresome, David! We are making our plans, and when they are complete we will tell you all about them."

"I only wanted to help," David said humbly.

Marigold turned away from him with an air of petulance. His devotion bored her.

She liked David. She had at times found him useful both as a friend and as a sort of adopted brother; but she did not find him attractive and she grew impatient when he wanted to identify too closely with her interests.

Sally, watching them, wished David would assert

14

himself more. Marigold was rather inclined to be unkind to people who bored her.

"If David would pay attention to someone else," Sally thought, "Marigold would be more interested in him."

David was clever. Sally believed, as his father did, that he would go very far and would one day become a great man in his own chosen career; but, an only child, he was not experienced where women were concerned.

They frightened him and he was too humble with them and especially with Marigold. Sally thought sadly that David was far more fun before he fell in love.

"I'm so excited about your new appointment, David," she said to bridge an embarrassing moment. "Isn't your father thrilled?"

"He is as happy as a sand-boy," David answered. "It is all through him of course that I have had the offer. He has been pulling strings through one of his old friends for a long time; I knew it, but I didn't think anything would materialise. Now that something has really come off, you would think someone had given the old man a V.C. or left him a million, he is so delighted."

"We are delighted, too," Sally said, and he smiled at her a swift, spontaneous smile which made him suddenly very attractive.

"Thank you, Sally. I came along here to tell you all about it, but I was going to break it gently to Marigold first if she would come out for a drive with me."

"Expecting me to cry on your shoulder?" Marigold said unkindly.

"Well, I did think you might be a little sorry at losing me."

"I don't suppose it would have been for long. I expect they have holidays, even in hospitals."

Sally knew that Marigold was hurting David. Quickly she intervened.

"Well, we needn't worry about that now. You may

15

be going to London, David, but you are taking three little maids from Cornwall with you!"

"You know I am glad about that," David said.

Sally looked at the clock.

"It is tea-time, I'll go and get some tea."

"I will come and help you," Anne said, following her from the room.

Marigold and David were alone. Marigold curled herself up on the sofa and stared into the fire. David got up from his chair and moved across.

"Marigold!" he said, and there was an urgency in his voice.

She turned to look at him.

"What is the matter?" she asked.

"Do you know why I came here today?" he said.

"I thought you had just told us why," Marigold replied.

"I really came to ask you something," David said. "When I knew I was going away there was only one thing I wanted. I wanted you to marry me."

"But you knew I wouldn't do that!"

"But why?" David asked. "Why, Marigold? I have got a little money of my own which my grandmother left me and now I shall be getting quite a good salary at the hospital. I can afford to keep a wife, and, Marigold . . . I want you so!"

Marigold put out her hand and patted his arm.

"Poor David! I am sorry! But I should hate to be a doctor's wife and I am not in love with you."

"I could teach you to love me!" David said forcefully. "If you would only give me the chance."

"I do not think you can make someone love you," Marigold replied. "I do not think things work like that. I think you either fall in love or you don't; and quite frankly, David, I am not in love with anybody—I never have been!"

"But a lot of people will fall in love with you when

16

you get to London," David said bitterly; "then I shall not get a chance."

"Poor David," Marigold said again.

He got up abruptly from the sofa and stood with his back to the room, his arms on the mantelpiece.

"It is all very well to say 'Poor David'," he said roughly. "But I love you, Marigold, and it hurts."

"I am sorry," Marigold said.

He turned to look at her. Her face was raised to his.

She was almost breathtakingly lovely as she looked up at him, her eyes wide with compassion, a smile of sympathy on her lips.

There was no mistaking her beauty, David was not a fool—he knew that she did not love him, that emotionally Marigold was unawakened. With a sigh that was almost a cry he turned towards her and, taking both her hands in his, stared down at her.

"I want you to promise me one thing, Marigold."

"What is that?"

"That if when you get to London you are ever in any trouble, whatever it is you will come to me for help."

Marigold gave a little laugh. She was in reality slightly embarrassed by the seriousness of his tone.

"I hope I shall not get into trouble, David."

"But if you do . . ."

"Then of course I'll ask you for help, but I warn you, it will very likely be an S O S to save me from bankruptcy."

"Then I shall do my best to save you," David said.

He held both her hands very tightly in his, then relinquished them just as Anne and Sally came into the room carrying trays. It was a light-hearted, enjoyable meal and when it was over David got to his feet.

"I must go," he said. "I have got to pick up the old man at Hayle Hospital."

He moved reluctantly to the door and Sally knew he

was hoping that Marigold would go and see him off, but Marigold made it clear she had no intention of moving.

In the end Sally saw him to the door and into his car. The mist was rising now and a pale shaft of evening sunlight was coming throuth the clouds. There was a freshness in the air and Sally, looking out towards the sea, sighed.

"We are going to miss this, David."

"Terribly," he agreed, and then added: "I suppose you are right, Sally, it is best for you all to go to London. Though I somehow cannot imagine you there; you have always seemed to belong here."

Sally made a little helpless gesture with her hands.

"What else is there we can do?" she asked. "I have thought and thought, but there is just nothing. You cannot see Anne serving in a shop in St. Ives or Truro, or Marigold helping in an arty-crafty tea-room in Penzance, and there is nothing else, just nothing!"

"No you are right," David said hastily. "But, Sally, look after yourselves."

"We will," Sally said.

He got into this car and waved to her. It suddenly struck him that she was very small and rather pathetic as she stood there on the steps of the old-fashioned Vicarage. The actual house was badly planned and was architecturally an eyesore, yet to David it had always been one of the most attractive places he had ever known in his life because of the people who were in it.

Sally stood on the steps watching him out of sight and then, instead of going back into the house, she shut the door behind her and walked across the untidy, ill-kept garden and out on to the cliff-side. She walked on across the coarse grass, climbing gradually until she stood high above a small sandy cove. The sea was calmer than it had been earlier in the day, but the waves were still breaking in silver spray against the rocks at the end of the bay. Sally stood listening to them. Suddenly there were tears in her eyes, overflowing and falling softly down her cheeks. This was her world and she must leave it all behind. She threw out her arms in a gesture of despair.

"Oh, Daddy, Daddy!" she whispered. "How can I bear to go away?"

Two

"Goodness, I am tired!"

Anne put her bag and shopping-basket down on the table and pulled off her hat, passing her fingers through her flattened hair.

Sally looked up from the other side of the room where she was painting the skirting board.

"Any luck?"

Anne shook her head.

"No, and I've walked till my feet feel double their usual size."

She made a movement as though to sink exhaustedly in the nearest chair but was arrested in mid-air by a scream from Sally.

"Don't sit there, it's wet!"

"Heavens! Why on earth didn't you say so? Put a notice on it or something."

She turned round to try to catch a glimpse of the back of her dress.

"I haven't touched the paint, have I?" she asked. "This is the only decent get-up I have and that's not saying much!"

"If you are talking about clothes," said a voice from the doorway, "I've got a good deal to say on the subject."

"Hullo, Marigold!" Sally exclaimed. She got up from the floor, wiping her forehead with the back of her hand. "I've been working like a Trojan and I am so hot I think I shall have to have a bath."

"What? Climb down three floors?" Anne exclaimed. "I wouldn't have the energy!"

Marigold crossed the room and, as Anne had done, pulled off her hat. She held it in her hand looking at it disgustedly.

"Do you know what this thing is?" she asked.

The others stared at her.

"It's a museum piece," Marigold went on, not waiting for an answer to her question. "Either that or a relic from the Ark. I feel positively antediluvian walking about London in it. Have you seen what other people are wearing?"

"We haven't time to fuss about clothes," Anne said wearily. "When we have got ourselves jobs we can begin to think about spending money. In the meantime, we . . ."

"In the meantime, we shan't get a job," Marigold interrupted. "Not dressed like this. I have been looking in the shop windows and at other women and at last I have realised what is wrong with us, all three of us. We look exactly what we are—country cousins—nice innocent little girls from a country vicarage."

"Well, I don't see that there's anything wrong with that," Sally exclaimed.

"Don't be ridiculous," Marigold said sharply. "If we want to get jobs in London, we have got to be sophisticated and smart. You should have seen the way the woman looked at me today when I suggested that I might get a job as a mannequin. She very nearly laughed in my face. It was then I realised what fools we had been."

She threw her hat down on the floor.

"We have got to alter our whole appearance," she added dramatically. "Sally, how much money have we got?"

"None for clothes," Sally replied.

Marigold opened her mouth as if she were going to argue, then she shut it again.

"I expect Marigold is right," Anne said reflectively. "I've tried four different agencies today and they offered me nothing except a job as a kitchen help."

"Kitchen help!" Sally exclaimed.

"Yes. I couldn't say I was good enough to be a cook, so they suggested I might like to help the chef at some woman's house—I forget her name—Lady something-or-other!"

Sally sat down on the floor.

"Oh, darlings, and I brought you here! It is all my fault!"

"Oh no, it isn't," Marigold answered quickly. "You know quite well it was I who suggested London."

"Yes, but I knew you would once I said we should seek jobs away from home." Sally sighed.

"That doesn't matter," Marigold said; "you're not going to take all the responsibility. If anyone is to be blamed, we'll all take our share, won't we, Anne?"

"Of course," Anne replied. "And don't let's be depressed. After all, we have only been trying to find something for three days."

"What is more, we have tried in the wrong way," Marigold exclaimed. "I am certain of that. I am going to turn the hem of my skirt up at least three or four inches and I am going to buy a rose and two yards of ribbon, throw them together and perch the result on top of my head. We can afford that, can't we Sally?"

"We'll have to," Sally said and laughed.

Nevertheless, her face was serious again as she looked up at her sisters.

Sitting cross-legged on the hearth-rug in an old white overall which was streaked with paint and with a smear of paint on her cheek, she looked absurdly young, and yet the older girls left unchallenged her position as their leader.

It was Sally who decided what was to be done, Sally who had so far taken command in this, the greatest adventure of their lives.

Ever since she had been a baby, Sally had made friends wherever whe went, with everyone with whom she came in contact, and it was through one of Sally's friends that they had found their present accommodation.

Old Fred, the boatman at St. Chytas, who had known the girls since they were babies and had been a close friend of Arthur Granville, although he was a chapel man, had suggested that they should look up his wife's brother when they got to London.

Anne and Marigold had taken very little notice of the many suggestions that they should visit this person or that on their arrival in London.

Like many pioneers and adventurers their one idea was to get away from their old ties, and entering a new world, they wanted everything about it to be new.

Although they smiled sweetly and thanked everyone for the advice they were offered, it went in at one ear and out of the other and they had no intention of following any of it.

Sally, on the contrary, took particular note of everything she was told.

She kept a note-book and put all the names and addresses down in it; and while the others teased her, they found as usual that Sally's plans were far more sensible than theirs.

Old Fred's wife's brother had greeted them with open arms. He kept a pub called the Saracen's Head in Chelsea and having invited Sally into the private bar had been disappointed when whe would not partake of a small port or a glass of sherry.

He had also been most obligingly helpful when she told him the real object of her visit.

"We have come to London to look for jobs, Mr. Jarvis. The first thing we have got to do is to find somewhere to live," Sally said, "and I don't think I need to tell you that it's got to be cheap."

Mr. Jarvis scratched his head.

"You are setting yourself a problem, Miss, and no mistake."

"Yes, I know," Sally answered. "I feel sure, however, that you with your knowledge of London will be able to help me."

Mr. Jarvis was obviously flattered, but he said:

"I'm jiggered if I know where to tell you to go first."

After some moments of thought accompanied by heavy breathing he suddenly went to the door of the bar and, opening it, yelled:

"Hi, missis!"

Mrs. Jarvis was as genial and as pleasant as her husband.

She was a very large woman who must have been attractive in her youth but was now like an over-blown peony. She had a naturally florid complexion which was not improved by being plentifully befloured with a very white powder.

Her hair, dressed high on her head, was a fiery red on top and a dark brown at the roots. Nevertheless, there was a smiling good-humour in Mrs. Jarvis's face which made Sally take to her at once.

Sally told her story once again of how she and her sisters decided to come to London and how they were looking desperately for accommodation at the right price.

"I tell her, missis, it's a dickens of a problem," Mr. Jarvis said.

"That it is, Bill, but you ought to be able to think of

something. What about that Mrs. Jenkins down the road?"

"Yes, she takes in lodgers, but not always the right type."

"No, I remember now, Mrs. Jenkins would not do at all," Mrs. Jarvis said, "not for three young girls." Suddenly she put her hands on her hips. "Bill! What about the attic? You have never had it done up as you said you were going to."

"The attic? Why, God bless my soul, that wouldn't be good enough."

"Well, it's dry and airy, and if the young ladies were not too particular I dare say they could make it do, and whatever other disadvantages they may have to put up with, this house is at least respectable—anyway, while I'm in it!"

"That's true enough," Mr. Jarvis said. "At the same time it isn't much of a place, but if you would like to see it, Miss . . .!"

Sally was only too anxious to view the attic, and having seen it she made up her mind instantly.

It was both dirty and untidy, but she saw that there was nothing wrong that could not be put right by a good scrubbing and a touch of paint. It was a long room with a low ceiling, partly sloping, and had three small gable windows which looked over the housetops.

From one of them there was a glimpse of the river, and it was that, perhaps, which decided the issue quicker than anything else.

The mere sight of that silver water made Sally think of home although the grey Thames was a poor substitute for the blue-and-emerald ocean she knew and loved so well.

"It's perfect, Mr. Jarvis," she said enthusiastically, turning from the window with her eyes bright and shining with excitement. "We can be very happy here and it will be wonderful to think that you will be our land-lord."

Mr. Jarvis, mopping his forehead after the stiff climb up the stairs, beamed at her.

"I am glad you like it, Miss," he said. "I'll have to try and get it cleaned up for you, of course."

"No, you are not to bother," Sally said, "we will do that ourselves. It won't take us long. The only thing, Mr. Jarvis, is—what about furniture? We could get some things sent up from home, of course, but I am afraid it would be rather expensive."

Mr. Jarvis considered.

"I have not got much that I could rightly spare," he said, "but I'll tell you what I could do. I've got a friend who often has a lorry going down to Penzance. If there wasn't too much, I dare say he could bring the things back for you."

"But that would be marvellous," Sally said. "The new Vicar has let us store our things in the stable until we find somewhere to put them. I can write to someone in the village who knows where everything is to sort out the things we want and if your friend could bring them up . . ."

"I'll make the arrangements for you, Miss. In the meantime, if you like to come here and get on with the cleaning, that will be O.K. with us. I don't like to ask ladies such as you to do it for yourselves but, at the same time, the missis is hard put to get help in the bar, let alone for anything else."

"Of course we will do it ourselves. Now, Mr. Jarvis, what are you going to charge us?"

There was some argument over this. Mr. Jarvis was all for giving them the attic for practically nothing, but Sally was determined to be businesslike.

"We hope soon to be making good money," she said, "and we must pay what is right and fair."

25

In the end Mr. Jarvis offered it to her for three pounds a week and both sides were entirely satisfied.

It took a week to get their furniture up from St. Chytas and during that week all three girls worked from early morning until evening.

They were staying in a respectable boarding-house in Bloomsbury which had been recommended to them by David's father. David had lodged there when he was a student at the London University.

It was squalid and uncomfortable and its only advantage was its cheapness. In contrast the attic had immense possibilities and the girls were determined to make it as attractive as possible.

Sally had made a list of all the things she wanted from St. Chytas and this included two armchairs, a table and some book-shelves, for they had decided to make one end of the attic their bedroom and the other a sitting-room.

They had got a local carpenter, who was ready to oblige any friend of Mr. Jarvis, to run a long curtain rail across the centre of the room so that it would be possible to curtain off the beds if they ever wished to entertain.

"We may have friends coming to see us," Sally said, "and I hate the look of beds about the place. Even if you try to make them into divans, they always look 'beddy', and besides, who ever heard of three divans in one sitting-room?"

The result when it was divided was not too bad although the so-called "sitting-room" was very tiny and, as Anne pointed out, it would not be possible to entertain many friends at the same time.

"If our prospective husbands all call at once," Marigold said, "it is going to be rather a crush."

"They'll have to take it in turns," Sally answered,

laughing. "That will give us two days a week each and we'll toss for Sundays."

As soon as they had actually moved into their new home Sally sent Anne and Marigold off job-hunting while she put the finishing touches to the attic.

"I've only got to paint the skirting boards," she said, "and the hard chairs, and then we have finished. It really does look nice!"

It was by no means an over-statement.

They had scrubbed the boards as clean as they could get them and then stained them a dark oak colour. They had distempered the walls a pale primrose-yellow and painted the window-frames and skirting-boards and chairs a lovely shade of blue; this matched the flowers on the chintz curtains and chair covers which had been sent up from St. Chytas.

There was a gilt-framed mirror over the fireplace and a picture which had always hung in their father's study.

It was of a flight of birds coming homewards across the evening sky, with the sea below them. Sally would stand and look at that picture and when she did so she could always hear her father's voice saying:

"What a wonderful instinct the birds have, Sally! Have you ever thought how much wiser humans would be if like the birds we followed our instinct rather than our convictions which are so often wrong?"

When the picture was hung on the wall, Sally had said a little prayer in her heart that her instinct had been right in bringing them all to London. She had not realised until she got there how big and overwhelming a city could be.

When she walked about the streets, she felt very small and unimportant.

Sometimes she had an overwhelming desire to go home, to be back again amongst the people she knew and loved and who she knew would always extend to

Arthur Granville's daughter the helping hand of friendship. Here they were nobodies!

No one knew them, no one cared what became of them. Sometimes when she was alone in the attic and the other two girls were out, Sally would feel an unreasoning panic sweep over her.

Suppose things went wrong; suppose they found nothing to do and all their money was swallowed up—what would happen to them then? They had so little!

When she felt like that, she would rise, go to the window and look out at the river. The shimmering water would bring her comfort. It gave her a sense of security, even as the sight of her beloved waves had always brought her a sense of belonging, of being an intrinsic part of the great universe.

"It is all right, be of good cheer. Be not afraid."

That was what the river said to Sally and she would go back to her work comforted and reassured.

But now, as she looked up from the floor at Anne and Marigold, she felt afraid.

They were both so attractive—they were both so helpless. They were not equipped to fight for a place in the hard commercial world—and yet, Sally thought, surely there was something all three of them could do?

"The room's finished now," she said. "Tomorrow I'm going to try and see what I can find. There is no need for us to get upset—we haven't been in London a fortnight yet."

"What are you going to try for?" Anne asked. Sally smiled.

"I have an idea, but I don't want to tell you about it in case I fail."

"I haven't got any pride left," Marigold said; "I will do anything!" Then she laughed. "That isn't true—I'm only saying it for effect! Actually I feel very particular; besides, I don't want to let London beat me. If other girls can get jobs, so can I."

"That's the spirit," Sally said. "By the way, Anne, did you bring back a newspaper?"

Anne went to the table and opened her shopping-basket.

"Yes, and I remembered the bread and I actually bought a cucumber. Was that extravagant of me?"

"No, it's lovely," Sally said. "We will have cucumber sandwiches for tea. Whose turn is it to go downstairs? No, don't answer, I'll do it. You are both tired out."

Mrs. Jarvis allowed them to boil a kettle in her kitchen for breakfast and tea. For other meals, they went out to one of the many little restaurants round about. The only disadvantage of meals at home was that they had four floors to climb down before they reached the kitchen.

Sally hurried downstairs kettle in one hand, the tea-pot in the other and the canister containing the tea under her arm. Mrs. Jarvis was not in the kitchen. She filled the kettle and put it on to boil.

On the table was a newspaper, and while she was waiting Sally turned the pages over attentively. It was the *Daily Telegraph* and she began to look down the columns of "Situations Vacant." Suddenly one advertisement caught her eye. She read it two or three times and, having done so, waited impatiently for the kettle to boil. She made the tea and hurried up the stairs as quickly as she could, the *Daily Telegraph* under her arm.

She burst into the attic breathless both with her haste and the stairs.

"I say, Anne, I've found something in this paper which I think will interest you."

Anne, who was sitting in the armchair, looked up.

"What is it?" she asked.

"It's here—the *Daily Telegraph*," Sally said, putting down the tea pot.

"Daily Telegraph!" Anne exclaimed. "But I bought the *Daily Sketch*. I adore Blondie and Pop."

"So do I," Sally said. "But this isn't our paper—it's Mr. Jarvis's—I've borrowed it for a moment. Look here!"

She pointed to the small advertisement and Anne read aloud:

"Titled lady requires daily companion. Must be young and educated. Apply: Box 'X'."

"There you are," Marigold exclaimed, "a titled lady is just your cup of tea, Anne: you may even meet your Duke there!"

"Young and educated. Do you think I'm educated?" Anne said.

There was a tone of doubt in her voice, but she was obviously excited by the advertisement.

"Of course you are," Sally said. "Sit down and write at once. I expect they will have lots of applications."

Anne jumped up and went to the table where they kept their writing materials.

"Write on the Vicarage note-paper," Sally said; "at least it's printed and personally I don't think that the Saracen's Head sounds a very good address!"

"Why not put just the number of the street?" Marigold suggested.

"But of course!" Sally exclaimed. "How silly of me! That's a good idea, Anne . . .92 Medway Street sounds much better than the Saracen's Head."

"How do I start!" Anne enquired.

They spent some time arguing as to what was the best way to address the advertiser and twenty minutes passed before Sally remembered that Mr. Jarvis might be wanting his paper.

"Hurry up and address the envelope," she said, "and I'll post the letter and put the newspaper back at the same time."

"There it is," Anne exclaimed. "Oh, bring me luck, please!"

"I feel in my bones that something will come of this," Sally said reflectively, and picking it up she put the newspaper under her arm and ran downstairs.

There was still no one in the kitchen, so evidently the paper had not been missed. She put it back on the table and opening the door let herself into the street.

There was a pillar-box on the corner and she inserted the letter into its gaping mouth she gave a little sigh which was half a prayer that something might come of it; and then, turning round swiftly, she knocked into a tall man who was standing behind her.

"I'm sorry," Sally exclaimed.

The man was bare-headed so he could not take off his hat, but he smiled at her.

"It's all right," he said, "it was my fault. I was crowding you."

Sally smiled in reply and was just turning away when he stopped her.

"Excuse my asking you," he said, "but aren't you staying at the Saracen's Head?"

"Yes," Sally answered.

"Then you are one of the Miss Granvilles, aren't you? Jarvis was talking about you the other night when I was having a drink. I wonder if you would think me very impertinent if I asked you something?"

"What is it?" Sally asked.

She was taking stock of the young man as she spoke. He was rather nice looking, clean shaven and fair, but his hair was too long and he dressed rather unconventionally in a deep wine-coloured sweater and baggy corduroy trousers.

"I'm an artist," the young man began.

"Of course!" Sally exclaimed. He looked at her enquiringly and she blushed, embarrassed by her own impulsiveness. "I only mean . . ." she stammered, "that you look like one."

"Is it so obvious?" the young man asked, then added: "Yes, I suppose it is. Well, now you know what I want to say. I wondered if your sister, the one with the wonderful hair, would sit for me."

"I wonder if you mean Anne or Marigold?"

"I'm sure it must be Marigold," the young man answered; "the name describes her."

"I'll ask her," Sally said, "but the point is we are all rather busy at the moment looking for jobs."

"Well, look here, I'm perfectly willing to pay. She is exactly the model I have been seeking for some illustrations that I am doing for a magazine."

"Oh, I thought you wanted her to sit for a proper portrait," Sally said in a disappointed tone.

The young man smiled.

"I would like her to sit for that, too, but I usually have to wait for those to be commissioned. Illustrations pay well and portraits—well, I haven't got to the stage when a rich financier's wife offers me a cool thousand for her face on canvas."

Sally laughed. She liked this young man, there was something frank and ingenuous about him. She hesitated a moment, then suggested:

"I suppose you would not like to come back with me now and meet Marigold?"

"I'd simply love it," the young man said instantly. "By the way, you did not ask my name. It's Peter Aird."

"Come on," said Sally. "Incidentally, you will be our first guest."

"This calls for a celebration," Peter Aird said. "We ought to have champagne at least, but instead, what about those strawberries?"

He pointed to a street vendor who was coming down the road pushing a barrow, and without waiting for Sally's reply he walked across to him. He was a moment or two choosing a basket, then he came back with it.

"All the big ones are on top as usual," he said. "These men are always rogues, but at least I can lay them at Marigold's feet as a tribute to her beauty!"

"It would be much better if you put them on the table and we all ate them," Sally said almost sharply.

She hoped this young man was not going to flatter Marigold too much. Already she was half regretting having invited him to come back with her.

Artists were impecunious, and although he had offered to pay Marigold, Sally had an idea that the pay would not be big. Then, as she turned her latch-key in the door, she heard him say humbly:

"It's awfully good of you to ask me, Miss Granville."

Somehow she found herself smiling up at him. He was rather a nice young man and after all they hadn't many friends in London.

"It is rather a climb up the stairs," she said. "Would you mind waiting a moment just while I go up and tell the others you are coming? We would like to have everything spick and span for the first visitor."

"Of course I will wait," he said. "Give me a shout from the top when you are ready."

"I will," Sally promised.

She hurried up the stairs, two steps at a time, opened the door and rushed in breathlessly.

Anne was sitting staring out of the window. Marigold was on the floor, her sewing things scattered all round her, her scissors in her hand. She was chopping several inches of material off the end of her skirt.

Sally slammed the door behind her and pulled the curtains to divide the sitting-room from the three divans which always reminded her of the Three Bears side by side at the end of the room.

"Quick," she said. "Tidy the place and look nice, I have brought you a visitor—our first visitor."

Marigold looked up, her mouth full of pins.

"Bother," she muttered. "Can't you see I'm busy?"

She had changed from her coat and skirt into a green linen frock. It was old and faded, but it threw into relief the whiteness of her skin and the curly burnished glory of her hair.

She was frowning and yet she looked ridiculously lovely.

Anne turned round eagerly.

"A visitor?" she said. "Who is it?"

Suddenly Sally felt her heart contract.

Anne was lovely, too—lovelier perhaps in many ways than her younger sister, and yet Peter, like David, was attracted by Marigold.

Three

Marigold was brusque with Peter Aird the first time she met him.

She informed him quite frankly that she was not interested in sitting for his illustrations and she was not going to model for artists.

"What future is there in it?" she asked scornfully later when the girls were alone. "Painters are always impecunious—I'm sure Daddy would not have approved of our associating with them even if we do live in Chelsea."

Sally felt guilty and she blamed herself for letting her invariable knack of making friends lead her astray.

She told herself severely that she should not have asked in a strange young man to meet her sisters, but despite his appearance and Marigold's criticisms she knew that she liked Peter Aird.

On acquaintance he was by no means what she had expected of a Chelsea artist. His clothes were misleading for there was nothing sloppy or Bohemian about his speech and she found herself longing to argue with Marigold and defend Peter against such scornful disparagement.

However, two evenings later things were much altered. Peter called unexpectedly bringing with him another basket of strawberries and some peaches.

Marigold and Anne had spent two more unsuccessful days looking for jobs and were therefore inclined to welcome any friendly face even if it was that of an impecunious artist. Marigold told them of the various places she had tried during the day and added:

"It's extraordinary to think how unsuited we all are to earning our own living. When I have daughters I shall bring them up to be really efficient at something."

"What exactly do you want?" Peter asked.

"At the moment," Marigold answered. "I want any job that will bring me in six or seven pounds a week regularly every Friday. I would prefer to model or be a mannequin for the simple reason that I am untrained in everything else, but I really believe I would take a position as a crossing sweeper if it was offered to me."

"If you want to be a mannequin," Peter said, "I might be able to help you."

Marigold raised her eyebrows and looked at him enquiringly.

"Why on earth didn't you tell me so before?"

"For the simple reason that you did not condescend to tell me what you wanted to do; you were far too intent on telling me what you didn't want to do."

"All right, I apologise. Now please be magnanimous and help me."

"I don't promise anything will come of it," Peter said, "but a friend of mine works at Michael Sorrell's; you've heard of him, of course?"

"What? The big dress designer?"

"Yes."

"And you will give me an introduction?"

"Of course I will."

Marigold jumped to her feet in excitement.

"But it's too wonderful! And to think I was so beastly to you when you asked me to sit for your illustrations. If you will give me a letter of introduction to your friend, I will sit for however long you like in whatever position."

"Thank you," Peter answered, "but I don't want to be paid for my magnanimity. I would like to give you an introduction. My friend's name, by the way, is Nadine Sloe."

"Oh, it's a 'she', is it?" Marigold said. "A girl friend of yours?"

"Not exactly, but I have known her for a great many years," Peter answered.

"You will write the letter now, at once?" Marigold asked. "Can I take it there tomorrow morning? I can't wait."

"Don't get too excited," Peter begged; "they may be full up or you may not be the type they want. I would hate you to be disappointed."

"Not half as much as I should hate it."

"I think you are very lucky," Anne said enviously. "I wish someone would come along who could find me a job."

"You haven't had an answer to your letter yet?" Peter asked.

He had already heard about the advertisement that Anne had answered.

Anne shook her head.

"Hope is beginning to die hard."

"Oh, something else will turn up," said Peter. "I've often felt like that myself and then the unexpected has happened. There have been days when I have looked in the letter-box every five minutes to see if the postman had called."

"Talking of that," Sally said quickly, looking up from the net curtain she was hemming, "there ought to be a delivery about this time. Shall I go down and see if there is a letter?"

"Yes," Anne said. "I would go myself only I know if there isn't one I shall burst into tears on Mr. Jarvis's shoulder."

"He wouldn't mind that, he would like it," Sally said, jumping to her feet.

"Yes, but would Mrs. Jarvis?" Anne asked.

Sally turned from the doorway.

"You flatter yourself. Old Bill thinks there is no one like 'his missis', and I'm certain he is right."

She ran downstairs hoping desperately as she went that there would be an answer to their application. Anne, who was usually so placid and calm, had been quite nervy for the last twenty-four hours, Marigold was short tempered and Sally felt it was time one of them had a lucky break.

Although she had not yet told the others, she had also been disappointed in her search for a job.

She had made up her mind when she first came to London that she would like to look after children—to be an assistant in a children's nursery or something like that; but although she had applied to three different addresses, she had found at each one that they required no further helpers.

There were other places of course, Sally told herself courageously, but all the same, too, felt a little downcast. She reached the little hall and saw with a sudden sinking of her heart that there were no letters.

She hated to go back to the attic and break the dismal news to Anne, so to make certain that the postman had come and gone, she opened the kitchen door.

Mrs. Jarvis was sitting in the armchair with her feet up and the cat purring comfortably in her lap.

"Has the post been, Mrs. Jarvis?" Sally asked.

Mrs. Jarvis turned her head round quickly.

"Dear, dear, what a start you gave me! I was just having forty winks. The post did you say? No, I haven't heard him. What's the time?"

"Oh, I'm so sorry if I woke you!" Sally exclaimed. "It's six o'clock."

"Well, he usually comes about this time, but I haven't heard him and if there is anything for us that letter-box makes a noise fit to wake the dead. Any news of a job?"

"That is what we are hoping for," Sally answered. "We have answered an advertisement for Anne, and if they are going to send us a reply it is nearly overdue."

"I wish I knew of something myself that would suit you," Mrs. Jarvis said, "but all I want is a woman who can wash up the glasses decently. That girl I got in last week is hopeless. She has no more idea of work than a block of wood. As I said to Bill this morning, 'She'll have to go!' It gives me double the amount of work having to do hers after her than if I did it all myself in the first place."

"You work too hard, Mrs. Jarvis."

"We both do, dear," Mrs. Jarvis sighed. "Between ourselves, I think it is about time we retired. I've often dreamed as how we'd have a cottage in the country with our own chickens and a little bit of garden. It wouldn't cost all that much and we've got a bit put by."

"I know just the sort of cottage you'd like," Sally said. "A friend of mine has one in our village at home. It is a dear little thatched place, but she has got electric light and her garden is a dream in the summer. She keeps bees, chickens and a goat and all through the war she has always managed to give one a really good meal. I often think that when I'm old that's what I would like —a cottage of my own and a garden with a view of the sea."

Sally's eyes grew dreamy—she was thinking of how

38

St. Chytas would look at this moment in the evening sunlight. The fishing-boats would be putting out to sea, their sails silhouetted against the evening sky.

In the old days she and her father would have been sitting on the cliff. It was their favourite spot at that time of the day when the weather was fine.

Sometimes they would sit in silence, but at others they would talk—of life, of death, and of things which really matter. Sally sighed; she felt very alone without him.

"I can't think why anyone wants to live in London," she said.

"You are feeling home-sick," Mrs. Jarvis answered; "but don't you worry, dear, you'll find your feet! London's a grand place for the young. I don't mind betting you half a crown to a bent pin that you will all be having the time of your lives in a month or so."

Sally gave her shoulders a little shake as though to throw away her dreams.

"I expect you are right, Mrs. Jarvis," she said with a wistful smile, "and I oughtn't to complain seeing how good you and Mr. Jarvis have been to us."

"Go along with you," Mrs. Jarvis replied; "you're no trouble and that's a fact, and you have made that room of yours really charming. I wouldn't have believed it could look as nice as it does."

At that moment there was a rattle and a crash. Sally gave an exclamation.

"There's the postman!"

She ran from the room to find three letters and a circular on the floor inside the door. She picked them up. Two of the envelopes were addressed to Mr. Jarvis and the third was for Anne.

The writing was clear and upright and the envelope was of very good quality paper with a crest on the flap. Sally rushed back into the kitchen with other letters and the circular.

"It's come, Mrs. Jarvis! The letter has come!"

"Well, I am glad," Mrs. Jarvis said. "I only hope that it is good news."

"Oh, I hadn't thought of that." Sally stood quite still with the letter in her hands. "Suppose they have written to say that they are already suited. Oh, Mrs. Jarvis, Anne will be so disappointed!"

"Well, I only hope for your sake that they're not," Mrs. Jarvis said. and added philosophically, "Anyway, there are other situations in the world, don't you forget that!"

"I won't," Sally said soberly, but she rushed upstairs three steps at a time and burst into the attic. "Look, Anne!" she cried holding out the letter.

Anne jumped up from her chair, took the envelope from Sally and stood looking at it.

"Do you know," she said after a moment, "it is silly, but I just daren't open it."

"I'll do it for you." Marigold cried.

She picked up the scissors from Sally's open work-basket and slit the envelope along the top.

"Now!" she said dramatically and took out the letter. For a moment she hesitated and then read aloud what was written on the sheet of paper:

Dear Miss Granville,

I was very interested in your letter and would be grateful if you would call to see me tomorrow, Thursday, at 10.30.

Yours truly,
Catherine Barfield.

Anne gave a little scream.

"Is that all? Oh. how wonderful! What shall I wear? And what is the address?"

"Halstead House, Berkeley Square!" Sally answered. She had been peeping over Marigold's shoulder.

"Berkeley Square? That sounds rich!" Marigold said, and her voice held a note of envy.

"What did you say the name was?" Peter asked.

Marigold examined the signature again.

"It looks like Barfield or Burfield."

"Burfield," Peter said. "That's who it is—Lady Catherine Burfield. She married the colonel commanding the Grenadiers."

The three girls looked at him.

"Are you sure?"

"Yes, quite sure."

"Is she nice?" Annc asked.

"I don't know what you call nice," Peter prevaricated.

He spoke rather diffidently as if he was not anxious to continue the conversation, but only Sally noticed this; Anne and Marigold were too busy poring over the letter.

"I am sure they are rich if they live in Berkeley Square," Marigold said. "Don't ask for too small a salary!"

"But how do I know what to ask for?" Anne questioned.

"I should wait and see what she offers you," Sally said quietly.

Anne was to remember this advice the next day when she sat nervously in the big library at Halstead House being interviewed by Lady Catherine Burfield. From the moment when she put up her hand to ring the bell of the large, imposing front door Anne had found herself shaking with nervousness.

The imposingly dignified butler who opened the door and the dismal grandeur of the library added to her feeling of shabby inferiority.

But when Lady Catherine came into the room she felt calmer and less afraid. Simply but expensively dressed, Lady Catherine gave an impression of being lovely although her face was in reality quite ordinary.

She had an unaffected, well-bred grace and she had, too, a charming way of speaking which was calculated to put anyone, even someone as nervous as Anne, at ease.

"It is nice of you to come and see me, Miss Granville," she said. "Won't you sit down?"

Anne did as was suggested feeling as awkward and ungainly as a schoolgirl meeting her headmistress for the first time.

"Shall I just explain what we want," Lady Catherine began, "and then you can tell if this is the sort of position you are requiring?"

"If you would," Anne murmured.

"What I advertised for," Lady Catherine began, "was a companion for my mother, the Duchess of Cheyn. I am going to be quite frank with you, Miss Granville, and say that my mother is not a very easy person to get on with, but she is rather a wonderful person with an outstanding personality and a very active brain.

"She is nearly eighty, yet somehow it is difficult to think of her as being very old. She likes young people and she insists that anyone who is with her should be young. We want someone to talk to her, to read to her, to do all the innumerable errands which have to be done because she is confined to her rooms.

"She has a nurse, of course, and that is why there is no reason for her to have a resident companion. The house is full at the moment and we prefer to have someone who lives out."

"I would prefer that, too," Anne said quickly.

"Well, that's splendid. Of course, I ought to add that there are my mother's letters to be written. She finds them too much for her to do herself and she prefers them written in longhand. She is of the old school who thinks it is rude for anyone to receive a typewritten letter."

Anne heaved a sigh of relief. At least she would not have to type.

"It is rather difficult for me to explain in detail," Lady Catherine went on, "what all your duties would be. My mother has all sorts of ideas of what she wants and what she doesn't want and we humour her.

"She entertains quite a lot and when she has guests she would want you to pour out the tea and things like that. She has a suite of rooms on the first floor so that it is convenient for her to see as many people as she wishes and her health permits."

Lady Catherine paused.

"I don't think there is anything else. If you are interested and would like to come here you must see my mother, for the final decision really rests with her. She takes very strong likes and dislikes and nothing I or indeed any of her children can say has any influence with her. Now what do you feel about the position?"

"I would try to please the Duchess," Anne said quietly.

"That's splendid," Lady Catherine approved. "Well then, you must come and see my mother. Oh, there is one other thing—what salary would you require?"

Anne remembered Sally's injunction.

"Perhaps you would tell me what you are offering."

Lady Catherine hesitated.

"We hoped to get someone for about six pounds a week," she said tentatively. "You see, we've had a lot of expense lately and I am afraid we could not afford any more. Of course, you would be here for luncheon and tea."

"That would be perfectly all right," Anne said, "if you want me."

"That depends on my mother," Lady Catherine smiled. "Shall we go up and see her?"

She led the way up the wide staircase and Anne, following her, had time to note the heavy brocade curtains which hung on each side of the high windows and the big, gilt-framed family portraits which decorated the walls.

Lady Catherine opened a door which led from the wide landing on the first floor and Anne following found herself in the most extraordinary room she had ever seen.

It was very large, high and light, but every square inch of the carpet seemed to be decorated with small polished tables. The tables all held photographs and tiny *objets d'art*—little china boxes, silver figures, filigree ornaments, scent bottles, miniatures, cameos—there was no end to them.

There were photographs everywhere, hundreds of them in wide, silver frames, many of which were surmounted by a crown.

There was a grand piano—which was also covered with photographs arranged on a Spanish shawl embroidered in many colours—and the walls were almost completely hidden by pictures, oil paintings, water colours and etchings, all jumbled together.

The chairs and sofas of an old-fashioned shape were dressed in shiny chintz covers patterned with large, overblown pink roses.

Lady Catherine walked straight across the room and Anne followed, gazing about her in amazement. They reached another door. Lady Catherine turned back to smile.

"These are my mother's most precious possessions," she said, "the collection of nearly a century. I'm afraid you will find that one of your chief occupations is finding some knick-knack which has been displaced by the housemaids. Mother knows them all and exactly where each one should be."

She knocked on the door and entered. The sun was

44

streaming in through two high, narrow windows and for a moment Anne felt dazzled and bewildered; then she heard an authoritative voice.

"Is that you, Catherine? What do you want?"

"I have brought Miss Granville to see you, Mother. You remember, I asked her to call this morning."

Lady Catherine moved forward and at last the room took shape and Anne saw a huge four-poster bed hung with dark damask curtains in the centre of which, propped up with pillows, lay the Duchess of Cheyn.

Anne's first impression was that she was tiny; then, as she met the Duchess's eyes, she knew there was nothing small or insignificant about her.

Once she had been an amazingly beautiful woman. Now, she was old and wrinkled and her skin was yellow as parchment, but her hair was still lovely, although snowy white, and it was piled high on her head as if it were a crown.

The bed was covered with a bedspread of old lace lined with deep violet satin. The Duchess wore a dressing-jacket of the same colour made of velvet and trimmed at the neck and wrists with bands of dark sable.

There were books, magazines and papers and a pile of letters lying on the bed, and Anne thought swiftly that here was no old lady content to lie back on her pillows but someone active and interested in all that went on around her.

"How do you do, Miss Granville," the Duchess said, holding out her hand, thin and bony, the fingers of which glittered with several diamond rings.

"I will leave Miss Granville with you for a little talk," Lady Catherine said. "Perhaps you will ring when you want me."

"Yes, I will ring if the bell isn't out of order!"

"Why, has it been out of order?" Lady Catherine asked.

"Out of order? It is always out of order! I ring and ring, but no one comes. One day I shall be found dead in my bed and then you will all be sorry."

"I will have it seen to at once," Lady Catherine said, but Anne got the idea that this was an old complaint.

"Sit down, Miss Granville," the Duchess said, pointing to a chair beside the bed.

Anne did as she was told.

"So you think that you would like to be my companion? Why?"

Anne was startled by the abrupt question.

"I need a job," she said.

"And is this the best thing you can do?" the Duchess enquired.

"I'm afraid I'm not qualified for many positions."

"Why not? Where were you educated?"

"At home," Anne answered. "We had a governess and then later on my father taught us. I am afraid it wasn't at all practical."

"It sounds to me more sensible than many I've heard of," the Duchess remarked. "Who was your father and where was 'home'?"

"My father was the Vicar of St. Chytas," Anne answered. "It is a little village near St. Ives in Cornwall."

"He is dead?"

"Yes," Anne answered, "and that is why we have come to London."

"Who is 'we'?"

"My sisters—Marigold and Sally. I am the eldest."

"So you've come to seek your fortunes, have you?"

"We have come to seek work," Anne corrected, not without dignity.

"And you all hope you will get married," the Duchess said with a chuckle and added before Anne could answer: "Well, I don't blame you, it is still the best career for any woman. Find a man who is fool enough to marry you and he has to keep you for the rest of your lives. It is better than all your fancy jobs as typists or getting varicose veins from standing behind shop counters."

The Duchess spoke in a deep voice that somehow had a humorous ring as if even while she was speaking she was mocking at herself. Anne had no idea if a comment was expected of her and remained silent. The Duchess looked at her with a smile.

"You are pretty, child; you will get married right enough. Are you in love?"

Anne flushed faintly at the question.

"No, I have never been in love."

"But you will be. Don't tell me that the men don't run after you with a face like that. What are your sisters like?"

"Marigold is lovely," Anne answered; "at least, we think so. And Sally—she is the youngest—is the sensible one of the family. She looks after us all."

"And what are they going to do?"

"Marigold is trying to get a job as a mannequin. She has gone off to see about it this morning. A friend has given her an introduction to Michael Sorrell."

"Michael Sorrell?" said the Duchess. "I know his clothes. He makes a duchess look like an actress and an actress look like a duchess. He is a clever young man, but his prices are ridiculous. And what about the youngest sister?"

"Sally has got some idea of what she wants to do, but she won't tell us what it is until she gets it," Anne answered. "She is sure to be successful because somehow Sally always gets what she wants."

The Duchess had no comment to make on this. She said nothing for a moment, only looked reflectively at Anne before she said:

"Well, will you be my companion or have you changed your mind since you have seen me?"

"I would be very grateful if you would give me a trial," Anne said.

"I don't suppose you will like it," the Duchess said. "You will find me difficult to get on with. Most companions sooner or later irritate me. They are slow and stupid; they simper at me. 'Oh, Duchess!' 'How could you, Duchess?' It makes me want to throw things at them. You don't appear to simper."

"I hope not," Anne said seriously.

"Well, if you want to come you had better come at once before you get married," the Duchess said.

"I don't think there is any likelihood of that, not for a long time at any rate," Anne replied with a smile.

"I should not be too sure," the Duchess warned, "but anyway, we'll try you out."

She rang the bell and a moment later the door opened and Lady Catherine came in.

"Well, it is settled, Catherine," the Duchess said. "Miss Granville will try to put up with me, so you can stop fussing for a few months and go and look after that husband of yours."

"When do you want Miss Granville to start?" Lady Catherine asked.

"Tomorrow," the Duchess said. "As I have just told her, there is nothing to be gained by waiting."

She looked at Anne with a smile that was somehow slightly mischievous.

"What time would you like me to be here?" Anne enquired.

"Nine-thirty," the Duchess said, "and don't be late. I like to get my letters done before the doctors arrive. One never knows when they will turn up. They always upset my morning."

"I'll be punctual," Anne said, and added, "thank you for saying I can come."

The Duchess seemed surprised.

"You oughtn't to be thanking me; the modern young

women expect me to thank them. You are old-fashioned, my dear, but you will soon learn to be the other way if you are in London long enough. Good morning."

Anne said good-bye to Lady Catherine and walked out into Berkeley Square. She felt strangely happy about her new situation.

In some peculiar way not easy to define the Duchess reminded her of her father. He, too, had had a sharp, rather amusing way of talking; he, too, had said just what came to his mind.

"I am not really afraid of her," Anne thought, and hoped it was the truth. She could imagine what some of her predecessors had been like—timid, shrinking little women who had been terrified of the Duchess's sharp tongue and her clear, penetrating eyes which seemed to look through one.

"I think I am going to like my first situation," Anne told herself. "Companion to the Duchess of Cheyn . . . I wonder if there is a Duke!"

Four

Marigold handed Peter's letter to a superior young woman dressed in pale grey and waited in the palatial hall of Michael Sorrell's shop while she took it to Miss Sloe.

The wide staircase of what had originally been an important London mansion was covered with grey carpet and up and down it hurried attractive young women dressed in neat dresses of the same shade of grey, looking all somewhat alike with their hair elaborately dressed and burnished, their lips vividly crimson and their eyelashes heavy with mascara. They looked happy.

Marigold thought, and she longed with a sudden

intense longing to be one of them. She could imagine herself slim and attractive in an identical grey dress.

She thought of a new way to do her hair which would call attention to the loveliness of its natural red-gold lights which other women tried so ineffectively to copy.

The telephone was ringing, customers with fantastic and amusing hats perched on their heads came and went through the front door. A girl at the desk was kept busy on the house telephone.

"Hello work-room—tell Mme Yvonne that Lady Sainsford is here."

"Hello tailoring, tell Monsieur Henri that Mrs. Cardew has called for her fitting."

"Hello . . . ask Miss Helena to come to the show-room. Lady Jenkins is waiting."

On and on it went while Marigold looked, watched and listened. Ten minutes passed before the girl to whom she had given the note came hurrying down the stairs.

"Miss Sloe will see you," she said. "Will you come this way, please?"

Marigold followed her down the corridor to where there was a lift and they shot up several floors of the building. As they went Marigold looked at the girl beside her. She was pretty in a sophisticated, rather sullen fashion.

Marigold longed to talk to her, to ask how she liked being part of this great establishment, but something about her polite indifference kept her silent. They travelled on in silence until the lift stopped with a sudden jerk. The girl opened the gates and Marigold stepped out.

"This way, please."

A door was opened and Marigold found herself in a small, exquisitely furnished room. Seated at a desk writing was a woman with her back to the window. Marigold advanced shyly, hearing the door close behind her.

There was a moment's pause and then the woman at the desk looked up. She raised her head and Marigold saw that her face was extremely attractive.

Her dark hair was swept back from a square, wide brow and her eyebrows, beautifully marked, were like wings over a pair of surprisingly blue eyes. She rose and held out her hand.

"How do you do, Miss Granville? Won't you sit down?"

She indicated a chair at the other side of the desk and then sat down again, her long, red-tipped fingers playing with a pencil.

"So you are a friend of Peter Aird?" Nadine Sloe asked in a slow, almost drawling voice which Marigold somehow knew was not natural to her but assumed.

"Yes. He very kindly gave me a letter of introduction."

Marigold hoped that she would not be asked how long she and Peter had been friends. Nadine Sloe picked up the note which lay open on her desk and read it again.

"He tells me that you would like a job her as a mannequin. Have you any experience?"

"I am afraid not."

Nadine Sloe looked down again at the letter and Marigold fancied that there was an expression of disapproval on her face.

"That is a pity," she said, "but I should think that you are about the right size. Will you stand up?"

Marigold did as she was asked, feeling rather foolish.

"Now walk across the room," Nadine Sloe said, and waited in silence while Marigold obeyed her.

"Now back again. Thank you."

She leaned back in her chair and suddenly Marigold had the impression that Nadine Sloe was disliking the interview as much as she was.

"I wonder if she is in love with Peter," she thought, and then, apprehensively, because she wanted the job so badly, she said:

"It was very kind of Mr. Aird to give me the letter to you. I appreciated it very much."

"I am sure you did. Peter seldom does a kindness that is not in his own interest."

There was a sarcastic note in Nadine Sloe's low voice. Again she looked down at the letter and Marigold felt uncomfortable. She had an idea that the older woman was seeking some excuse to send her away, to refuse her application.

She watched the long, thin fingers moving restlessly as they fondled the pencil, turning it round and round, twisting it, tapping with it gently on the desk. At first it seemed Nadine Sloe made up her mind.

"As a matter of fact we have a vacancy in the show-rooms," she said. "If you would like to come on trial for a month, we could see how you shaped."

Marigold's heart leapt with excitement.

"Thank you! Thank you very much indeed! It is kind of you."

"There is no guarantee, of course, that we shall keep you," Nadine Sloe continued. "We expect a very high standard of efficiency here and also a tremendous amount of hard work from our mannequins. You will receive seven pounds ten shillings a week to start with. Your hours will be from nine in the morning until six in the evening."

"When would you like me to start?" Marigold asked.

"Next Monday. You had better be here a little before nine and ask for Madame Marie—she is in charge of the mannequins."

"Thank you. I am grateful."

Nadine got to her feet.

"I hope you will like being here," she said without any warmth in her voice. "You will be seeing Peter, I expect? Tell him I always do my best to oblige an old friend."

"I will give him your message," Marigold replied.

Nadine stood up and pressed the bell on her desk. The door opened and the same girl who had escorted Marigold upstairs was waiting.

"Good-bye," Marigold said again, "and thank you."

Nadine Sloe obviously did not intend to shake hands.

"Good-bye, Miss Granville," she said coldly.

Marigold got into the lift and the girl in grey closed the gates. Now that she had left Nadine Sloe Marigold's enthusiasm burst through her shyness.

"I am going to work here," she told the girl on the lift.

The girl glanced at her without interest.

"I hope you will enjoy it; I am leaving."

"Oh, I am sorry."

"I am not," the girl replied. "Miss Sloe's had her knife into me for ages. When she gets like that there is nothing you can do about it."

Marigold felt a little shiver run over her. She was well aware that Nadine Sloe did not like her and had grudgingly given her a post simply because of Peter. She wondered almost apprehensively what the future held.

All the same, it was impossible for her to be downcast for more than a few minutes.

She hurried homewards as though her feet had wings, to remember only when she actually reached the Saracen's Head that both Anne and Sally would be out. She looked at her watch.

It was just eleven o'clock and they had not arranged to meet until lunchtime at a small, cheap café on the Embankment where they had their meals.

Marigold decided to telephone to Peter and tell him the good news. She went to the call-box at the end of the road, inserted her pennies, waited while the telephone rang and rang, but there was no answer. He must have gone up to the City to sell his illustrations.

On an impulse she dialled St. Anthony's Hospital. David had written to her nearly a week ago to say he was coming to London and that he would call and see them as soon as he could get away from the hospital, but he had not turned up.

Although Marigold had not minded his absence, she now longed for someone to talk to, someone to whom she could tell her good news.

She got through to the hospital and waited a long time before they finally put her through to David. When he spoke he sounded a little breathless as if he had been hurrying.

"Hullo!"

"Hullo, David, it is Marigold."

"Marigold! I never thought it might be you. How are you and what have you been doing? I have been hoping I should be able to come and see you this evening."

"Why haven't you been before?"

"I've been so frightfully busy. I had to settle in and we are short-handed at the moment. I've not been free any night until long after your bed-time, but I shall be free this evening. I want to hear everything—all that you have been doing."

"I have got a job!"

"Good for you. What is it?"

"A mannequin at Michael Sorrell's."

David whistled.

"You are aiming high, aren't you?"

"Only the best is good enough," Marigold laughed.

"Good pay?"

"Not so bad."

There was a moment's pause and then David said:

"Marigold, have you missed me?"

Marigold hesitated before she answered and then she decided to be kind to David for once.

"Yes, very much," she lied.

"That is wonderful! I have missed you terribly! I have been thinking about you every moment since you have been away."

"Well, we will see you this evening," Marigold said abruptly. "Good-bye, David."

She hardly waited for his reply before she put down the receiver. As she walked away from the telephone box she asked herself what was the point of encouraging David when she knew she was not really interested in him. She only rang him up because she wanted someone to talk to!

She walked on through the quiet, sunlit streets until she reached the river. There she put her arms on the parapet, looking at the water silver in the sunshine, the little boats and barges chugging up and down.

"This is London!" she thought. "And I have begun to find my feet, but I want so much—so much more! I want to get on. . . . I want to be successful. . . . I want to be somebody!"

She threw back her head and looked up at the blue sky.

"The sky's the limit!" she whispered, and laughed at herself.

She was in high spirits that evening when David arrived to see her. Peter had also come in to hear the result of his note and, as Sally said, the room was congested with people but at least it was cozy.

There were not enough chairs for so many so they put the cushions on the floor and sat on them.

"Tell me all about everything," David commanded.

Having been introduced to Peter he stared at him suspiciously as though he resented a stranger being friendly with the three girls he had known since childhood.

Marigold and Anne both wanted to talk at once, but Marigold won of course. She began her story, slightly exaggerating her interview with Nadine Sloe to make it sound exciting.

"Why didn't you tell me she is in love with you, Peter?"

"Because she is not!" Peter replied.

"Nonsense!" Marigold contradicted. "She would not have behaved like that unless she had been crazy about you. I expect she will do her best to get me thrown out so that she can tell you how awful I was!"

Peter looked cross.

"I have known Nadine for years," he said, "and if she is beastly to you I shall have a good deal to say about it."

"I am sure no one could be beastly to Marigold for long," Sally said gently, and David smiled at her as if she had anticipated the words he had been about to say.

"Now, I want to tell you about my job," Anne began.

They all listened intently while she described the Duchess and Halstead House. Only when they had laughed and exclaimed and teased her about her important connections did David turn to Sally and ask:

"And what about you, Sally?"

"That is what we want to hear," Marigold said. "Sally has been out all day. She missed her luncheon appointment with us, and only came in a moment before you arrived, so we have not had a chance to ask her what she has been doing. Come on, Sally, tell us! No more secrets!"

Sally, sitting on the floor on a cushion, looked up and smiled.

"It is not a secret," she said. "I, too, have got a job!"

Her two sisters gave an exclamation.

"Why didn't you tell us?" they said. "What is it? Go on, Sally, we can't wait to know!"

Sally began from the beginning. She told them all how she had wanted to look after children.

"I have always loved them," she said in her quiet, sweet voice. "Don't you remember how Daddy and I used to plan the sort of family I would have when I got married? Three boys and two girls I think was the number we had decided on just before he died.

"He always said I was good with children. Your father said so, too, David. He has often asked me to go with him to play with a child to whom he had to give an injection or something like that. So I felt that looking after children was the career I should choose, but it was not nearly as easy as I had anticipated."

She told them how she had tried the various day-nurseries only to be told that they were full up or she was not experienced enough.

Finally, she had gone to a well-known agency which catered especially for nurses and nursery governesses.

"It was all rather awe-inspiring," Sally laughed. "There were two old-fashioned nannies waiting there when I arrived. They looked at me so severely that I felt as though I was a child again and that at any moment they would tell me to tidy my hair and pull up my socks.

"There was an elderly, grey-haired woman like a thin spider seated at a desk who was dealing with everything and she disposed of the nannies quickly in what seemed to me to be a manner that would stand no nonsense.

"One was told to go off and interview a lady in Grosvenor Square immediately, the other was informed that a lady was waiting to see her in another room and that she was late! When my turn came, I was so frightened I felt that my voice had vanished altogether and only a little squeak came out when she asked my name.

" 'What do you want to do?' she asked.

"I told her that I wanted to be with children. She asked me all sorts of particulars about my home and my education; in fact, at any moment I expected to be told that I had to show my birthmarks, and then, while we were sitting talking, the door was thrown open. . . ."

Sally told them how she had been feeling as if all her confidence in herself was ebbing away and that her chances of getting a job through this particular agency were negligible when the outside door opened and a tall, agitated woman came rushing into the room.

She pushed Sally on one side and standing in front of

the desk she said in a high-pitched, almost hysterical voice:

"I've had enough, Mrs. Bellows!"

Mrs. Bellows, who had been writing down Sally's particulars, looked up in surprise.

"Oh, it's you, Miss Harris," she said, "and what is the matter now?"

"I tell you I've had enough," Miss Harris said, thumping her fist on the desk, and Sally saw that she was trembling and not far from tears. "I wanted to give in my notice last week," Miss Harris went on, "but you would not let me; you persuaded me to stay because the child's father was away in Paris.

"Well, I don't care if he is in Timbuctoo, Im going now, at once! The whole household is impossible— quite impossible. The nurse panders to the child and spoils her and then I am expected to deal with her. I can't go on, it is getting on my nerves.

"I have never been in such a place before and I do not intend to start. I've stayed on to oblige you, Mrs. Bellows, and now I'm going home to oblige myself, today, at once!"

Mrs. Bellows sighed.

"Very well, Miss Harris, if you feel like that you must do as you think fit. You will understand of course that by leaving without giving proper notice you will forfeit a week's wages."

"I would forfeit a year's rather than go back there!" Miss Harris said.

"I do not know whether Mr. Dunstan will give you a reference," Mrs. Bellows said. "If he does, I will post it on to you, Miss Harris. I have your home address."

"Thank you, Mrs. Bellows."

Miss Harris's voice was lower now. She seemed to sag and become deflated as if her anger in passing had left her empty and exhausted.

She hesitated a moment, touching her worn leather

handbag as if the sight of it had suddenly recalled something to her mind.

"I should be glad, Mrs. Bellows," she said, "if in a week or so you would look out for another situation for me. I cannot afford to be out of work indefinitely."

"I will see what I can do," Mrs. Bellows replied. "I had hoped that you would settle down in your present post, but if you find it impossible . . ."

"Impossible! Of course it is impossible!" Miss Harris said passionately. "Quite frankly, Mrs. Bellows, my nerves will not stand it. I cannot put up with rudeness and insolence all day long."

"Well, there it is," Mrs. Bellows said, "I will write to you, Miss Harris."

"Thank you."

Miss Harris turned and walked towards the door and suddenly Sally felt extremely sorry for her. She saw her for what she was—a tired undernourished woman whose nerves had got the better of her.

She looked shabby and down-at-heel and terribly pathetic. Sally wanted to run after her and say something kind and friendly, something that would give her courage, something that would take that expression of anxiety and unhappiness from her eyes.

But she was too shy to make the movement and in a moment Miss Harris had gone and the door had closed behind her.

Mrs. Bellows pressed a bell by her desk. The door on the other side of the room opened and a woman appeared.

"Bring me the Dunstan file, please, Miss Lane," Mrs. Bellows commanded and turned to Sally. "I'm afraid you will have to wait, Miss Granville."

"Of course," Sally said.

Miss Lane brought the file and Mrs. Bellows turned it over.

"Miss Harris has left," she said.

Miss Lane gave an exclamation.

"Gone? Already? That will be the sixth in three months!"

"Yes, I know," Mrs. Bellows said irritably, "and I cannot think whom we are going to send there now. Mr. Dunstan relies on me, as you know."

She turned over the papers, her brow furrowed.

"What about Miss Webster?" Miss Lane suggested.

Mrs. Bellows shook her head.

"No, she is suited. I had a letter from her this morning."

"Well, there's no one else at the moment," Miss Lane said. "Miss Tomlinson is ill. She rang up last night to say that the doctor will not let her take a place for at least six weeks."

"Dear, dear, how worrying!" Mrs. Bellows sighed. "I really do not know what to do."

It was then Sally spoke.

"Couldn't I take Miss Harris's place?"

Mrs. Bellows looked at her in a startled fashion while Miss Lane's mouth dropped open.

"Oh, I am afraid you are much too young," Mrs. Bellows answered.

"I gather the child is rather difficult," Sally went on, "Perhaps a young person would be more successful with her."

"Well, I don't know." Mrs. Bellows looked at Miss Lane.

"It—is an idea," Miss Lane said.

Mrs. Bellows looked back at the file.

"Well, Mr. Dunstan will be back from Paris at the end of the week, but in the meantime . . ." She stopped. ". . . no, I don't think it would work, Miss Granville; you see, this is a very difficult position—in fact, if I may say so, it is one of the most difficult we have ever had to cope with in this office."

Miss Lane nodded her head solemnly.

"That's a fact, Mrs. Bellows, quite the most difficult!"

"Well, then, you have everything to gain if I succeed," Sally said cheerfully, "and nothing to lose."

Mrs. Bellows looked at her again and a faint suspicion of a smile crossed her severe features.

"It certainly seems as if you might be the solution to the problem at the moment," she said. "With Miss Harris having walked out at a moment's notice and Mr. Dunstan in Paris . . . I promised him I would arrange for someone to be there with his little girl."

"How old is the child!" Sally asked.

"She is nearly ten, I think," Mrs. Bellows said.

"And a little horror!" Miss Lane interposed.

Mrs. Bellows looked at her sharply as if in rebuke.

"A little difficult, shall we say?" she corrected. "At least, her governesses seem to find her so, but she is Mr. Dunstan's only child and he dotes on her. Nothing is too good for her and it is very important that Mr. Dunstan should be pleased."

"Who is he?" Sally asked curiously.

Mrs. Bellows looked at her in surprise.

"Haven't you heard of him—the great financier, Robert Dunstan? His name is always in the papers!"

"No, I've never heard of him," Sally said, "but I suppose that money is no object."

Mrs. Bellows sighed.

"Not even money will buy the right governess for Elaine."

"Is that her name?" Sally asked.

"Yes, Elaine," Mrs. Bellows said, making it sound rather like an epitaph.

"Let me try to manage Elaine," Sally said. "If I fail I can only come back and apologise and ask you to find me something easier."

The telephone rang sharply at that moment in the

adjoining room. The clerk ran to answer it and came back wide-eyed.

"It's the old Nanny," she said. "She's in a terrible state."

"Put her through to me," said Mrs. Bellows.

Nanny apparently seemed to have plenty to say and it was some time before Mrs. Bellows could get a word in.

"Yes . . . yes . . . yes . . . I quite understand. . . . Yes, I am sending someone along right away . . . Yes, I can assure you you will find her very suitable. . . . Yes—I am very sorry about Miss Harris, but she is not very well. . . . Yes, Miss Granville—that is the name —is coming along now."

She raised her eyes in interrogation to Sally, who nodded her assent.

"Yes, at once. . . . Yes, I'm very sorry. Of course . . . I will telephone Mr. Dunstan as soon as he returns."

She put the receiver down.

"The Nanny is very upset about Miss Harris walking out like that. Can you really go along straight away?"

"Yes," said Sally, "but there is one thing I ought to have explained. I do not want to live in."

Mrs. Bellows turned the letters over in the file.

"Oh, I don't think that will matter. Miss Harris lived in but Miss Jackson didn't. It is not compulsory. The child's Nanny gets her up in the morning and puts her to bed. If you are there during lesson hours I am sure it will be all right."

"Very well," Sally said, "and what is the address?"

"Eight hundred and seven Park Lane," Mrs. Bellows said. "I do hope you will be able to put things right, Miss Granville."

She spoke as though she was not very optimistic that such an achievement was likely to be accomplished, but she held out her hand almost genially.

"Good-bye, Mrs. Bellows, and thank you," Sally said.

She felt like asking Mrs. Bellows to wish her luck but thought it would sound too frivolous, so she wished it to herself as she ran down the stairs into the busy street.

Eight hundred and seven Park Lane was a block of flats. A green-liveried porter escorted Sally to the lift and took her up to the top floor.

The door of Mr. Dunstan's flat was opened by a footman in livery. Sally explained who she was and she thought she saw a look of surprise and incredulity cross his countenance, but he led her with dignity across the hall and down the passage.

There he opened a door and announced:

"Miss Granville!"

Sally found herself in a large, light room which was furnished as a nursery. There were big windows overlooking the park and there were toys of every description round the walls.

Sally thought she had never seen such a large dolls' house or so many beautiful and expensively dressed dolls. There was a rocking-horse, too, and every sort of woolly animal, all in out-sizes and all looking as if no one ever cared to play with them.

A grey-haired woman, obviously a Nanny, was sitting in an armchair by the fireplace and a small girl with her back to the room was kneeling on the window-seat staring out of the window. Nanny rose from her chair.

"How do you do?" she said. "I presume you are Miss Granville from Mrs. Bellows."

"Yes," Sally said; "Mrs. Bellows asked me to come along at once."

"Well, I am so glad you could manage it," Nanny said. "It has given us all a turn, Miss Harris walking out like that. I can't get over it, I can't really! Just because she and Elaine had a few words at breakfast she packed her bags! It's not right, as I said to Mrs.

Bellows, it's not a right thing to do—and I shall tell Mr. Dunstan so when he returns."

"I don't think Miss Harris was very well," Sally said soothingly.

She glanced towards the child, who had not looked round from the window. Nanny looked in the same direction.

"Elaine, come and say 'how-do-you-do' to Miss Granville. Come along, dear, there's a good girl."

Elaine made no movement.

"Now, Elaine, don't be tiresome—come and say 'how-do-you-do'! She has got such pretty manners when she wants," she said in an aside to Sally.

Elaine still made no movement. Nanny got impatient.

"Come along, Elaine, it is lesson time and you know it! Now be a good girl and don't show Miss Granville how naughty you can be as soon as she arrives."

"I am not going to do any lessons," Elaine said, speaking slowly and distinctly.

The hard, high-pitched, childish voice seemed to Sally to echo down the ages. She had heard Marigold speak like that often enough when whe was upset or put out about something. She felt impatient with the old nurse for arguing with the child.

"Don't worry, Nanny," she said quietly, "I expect Elaine doesn't feel like lessons at the moment."

Nanny looked nonplussed.

"Well, Miss Granville, I expect you would like to manage her in your way," she said. "I will leave you together to make friends and I hope Elaine is going to be a very good girl." She spoke meaningly with a glance at the child, but there was no response. "If you should want me, Miss Granville, you have only to ring the bell and either the footman or one of the maids will fetch me."

"Thank you so much," Sally said.

Nanny went out closing the door behind her and

Sally sat down in a chair by the fireplace. There was a newspaper lying on the floor. She picked it up and started to look at it.

After some moments the small figure kneeling by the window turned round. She made a quick movement with her head, saw that Sally was still there and looked away again.

There was a long silence and then her curiosity was too much for her and she turned round. Sally went on reading the paper. Elaine made a movement as if to attract attention and then, as Sally took no notice, she turned round completely and stood staring at her.

"I do not want to do any lessons," she said.

There was defiance in her voice. Sally looked up.

"I am so sorry," she said. "What did you say?"

"I do not want to do any lessons," Elaine repeated.

"I don't blame you," Sally said sympathetically. "I don't want to teach you, either."

Elaine looked at her in astonishment.

"You do not want to teach me?" she said. "Then what are you here for?"

"Because I have got to do a job of work," Sally said. "You see, I want money. I get paid for being here."

There was no disguising Elaine's interest in this unusual course of conversation. She came away from the window-seat and walked across the room to stand beside Sally's chair.

"Haven't you any money?" she asked.

Sally shook her head.

"No," she said. "That is why my sisters and I have come to London—to look for jobs so that we can make some money."

"Do you want to be a governess?" Elaine asked.

Sally shook her head.

"No," she said. "I want to look after children in a nursery, but they would not have me so I have to come here instead—to see if I like it."

Elaine took a deep breath.

"To see if you like it?" she said. "Governesses usually leave here because I don't like them. I couldn't bear Miss Harris. She was stupid and frightened of me. She was frightened of everybody, even Nanny and Bates."

"Who is Bates?" Sally asked.

"Our butler," Elaine said. "He is an awful old man —he drinks Daddy's port when he is away."

Sally made no comment; instead, she sighed and said:

"I'm sorry for Miss Harris."

"I'm not!" Elaine said scornfully.

"I saw her just now," Sally went on. "She is poor and old and she looked rather ill. I wished I had lots of money, then I would have fed her, looked after her and given her nice things to wear. She would have been quite a different person then. Being poor makes people frightened, you know, frightened of not having a roof over their heads, frightened of people being unkind to them."

Elaine seemed to digest this information for a few moments and then she said:

"But you are not frightened."

"No. But then I am young and there are such lots of things I can do. Besides, I have not been poor for very long, you see; my Daddy used to look after me and it was not until he died that we had no money."

"Did you love him very much?" Elaine asked.

"Very much," Sally answered, and there was a little throb in her throat.

Elaine was silent for a moment and then she said in a very quiet voice:

"I loved my mother and she died . . . died nearly three years ago. Nobody ever talks about her here. Daddy never mentions her."

Quite suddenly Sally knew that this was the secret of

the child's naughtiness . . . pent-up misery, loneliness and yearning for her mother.

Before she could say anything, the look of tenderness on Elaine's face had vanished and was replaced by a hard sulkiness which Sally guessed was characteristic of her in these days.

She was a pretty child but lacking in colour and her mouth turned down at the corners.

"You are making me talk to you," she said. "I expect it is a trick to make me like you. All the governesses when they come try some sort of trick. I have told you I am not going to do any lessons."

"And I have told you," Sally said, "that I can understand why you do not want to do any. Do you know, I had a governess once. She taught my two sisters and me. She was very old and rather cross.

"One day my sister, Marigold, said she was not going to do any lessons any more, so my father sent the governess away and he taught us himself, but first of all he made us want to have lessons."

"Made you want to have lessons?" Elaine echoed curiously. "How did he do that?"

"Well, you see," Sally said, "when Marigold said she would not do any more lessons and the governess went away, he just did nothing about it. We were rather surprised; we thought he would make an awful fuss. The days went by and we did nothing and then one day he started to talk to us about India and he was just making what he was telling us very interesting when he said:

'I don't believe you know where India is.' And Anne —that is my eldest sister—said,

'Yes, I do!'

"Marigold was not certain and I did not know at all. Then he said,

'Before we go any further, you had better find out about it.'

"We went into his study and got some books and pictures about India and then he showed us on a globe where it was and we read about it and became very interested and then he finished his story. It was only when he had finished that he said,

'There, that is the first geography lesson I have given you.'

"We laughed because it had not been like a geography lesson at all.

"The next day we wanted to go shopping and he made us work out exactly what our expenditure was going to be and add it all up before we went, and he told us that it was our first lesson in arithmetic.

"As days went on, it became rather fun. If a letter came from abroad, we learned about the place it came from; if someone who called at the house happened to mention some special place in England or talked about some part of the world where there had been a war or something like that, we read all about it from books in my father's study."

"And didn't you do any proper lessons?" Elaine asked.

Sally shook her head.

"Not what you would call proper lessons," she said. "But we learnt a lot all the same. The only thing our father was ever really fussy about was our writing. He hated people who wrote badly, and when we had to write down a telephone message or send a letter to someone he insisted on it being beautifully written and spelt correctly. I have sometimes had to write a note four times before he was satisfied."

"I think it sounds fun," said Elaine. "I wish I could learn like that."

"But you can," Sally said. "You see, it is the only way I could possibly teach you."

Elaine looked at her incredulously and then she clapped her hands.

"Oh, this is quite different!" she said. "When do we start?"

"Well, I will tell you what we will do," Sally said. "Before I come in the morning, you look up in the newspapers and find anything you want to know about, whether it is a place or a person, or something like that, and then if there are not the proper books in the house we will go to the public library—I expect there is one near—and we will find out all about it. A sort of research."

"Oh, this is fun," said Elaine, and then she hesitated. "I don't think we ought to tell anyone, do you? They are sure to say it is all wrong and that you are not a proper governess."

"I am afraid they might," Sally said seriously. "The only thing is, you will have to try and learn quite a lot in that way, otherwise they will stop us and make you go back to the old-fashioned method with someone else."

"We will get round it somehow," Elaine said. "I like you and if they try to take you away I shall scream and scream. That will stop them."

"Yes, but it might stop my coming," Sally said. "I hate people who scream."

Elaine looked at her in sudden fear.

"Do you mean to say that you might not want to stay with me?"

"I have not decided yet. You must give me time. You see, you are the first person I have ever taught and I must make sure I can do it."

"But you can! I can learn . . . I can really!"

"All right, we'll try. Here is the newspaper. You look and see if there is anything you want to know about and if I can't teach you, well, I shall just have to go. You understand that, don't you?"

"You will be able to teach me," Elaine said. "I can do anything I want to do. Don't you understand?"

"It ought to be all right then," Sally assured her.

All the time it had not been too easy even after her initial conquest. Elaine was spoiled and very out of hand. She was rude to the servants, argued with her old Nanny, who had no control over her, and was in many ways a thoroughly unpleasant little girl.

When it was time for Sally to go home she had clutched her arm and whispered:

"You will promise you will come tomorrow, won't you?"

Sally nodded.

"Yes, I promise," she said.

"And you will come every day?" Elaine insisted.

"We will wait and see," Sally said.

She felt it would not hurt this young thing who had always had everything she wanted in her life to be apprehensive for a while, to be uncertain whether she was going to get what she wanted.

At the same time, she felt sorry for the child, left in that big, luxurious flat with only servants to care for her.

She told the others what had occurred lightly and humorously. They laughed and told her that she was extremely clever, but David looked at her appreciatively, having a greater understanding of what she had achieved than the others.

"Where did you learn your psychology, Sally?"

"From Daddy, of course. There was no one like him when it came to understanding people. He said everyone had a kink and the way to get along in the world was to recognise and be decent about each other's kinks."

The others laughed.

"I wonder what mine is?" Marigold said.

It was Peter, surprisingly, who answered her.

"You are greedy!" he said.

"Greedy?" Marigold sounded indignant.

71

"Yes," Peter replied. "You want to snatch things from life, to gobble it all up without waiting to see if it's digestible or not. That is the difference between you and Sally."

"I think you are being very unkind to me," Marigold said sharply.

She looked at David as if for championship. But for once he failed her; he was thinking of Sally's story with a little smile of appreciation on his lips.

Five

Elaine was waiting for Sally in the hall when she came up in the lift on the following Monday morning.

"My Daddy's here!" she cried excitedly. "He got back from Paris last night. He is terribly angry about Miss Harris . . . simply furious with her . . . but I told him that I would much rather have you and he is going to see you this morning."

Sally felt her heart sink.

She was not looking forward to meeting Mr. Robert Dunstan. She had heard so much about him during the last few days that she wondered now how she could ever have said to Mrs. Bellows that she did not know his name.

Apparently, he was the most formidable financial force the City of London had known for many years and he was also playing a big part in international economics, but every report that Peter or David brought to Sally to add to her knowledge of her employer merely confirmed her opinion that here was a man who knew a great deal about money but nothing about children.

The more she saw of Elaine's life in the luxurious Park Lane flat, the more she was horrified at the inadequate upbringing the child was receiving.

The servants might be attentive and reliable when Mr. Dunstan was about, but they were certainly slack and lazy when he was away. Elaine received her breakfast at all sorts of hours and food for luncheon was often ill-chosen and badly served.

Elaine's nurse was very old; in fact she confided to Sally that she was on the wrong side of seventy—"although it did not do one any good to let one's employers know it." She was therefore content to do as little as possible.

She loved Elaine, there was no doubt about that, even as she had loved her mother, to whom she had also been nurse; but she was too old for her job and too tired to make trouble with the servants when the nursery was neglected or forgotten.

"I am all for a quiet life," she said to Sally, nodding over her knitting. "There have been times, of course, when I have fought for my rights and for the rights of the children I have cared for, but these modern servants will not listen whatever you say and I have just ceased to trouble about them."

"That's all very well for you," Sally longed to say, "but what about Elaine?" But she knew it was no use making an enemy of Nanny and therefore decided to hold her tongue for the moment, but to tell Mr. Dunstan exactly what she thought of the whole household when she got the opportunity.

Bates, the butler, was another offender.

It was quite obvious to Sally that Elaine had been right when she said he drank her father's port.

He looked like a man who drank heavily and Sally found him mooching around the flat without a coat and usually unshaven; but from the surly way in which he greeted her she was certain he could not imagine her as a potential danger to his position.

Mr. Dunstan also kept a housemaid, a young and rather frivolous creature who spent her time giggling with Thomas the footman, and the cook, who was a fat, good-natured soul, but whose Irish temperament prevented her from ever considering that punctuality and cleanliness were essential parts of domestic service.

Elaine spent a good deal of her time in the kitchen gossiping with the cook and culling from her all the titbits of scandal about the other servants.

"Cook says that Nellie is no better than she ought to be," Elaine informed Sally one morning when she arrived. "What does she mean by that?"

Nellie was the housemaid, and while Sally privately agreed with Cook she felt that this sort of thing should not be a part of Elaine's education.

After a very few days she had a whole list of things which she wished to discuss with Mr. Dunstan on Elaine's behalf, but she was wise enough in the ways of men to realise it would do no good if she rushed at him baldheaded when she first met him.

She must get to know him and let him realise that she had Elaine's well-being at heart before she attempted reforms.

Despite all reports of his devotion to Elaine she thought the man must be rather a fool to leave a growing child to the mercy of servants. She questioned Elaine about her relatives.

"Have you any aunts or uncles?" she asked.

Elaine had shaken her head.

"Daddy was an only child," she said.

"And your mother?" Sally asked gently. "Had she any brothers or sisters?"

Elaine looked startled as she always did when her mother was mentioned. For a moment she did not reply, then she answered:

"I have never asked Daddy. I wish I knew, but he will never talk about her."

"Poor child!" Sally thought.

Impulsively, for the first time, she put her arms

round Elaine's shoulders and kissed her cheek. She felt a tremor run through her slim body, then suddenly Elaine flung her arms round her neck.

"I do love you, Miss Granville. I never let any of my other governesses kiss me; nasty wrinkled old things, it would have made me feel sick! But I love you, you are so pretty and soft!"

Sally laughed but at the same time she felt near to tears. This poor motherless child was all at sea with her emotions with no one to guide her.

After that Elaine got into the way of kissing Sally when she arrived and when she left in the evening, but this morning she was so excited that she had forgotten everything but the news of her father's return.

"Daddy came back in an aeroplane!" she chattered. "There were lots of important people on board. He told me all about them when he arrived, but now I can't remember their names."

"Try to remember," Sally said, "there may be something we want to learn about."

"Oh dear, how silly I am!" Elaine exclaimed. "I wish I had written it down, but I will ask Daddy later today."

On the table in the nursery was a large doll. It was a French doll, beautifully dressed, with every sort of accessory such as a handbag, hot-water bottle, a muff and even a tiny pair of glasses.

"What a lovely doll!" Sally exclaimed.

"Do you like it?" Elaine asked. "Daddy brought it for me from Paris, but I don't think I like dolls any more. They are awfully dull!"

Sally looked up at Elaine and understood. The child was ten—far too old for dolls. That was another thing Mr. Dunstan did not understand about his daughter— that she was growing up. She looked round the nursery with its panorama of magnificent and expensive toys.

"Do you know, Elaine," she said after a moment, "I

think you are too old for dolls. I think it would be a lovely idea if you sent all your toys to a children's hospital and then we could stop calling this the nursery. It could be the schoolroom and you could have a desk of your own to keep your own things in.

"A proper grown-up desk, not the school sort. And we could have some book-shelves put up and could gradually collect the books you like best, so you would have a library all your own."

"Oh, Miss Granville, what a lovely idea! I will tell Daddy at once, shall I?"

"Not perhaps at once," Sally said quietly. "It would be unkind after he has brought you that lovely doll from Paris, but we might gradually put the idea into his head that you are getting a big girl and too old for toys."

"But I want to tell him now, at once!" Elaine said impatiently.

"And hurt his feelings about the doll?" Sally asked, raising her eyebrows.

Elaine hesitated for a moment. Sally knew that it was the result of her teaching that the child should hesitate at all.

"All right," she said ungraciously after a moment, "but how long must I wait? Until tomorrow?"

"Shall we say the day after?" Sally said, deciding not to make the conditions too impossible.

Elaine brightened.

"That will be Wednesday, won't it?" she asked. "Very well, I will wait until Wednesday, but it will be terribly difficult!"

At that moment the door opened and Thomas stood there.

"Mr. Dunstan would like to see you, miss."

"Shall I come too?" Elaine asked.

Sally shook her head.

"No, Elaine, you had better wait until I come back.

What about looking through the newspaper and choosing something for us to find out about this morning? Unless you can remember the names of the people who were in that aeroplane?"

"I will think of the names," Elaine decided; "I will think terribly hard, but don't be long."

"I will try not to be," Sally said with a smile, and she followed Thomas to Mr. Dunstan's study on the other side of the flat.

It was a big room lined with books, rather dark and austere. Sally had been shown it by Elaine and had wondered then if it betrayed the personality of its owner. Now she felt it did.

Robert Dunstan advanced across the room to shake her by the hand, but she had a feeling it was an effort at politeness and that he would have preferred to interview her from his desk as if she were a clerk in his office.

He was tall, square-shouldered and heavily built, but Sally's first impression was that he was younger than she had expected. He looked grave and clever and she had a feeling as she looked at his face that it would be an effort for him to smile.

Some people might have thought him good-looking, but to Sally he was rather awe-inspiring and she felt that he somehow typified in the flesh the heavy and ponderous things she had heard about him.

"Good morning, Miss Granville," Robert Dunstan said in a deep voice which had a ring of authority about it. "Won't you sit down?"

He indicated a chair beside the fireplace and she obeyed him, feeling suddenly extremely young and inexperienced.

"I understand," Robert Dunstan went on, "that you were kind enough to come here at a moment's notice and take the place of Miss Harris, who behaved, I regret to say, extremely badly in leaving as she did."

Sally suddenly remembered the reference that Miss

77

Harris would want from Robert Dunstan and impulsively, without pausing to think of her words, she said:

"I was very sorry for Miss Harris, Mr. Dunstan. I saw her at Mrs. Bellow's—she looked ill, in a bad state of nerves. I hope that you will not let her leaving here prejudice her in the future in getting another job."

Robert Dunstan raised his eyebrows.

"You can hardly expect me to be pleased that she should walk out and leave my child alone."

"Hardly alone," Sally suggested. "Elaine had Nanny to look after her and I am afraid it was Elaine's fault the Miss Harris left as she did."

"Elaine's fault?" Mr. Dunstan asked the words sharply.

"Yes, Elaine's fault," Sally repeated. "She was very rude to her. The woman was not well and I gather that they had had continual rows and arguments for weeks. It got on Miss Harris's nerves. She was on the point of collapse when she ran away."

Robert Dunstan drew his brows together and the expression on his face was formidable.

Sally wished that this argument had not arisen, but at the same time she could see so vividly the thin, pathetic look about Miss Harris as she turned away from Mrs. Bellows's desk, the worn handbag, trembling hands, the out-of-date and shabby clothes.

It was not fair, Sally thought, that she should have to suffer for the rest of her life because she had been unable to handle a child like Elaine. It was not her fault that the child was spoilt.

There was a moment's silence and then at last Mr. Dunstan looked at Sally and said:

"Well, I have not really asked you here, Miss Granville, to talk about Miss Harris but about Elaine. I understand you have been able to get on with her very well. She certainly speaks enthusiastically about you."

"I am glad about that," Sally said, "but you do realise, Mr. Dunstan, that she is extremely out of hand and very spoilt?"

Sally had not meant to speak so forcibly, but somehow Mr. Dunstan was annoying her.

"He has so much," she thought, "money, position, big reputation—and Miss Harris has so little."

And yet he was prepared to crush that poor, pathetic little woman simply and solely because she had not fallen in with his ideas, had not managed to please him and control his spoilt child.

She had certainly managed to surprise and startle Robert Dunstan. He stared at her for a moment and then he said slowly, as if deliberately choosing his words:

"You are certainly unusually frank, Miss Granville."

"Unfortunately, I am speaking the truth," Sally replied.

"Inferring, I presume," Mr. Dunstan said, "that most people in the same position as yourself do not tell me the truth."

"You alone can decide that, Mr. Dunstan," Sally replied.

Robert Dunstan's lips twisted as if in a faint smile, then he sat down on the opposite side of the fireplace.

"Well, Miss Granville," he said, "suppose we talk this thing out. You have accepted the position of my daughter's governess and after a few days' acquaintance you inform me that she is spoilt and out of hand. Am I to gather from that, that you are suggesting a far stricter regime for Elaine?"

Sally shook her head

"Not stricter, but more sensible."

"What experience have you had, Miss Granville?"

Sally flushed.

"I have never been a governesses before, but I have had a certain experience of children . . . and people."

79

"You are very young," Robert Dunstan said pointedly.

"The elderly governess you have engaged in the past do not seem to have managed Elaine."

She did not mean to make her words sound like a retort, but when they were said she realised that she was fencing with this man, fencing superficially with words, while conscious of a strong emotional undercurrent to their conversation.

Abruptly, Robert Dunstan got to his feet and walked over to the window. Sally, looking at his back, thought:

"He doesn't like me. If he could he would sack me, but he daren't because he is afraid of Elaine."

Robert Dunstan stood at the window and then walked back across the room. Suddenly he looked at his watch.

"I am interested in what you have to say, Miss Granville," he said, "but unfortunately, I have an appointment in the City. I would like to talk this matter over further, but for the moment it must wait."

Sally rose from her chair.

"I understand," she said. "In the meantime I suppose you wish me to continue to teach Elaine as I think best?"

"Of course," Robert Dunstan said. "Of course. But now . . . if you will excuse me . . ."

He moved towards the door, holding it open for her to pass through, and then, following her into the hall, picked up his hat and rang for the lift. Sally had the idea he was glad to escape, glad that the interview with her was at an end.

"What a strange man he is!" she thought. "I should have imagined that he would have liked the truth."

She went back to the nursery and found Elaine waiting for her excitedly.

"I have remembered a name," she cried. "One of

them was the King of Arabia—at least I think that was what Daddy said."

"Oh, good!" Sally smiled. "It will be exciting to read about him. He is a very important person."

"How did you get on with Daddy?" Elaine asked, and added as Sally hesitated before replying: "You were an awfully long time. What were you talking about? My other governesses used just to go in and say 'yes' to everything that Daddy said to them and it was all over in a few minutes. They were far too frightened to say anything else. I used to listen at the door and they never said anything but 'yes'."

"You shouldn't listen at doors," Sally rebuked. "I am surprised at you, Elaine!"

"Well, I didn't listen today," Elaine said plaintively, "because I knew you wouldn't like it. I hope you have told Daddy I'm improving—I am, aren't I?"

"Yes—a little," Sally admitted.

She wondered whether Robert Dunstan would ask to see her again, but he had not returned to the flat when she left at six o'clock.

She had arranged to meet Marigold at the bus stop by Curzon Street and she hurried there thinking she would be late, only to find she had nearly a quarter of an hour to wait before Marigold arrived.

"I am sorry, darling," Marigold cried.

She came rushing up looking radiantly lovely in a new dress—a model of Michael Sorrell's she had been allowed to buy cheap as it had got slightly damaged in the work-room.

She linked her arm through Sally's and started talking quickly in a low voice.

"It has been so exciting today! I've such lots to tell you. Michael Sorrell came in when I was modelling one of his evening gowns and raved—yes, really raved—about my hair. I had seen him before, of course, but he had never spoken to me. It was awfully funny because

81

Nadine Sloe was there and she was simply furious! I'm certain she hates me. Michael Sorrell said to me,

'What is your name?'

'Marigold,' I told him.

"The mannequins are all called by their Christian names, you know.

'Your hair is the most wonderful colour I have ever seen!' he exclaimed. 'I will design a special dress for it in the next collection.'

'Marigold may not be here then,' Nadine Sloe said in a nasty voice as though she was hoping I would fall downstairs and break my neck.

'Not here?' Michael Sorrell exclaimed, flinging up his hands—he is frightfully theatrical.

'She has had no experience,' Nadine Sloe drawled, 'and Madame Marie is not certain if we can keep her.'

'Of course we can keep her,' Michael Sorrell said. 'You want to stay, don't you?'

"I smiled at him.

'I am simply longing to stay,' I answered. 'I love being here and I think you are wonderful, Mr. Sorrell.'

"Michael Sorrell purred with pleasure but Nadine Sloe just looked at me—if looks could kill, I would have fallen dead there and then! There was nothing she could say, but I quite expect to find arsenic in my tea one afternoon."

Sally gave a little cry.

"You don't think she would really hurt you?"

"Oh no," Marigold said. "Not really. But she hates me. She must be frightfully in love with Peter—I wish he would tell me about her."

"Does she ever speak about him to you?"

"No, she never speaks at all if she can help it. She just walks by as if I were a bad smell under her nose. The girls say she is often like that if she doesn't like anyone. It is all rather like being at school. If you get a pat from the headmistress you are one up on the rest of the class!"

The sisters laughed and at that moment their bus arrived. They got a seat right up in the front and continued their conversation.

"I cannot help feeling," Marigold said, "that Peter is a bit of a mystery. So is Nadine Sloe if it comes to that. I have asked several of the girls where she comes from and what they know about her, but they know nothing. She can't be more than thirty and yet she has an extremely responsible job. Michael Sorrell only does the designing—he has no idea of running the business and according to reports knows nothing whatever about finance."

"Perhaps you are only imagining that Miss Sloe dislikes you," Sally said.

"There's no imagination about it," Marigold answered. "She is longing to get rid of me and will do it on the first possible excuse. Anyway, I have got an ally now—the great Mr. Sorrell himself, and if there is any trouble I shall go straight to him."

Sally smiled at the defiant note in Marigold's voice, but her eyes were troubled.

Somehow all through her life Marigold had been a disturbing factor—there were always dramas, excitements and very often unpleasantness when Marigold was about.

There was no doubt that a lot if it was due to jealousy. Marigold was lovely and she had a knack of attracting men—there could be no question about that. But women could be dangerous enemies and Sally was worried about Nadine Sloe.

To change the subject she asked:

"When did David say he was coming to see us again?"

"Tonight," Marigold answered. "As a matter of fact I had promised to dine with him, but Peter has asked me to try a new restaurant he has discovered, so I shall chuck David. You and Anne can have dinner with him instead."

"He will not like that," Sally said quickly. "Oh, Marigold, won't you be a bit kinder to David?"

"What is the point?" Marigold asked. "I find him a bore, and I didn't come to London to go out with a boy from my home town. I want to meet real people—rich people, people who live in Mayfair—not a lot of impoverished doctors and artists!"

"I think people are much the same wherever they live," Sally said.

"How do you know?" Marigold asked. "You have never met anybody really important." She stopped. "Or have you?" she added. "Have you seen the great Mr. Dunstan yet?"

"This morning," Sally answered, and told Marigold about her interview.

"He sounds marvellous," Marigold enthused! "Oh, Sally, could I come to the flat one day and meet him? He might fall in love with me and settle all our problems. I would soon get rid of all those horrible servants."

"He is not a bit likely to fall in love with you," Sally replied. "He is only interested in finance. If you were a gold mine, or a Government issue, it might be different."

"How do you know?" Marigold asked. "Men are all the same where women are concerned. It is just an opportunity of meeting the rich ones that I want. Be a sport, Sally."

"Don't be silly, I only met him myself for the first time this morning, and our relations could hardly be called cordial."

"Well, I'm going to meet him one day," Marigold said. "Don't forget!"

"You will be very disappointed," Sally warned her, but Marigold was not listening.

"Oh, for money!" she sighed. "If you could see the dresses at Michael Sorrell's and the furs! Some of their winter consignment arrived today. The foxes and the sables were simply wonderful; I only wish you could see them—they just make my mouth water. I must be rich, I must have lovely things, and before I am much older!"

Sally did not answer. She was thinking at that moment that if she had any money the only thing she would ask would be to be back in Cornwall.

It was hot and stuffy in the bus, and in the streets the people hurrying home from work were looking tired and exhausted. Sally felt stifled.

She wanted the clean, fresh wind in her face; she wanted to smell the fragrance of the earth warm in the sunshine and the salty tang of the sea; she wanted to feel free and untrammelled.

Far away in the past she remembered standing with her father on the edge of the cliffs and looking down at the great waves breaking on the shore. There had been a storm the night before and the waves were galloping in, thundering in their violence against the rocks.

The wind, billowing around Sally, tossed her hair high above her head. There was something thrilling and exhilarating about it and she turned with a laugh to her father and slipped her arm through his.

He smiled at her and then threw back his head, looking up at the heavy, clouded sky and again down at the tumbling green and silver waves.

"Monarchs of all we survey," he quoted, and added, "Would you change this moment for all the riches in the world?"

Sally could hear his voice now. Yes, that had been a moment when she had possessed so much.

Marigold was still talking.

"I wish you would see the wedding dress," she said. "It is made of white tulle and caught with tiny bunches of orange blossom. It is lovely, Sally, and I do hope they will let me model it, but Madame Marie seems afraid of Nadine Sloe."

The bus stopped at the Chelsea Town Hall and the girls got out and turned down a quiet tree-bordered street.

"I wonder if Anne will be home yet," Sally said.

"She is lucky," Marigold answered. "She has a chance of meeting decent people with the Duchess."

"The Duchess's friends are too old for Anne," Sally replied.

"One never knows," Marigold said darkly.

There was an expression of envy on her face which frightened Sally. Quite suddenly she stopped.

"Marigold," she said intensely, "don't grow away from us. Don't want too many other things and too many other people besides us."

Marigold looked at her in surprise.

"Why, Sally, what do you mean?"

Sally had already begun to walk on.

"I'm just being silly, Marigold," she said, "but sometimes you seem to want to leave us behind you.

Six

Anne met the Duke of Cheyn and was illogically but understandably disappointed.

At heart Anne was an incurable romantic. She was quieter than either of her sisters and so reserved about things which concerned herself intimately that it was easy on first acquaintance with Anne to believe her the traditional brainless beauty.

This was untrue, however, for she was actually much cleverer at learning than either of her sisters; only unfortunately she had not been blessed with Marigold's flare for putting herself over or that warm-hearted friendliness which enabled Sally to make friends wherever she went.

Anne, calm and sweet as a quiet stream among the meadows, drifted through the years, spending a great deal of her time in dreaming dreams.

All her dreams were romantic but at times they seemed so real to Anne that she lived as it were in a world of her own which had no relationship to reality.

She had long ago planned the type of life she wanted for herself, and her wish to marry a Duke, uttered laughingly, nevertheless expressed the fundamental yearning within herself for the romantic world of her imaginations.

Arthur Granville had devoted most of his life to a research of Cornish history and Cornish customs, but the fact that these were connected with the history of many countries and of many different eras made his library at the Vicarage an extremely extensive one.

The girls were allowed to read what they wished in their very earliest years and Anne soon found a liking for the romances which flourished at the courts of the French kings and the drama and passion which coloured Spanish history.

Steeped in the past, it was not surprising that for her own future she craved for herself a position where she would have respect, peace and security.

In contrast to the books she enjoyed from her father's library she found modern novels almost frightening because they portrayed cheap, uncertain and tawdry emotions.

A love affair squeezed between a cocktail party and a night club or conducted casually with slangy familiarity filled Anne with horror.

There was no grace, no beauty, it seemed to her, in a world where men looked on their women as companionable fellows and thought of kisses as an easy way of greeting acquaintances.

Anne dreamed of love affairs conducted with grace and dignity and with all the magic of a traditional setting—moonlight on the terrace, while behind her in a great house men and women, beautifully dressed, glided beneath candle-lit chandeliers, and a violin, exquisitely played, throbbed a prelude to words of love.

That was the background while Anne held out her hands in surrender to a man who had courted her with an ardour which held no familiarity about it and who laid his heart at her feet humbly and with the conviction that in her he had found his ideal woman.

In her imagination Anne thought herself the chatelaine of a great and splendid mansion and waited on by old retainers who would give her the respect which their families had given her predecessors for hundreds of years.

There in perfect happiness she would live and be loved by a man whom she could honour and respect, and she would bring up her children amid the peace and beauty of the English countryside far removed from the ugliness of commercial cities and the striving and scratching of people who wanted only money and the cheaper forms of entertainment.

That was what love meant to so many, Anne thought, an entertainment.

For her it would be the blooming of her whole character and of her whole personality, a surrender of herself only that she might give and go on giving to someone worthy of her love.

It was not surprising therefore that, when Anne found herself through a chance advertisement the companion of a duchess, she should dream that here was her opportunity to meet a man whose background at any rate was all that she had been seeking.

But first of all she was to learn with somewhat of a

shock that it was no longer possible to keep up the fine estates which childishly she had imagined, whatever the economic troubles of the world, must always be in the possession of a duke.

It was the Duchess who disillusioned her when, after a week in her service, the household bills were brought at the end of the month to be checked over and paid. The Duchess, sitting up in bed, the blue-white diamonds glittering on her yellow hands, turned them over muttering:

"Disgraceful! Disgraceful!"

"What is?" Anne asked.

"These bills," the Duchess replied; "look what has been spent this month! It is not Cook's fault, we have got to live; but just look what they are charging for vegetables. Why, before the war our account came to half that for three months!"

Anne was interested and not a little astonished to find how much the Duchess knew about the cost of living, but this was only a part of her complaints against life today.

"Look at the wages!" she exclaimed as Anne presented her with a list and a cheque made out for her signature.

"When I first married," she went on, "housemaids used to be glad to come to us for eight pounds a year. We had our choice of half the girls in the county, and if one was not satisfactory there were always half a dozen others begging for the favour of serving us. Eight pounds a year! Now, a little chit of fourteen just leaving school expects at least five pounds a week. I don't know what the world is coming to!"

At first Anne imagined that the Duchess was being mean in her close attention to the accounts and wages, but she soon learned that taxation was slowly grinding such families out of existence.

With something like dismay she heard that Cheyn

Hall, the seat of the Dukes of Cheyn for five centuries, was shut up.

"We cannot afford to live there," the Duchess said bitterly, and added: "In fact, we can't really afford to live at all. We ought to sell this house, and my children will as soon as I am dead. As it is, my son-in-law pays the rent. Thank goodness one of my daughters had the sense to marry into trade. He is a brewer and I wish we had a few more like him in the family."

"And the Duke—where does he live?" Anne ventured to ask.

She had heard the Duchess talk of her eldest son but she had not yet seen him.

"Oh, Stebby! He has a flat in Westminster—it is small, poky and unpleasant, but Stebby finds it convenient and he is not in London much. By the way, he will be here tomorrow. He is coming to tea with me. You had better tell Cook. She always makes him some special scones."

Anne felt excited.

"I think the Duke is the only one of the family I have not seen," she said. "There is Lady Elizabeth, Lady Catherine and Lord Henry. That is all isn't it?"

"Yes, they are the only ones alive," the Duchess said; "my third baby was born dead, Adrian and his wife were killed in a motor accident ten years ago, and John, the youngest, was thrown from his pony when he was a little boy. Goodness me, how times flies! If John had lived he would have been forty this year. It seems strange to think of it."

"And how old is the Duke?" Anne asked.

"Forty-nine," the Duchess answered. "He is getting an old man. I tell him so whenever I see him, but he doesn't care. Poor Stebby, we never thought he would grow old."

The Duchess sighed, and although Anne was longing to ask further questions she felt they would sound impertinent. She could only possess her soul in patience until the following day, but then, when she saw the Duke, she understood.

He had arrived during the afternoon when she had gone to the Library to change the Duchess's books.

When she got back she heard voices in the sitting-room and knew he must have arrived.

In the afternoon the Duchess was usually carried from her bed to a *chaise longue* by the window. Here she could get the sunshine and watch the people and the traffic passing in the square.

When she had visitors, tea was laid on a small side table and it was Anne's duty to pour out the tea from the big crested silver pot and hand round the food.

Now, before she entered the room, Anne gave one fleeting glance at herself in the old gilt-edged mirror which hung on the landing.

The glass was ancient and distorted her face a little, but it could not dim the shining gold of her hair or the light in her eyes.

There was a smile on Anne's lips as she entered the room.

"Oh, here you are, Miss Granville," the Duchess said sharply. "We have been waiting for you to pour out."

"I am sorry if I am late," Anne answered quietly, "but the traffic in Piccadilly is very bad and I had to wait for a bus."

As she moved across the room she could see that someone was sitting beside the Duchess in the high wing-backed chair.

"Stebby, this is Miss Granville," the Duchess said. "She has been putting up with me for the past three weeks. Miss Granville—my son."

For a second Anne wondered why he did not get up; then she understood. She saw the twisted legs, the crutches and the thin face etched with lines of pain.

It was after the Duke had gone that she heard how

he had contracted infantile paralysis in the trenches early in 1918. The doctors had saved his life but that was all they had saved.

A helpless invalid, he could drag himself about with the help of crutches, wheel-chairs and attendants, but as a man his life was over.

It was later that Anne was to realise that inside that tortured, ungainly body was a brilliant mind and a man who had evolved a sustaining, sound philosophy to comfort and help him.

At the moment she was only concerned with the wreck of what had been at one time a fine, good-looking young man and the disappointment within her own heart.

It was ridiculous, of course, and yet who can help the dreams they dream in secret—or the hope of happiness which lies within each human breast?

"Can nothing be done?" she asked the Duchess passionately.

"We have done everything it was possible to do," the Duchess replied, and added, "Sometimes, when I see Stebby in such pain I think perhaps it would have been better if he had died."

Anne felt the tears prick her eyes.

"He was such a beautiful little boy," the Duchess went on quietly. "My husband and I wanted a son so much. I can remember now lying in bed at Cheyn and hearing the village bells ringing across the park.

"We have a great feast for the tenants too—fireworks—sports. Stebby was shown to them and they cheered him and talked of the days when he would inherit the estate and his sons after him.

"Oh well, those days are over. Now there is nothing to inherit—at least, little enough. Half the estate had to be sold to pay death duties and when Stebby dies only the house will be left for Henry."

"Has Lord Henry got a son?" Anne asked.

"Six daughters!" the Duchess replied, then she said brusquely, "Let me have my library books, Miss Granville, and I hope you have got something I like this time."

Anne knew the Duchess would talk no more. She loved to make her gossip of the family and usually she was willing enough.

The house, traditions and all that went with it were the whole of the Duchess's life and Anne knew that she clung to them passionately because now she had so little else to interest her.

The passing years had taken her friends one by one; her children had grown up and had their own families; income tax had shorn her of so much of what she had once thought essential to existence and now she was an old, old woman with nothing but her memories.

"Is there anything else I can do for you?" Anne asked, thinking that the Duchess looked exhausted and very frail.

"Nothing, thank you, dear," the Duchess replied.

Anne took her leave and went home, walking across the Green Park to Victoria as it was easier that way to get a bus at the rush hour. And as she walked she thought of the Duke.

He had talked interestingly at tea, but more than once she had thought she noticed an expression of pain on his face and when he had come to leave and she had watched him drag his wasted, useless legs across the floor, she had known a sudden revolt within herself against the cruelty and unnecessary suffering there is to be found in life.

Why couldn't things be as she had so often imagined them—beautiful and gracious? Why must disease and the bestialities of war torture mankind and destroy minds and bodies, peace and happiness?

"You are very serious," Sally said when Anne had been home for nearly a quarter of an hour and had sat listening to Marigold and Sally chattering but made no contribution to the conversation.

She wanted to tell them what had occurred, but somehow the words died in her throat and thinking it over she knew that all her life she had tried to run away from anything unpleasant.

She had even been reluctant to visit the elderly people in the parish because she hated to learn of their ailments or to see the poverty of their homes.

Suddenly she got up and crossed to the window, looking out over the rooftops.

"What is the matter with me?" Anne asked herself. "I do not crave money like Marigold, but I am afraid of things that are sordid and ugly."

She stood there and suddenly felt Sally's arm round her shoulder and Sally's soft voice in her ear.

"What is the matter, darling, has something upset you?"

Marigold left the room at that moment to fetch something from downstairs and Anne was able to confide in Sally. Badly, without elaboration, she told her about the Duke.

"Poor, poor man," Sally exclaimed, "how terrible for him—terrible, too, for his mother! Perhaps you will be able to help him, darling."

Anne moved restlessly.

"How?" she asked. "Besides, to be honest, I don't want to. It is awful of me, Sally, but I am not like you. I don't like people who are ill. Don't tell me it is wrong, because I am ashamed of myself; but that is the truth. I want a world where everybody is healthy and well, happy and contented."

Sally laughed.

"Darling, that would not be a world, that would be Heaven, but as we cannot have that we just have to do our best. Do you remember how Daddy used to say, 'You will never be perfect but you can try to be'?"

"It was different for Daddy," Anne said impatiently. "He was not like us—everything looked wonderful to him and he found goodness and beauty everywhere, even in the most impossible places."

"Yes, I know," Sally sighed. "I wish we were like him."

"You are," Anne said and turned to kiss Sally's cheek. "Don't worry about me, poppet, I shall never get what I want but I can still go on hoping."

Sally said nothing but her arm tightened round Anne's shoulder; then the door opened and they moved apart. It was Marigold who had returned, carrying a jug of milk in her hand and followed by Peter.

"Look who I found on the doorstep," she said gaily, "and he has asked me out to dinner. I've accepted with alacrity; I am sick to death of lentil cutlets, which is all we ever get at our restaurant. Wait while I get my hat."

She vanished through the curtains which divided the room. Sally turned round to greet Peter, then eyed him speculatively. He looked different somehow.

For a moment she could not think why and then she realised that instead of the usual corduroy trousers and pull-on sweater he was wearing a conventional and well-cut grey flannel suit and a collar and tie.

"You're all dressed up!" she exclaimed.

Peter smiled.

"Is that a compliment?"

Sally nodded.

"You look different, and I like it. I had no idea you were so good-looking!"

"Your words compensate me even for the discomfort of a tight collar," Peter laughed.

"It is true," Sally thought, "he does look different and far nicer."

She had always rather disliked the sloppy clothes he wore; they might be artistic but to her mind they looked queer on him as though they were deliberately affected and not his natural choice.

He was tall and broad-shouldered and there was something quite distinguished about him now that he was dressed conventionally.

Marigold came back through the curtains. She had perched on her head an absurd little hat made of white daisies, and she looked entrancingly lovely.

"Come on, Peter, let us go somewhere exciting! Are you feeling rich?"

"Rich enough to give you a good dinner," he replied.

"That's wonderful!"

They said good-bye to Sally and Anne and hurried down the dark stairs and out into the evening sunshine. Marigold was just turning down the street when Peter touched her arm.

"I have brought a car."

"A car? I didn't know you had one."

"It has been laid up."

It was a long, low, streamlined car and Marigold eyed it appreciatively.

"Fancy your not having produced this before," she said, "when we have all been struggling about in buses. Why have you kept it such a secret?"

"For reasons of my own," Peter said, but he smiled —which took the sting from his words.

Marigold shrugged her shoulders.

"Oh, well, if you want to be mysterious. . . . Where are we going?"

"The Berkeley Grill."

Marigold's eyes widened. She said nothing.

They had a good dinner and Peter made every effort to amuse her. Marigold was amused; she liked, too, the comfort of the restaurant, the attentive waiters and the knowledge that both her own appearence and that of her escort were entirely satisfactory.

When they came out into the street it was twilight.

They got into the car and without a word Peter drove swiftly through the emptying street and on to one of the great by-passes leading out of the City.

"Where are we going?" Marigold said after they had been travelling for nearly twenty minutes.

"To somewhere quiet," Peter answered. "I want to talk to you."

It was some time before he drew up the car. They were on top of a hill, and a valley, wooded and dissected by a small stream, lay beneath them.

The moon was rising, but in the soft summer dusk they could still see each other and the countryside.

Peter got out, opened the hood of the car and then climbed back into the car again. It was very quiet; there was only the chirp of the crickets and the soft rustle of dead leaves under the trees as a light wind moved them.

Neither of them spoke for a little while until at last Marigold broke the silence.

"Why have you brought me here?"

"To talk to you."

"What about?"

"Ourselves."

Marigold made a little gesture with her hands and then on an impulse pulled the little white hat from her head and tossed it on to the seat behind.

"What is the point?" she asked.

Peter slid his arm along the seat behind her shoulders.

"Look at me, Marigold," he commanded.

She made a slight move as if she would obey him, but then turned her head away.

"No, Peter! No!"

"You are afraid!"

She laughed a little nervously.

"Let us go back; I have enjoyed my drive, but I have got to get up early tomorrow morning so I want to go to bed early. Turn round Peter."

He shook his head.

"Not until you have heard what I am going to say."

It seemed as if a sudden panic shook Marigold.

"No, Peter, don't say it! I don't want to hear it!"

"So you know what I am going to say?"

"I can guess."

Quite suddenly he moved and taking both her hands in his held them firmly.

"Listen, Marigold, I love you—I love you with all my heart and soul and I believe that you love me."

Marigold tugged at her hands striving to free them.

"No, it isn't true! Let me go, Peter!"

"I won't!" he said grimly. "I won't ever let you go—I am going to marry you, Marigold."

"You are absurd!"

There was no scorn in Marigold's voice, only a cry, almost one of pleading.

"I am not absurd and you know it," Peter answered. "I love you and I am almost certain that you love me too."

"I don't—I don't!" Marigold cried.

Peter was silent for a moment, still holding her hands and then at last, in a voice deep and low and yet somehow commanding, he said:

"Very well, I will let you go on one condition—that you look me straight in the eyes and tell me that you do not love me. Do that and I will take you home right away and I will not trouble you any more."

"Let me go first."

"Very well."

He released her.

"You have hurt me!"

It was a complaint of a petulant child. Marigold was rubbing her hands together.

"Marigold, do as I have told you."

Peter was very still but he was leaning towards her

and she was conscious of his nearness, of the tension about him.

"Very well, if you insist!"

She turned her head up impulsively, looked up into his eyes and the words she was about to say died on her lips. For a moment they stared at each other both quiveringly conscious of the magnetism which held them, both aware of beating hearts and of a flame rising within them, leaping higher and higher . . . until suddenly the tension broke.

"Oh, Peter!"

His lips were on hers, his arms round her, holding her fiercely, tightly, possessively.

For a moment she surrendered herself utterly, giving him her very soul through her lips, and then widly she pushed him from her.

"Don't, Peter, don't!"

"You love me!"

It was a cry of triumph.

"I don't, I tell you, I don't!"

Peter laughed.

"Darling, you lie so terribly badly; besides, your lips betrayed you."

Quite suddenly Marigold seemed to crumple up; she turned her hands upwards in a gesture infinitely childish and pathetic.

"Don't make me love you! Can't you understand how impossible it would be?—I can't marry you! I can't marry anyone who is poor! I have got to have money —I must have the things I want in life. If you make me love you now I shall only hate you later on for what you have done. Let me go, Peter, please let me go!"

He was motionless a long second, then very quietly he said:

"Very well then, you are free."

A little shudder seemed to pass over Marigold as if she shook herself and she put her hands up to her face.

"Oh, why did you kiss me!"

"You silly child!"

There was a deep compassion and understanding in Peter's voice and once again he put his arms round her.

"I kissed you because you wanted me to kiss you, because you love me, Marigold—however much you may deny it, however much you may lie both to me and to yourself. I loved you from the first moment I saw you; I wanted you and I knew later that you wanted me."

"But it is impossible, Peter, you must see that. I can't love you."

"Why not?"

"You know the reasons."

"That you want money so much?"

Marigold nodded her head.

"So much! You don't know what it is like to be poor —I have hated it all my life. I've hated the clothes I've had to wear, the meals I've had to eat. We were happy, I suppose, in a way; but always I wanted more. I've felt as if I was a caged bird.

"Other children could go for expensive holidays but not us, we could not afford it. Other children had lovely things—ponies, parties—oh! a thousand and one things which we could not afford—and now . . . now I have grown up, I have got a chance—a slender chance but still a chance—of meeting someone with money, someone who would give me all those things I have longed for."

"And you don't think that love is important?"

"Of course it is important," Marigold answered, "but don't you understand, Peter? Can't you see that if I marry you I shall always resent that you are unable to give me the things I want so much? In time I should grow to hate you. What is the point of deliberately entering upon a life of misery with our eyes open?"

Marigold's voice died away, plaintive, unhappy. It

seemed as if the night closed in about them; then suddenly Peter held her more closely.

"You little fool!" he said softly. "Do you think money can buy you this—or this?"

He put his hand under her chin, tipped back her head against his shoulders and then his lips were on her mouth. He kissed her roughly, almost brutally, bruising her lips yet compelling her with an attraction which she could not deny.

For a moment she resisted, then she kissed him back, kissed him until the world swam round her and she felt herself throbbing beneath his hands. . . .

He freed her abruptly.

"That is my answer, Marigold," he said.

Without another word he started the car and drove home with a speed and a recklessness which would have frightened her had she not been beyond being afraid of anything save of the fear within herself.

The car drew up abruptly at the Saracen's Head.

"Good night, Marigold."

It seemed to her that there was something mocking in Peter's voice. Automatically she reached back for her hat, put her bag under her arm, and then stared up at him.

"Good night, Peter."

Then, with something strange in her voice, she asked,

"What are you going to do?"

"Marry you. Haven't I just told you so?"

Marigold got out of the car quickly as if she would wrench herself free from the spell he had cast over her. She slammed the car door behind her and taking her latch-key from her bag inserted it into the lock of the door.

She turned round and to her surprise Peter had not left the wheel of the car. Instead, he was sitting there looking at her.

She hesitated and some irrepressible part of her made her defy him.

"You will wait a long time!" she said, and opened the door.

As she crossed the threshold she heard Peter's answer.

"No, you will do that, my dear."

As she shut the door behind her she heard him drive away.

Seven

Sally found that Elaine was gradually beginning to lose her reserve about her dead mother.

It was obvious to anyone interested in the psychology of children that not being able to talk of her mother had given Elaine a strange complex.

Sally noticed when she first began to teach her that she shrank from hearing about mothers and children, and it was this which had alienated her from the few friends of her own age that she might have played with.

"They are stupid—I hate them!" she said sullenly when Sally enquired whether she would like certain children, whose names she had learnt from Nurse, to come to tea.

"But, Elaine, it would be nice for you," Sally protested.

"If you ask them I shall be rude to them," Elaine warned her.

At first Sally found this ostracism of other children difficult to understand until gradually it dawned on her that Elaine longed to be like other children with a mother to make a fuss of her.

Tentatively and with exquisite tact Sally set herself to break down the barrier which kept Elaine from being a normal child. It was difficult, for she realised on her very first acquaintance with Robert Dunstan that he was by no means a normal father.

She had had no conversation with him after their initial interview. He left the flat before Sally arrived in the morning and came home after she had departed. But she noticed his name often enough in the financial columns of the papers and she gathered that he was concerned with some great Government Amalgamation which kept him too busy to have time even for his only child.

She often wondered how much affection Elaine really had for her father, because she saw so very little of him.

But at last Sally began to understand that Robert Dunstan was the only stable thing in Elaine's small, barren life, and she clung to an idealised figure of her father, in unconscious self-protection.

Being Robert Dunstan's child, Elaine had a good brain and was quick enough to be critical of the people around her and to see their faults only too clearly.

She realised how old and incompetent her nurse had become and she knew, too, that the servants did as little for her as they dared. But for her father she had only praise and what appeared on the surface to be an emotional love.

It was only by degrees that Sally began to sense the truth when Elaine repeated to her remarks supposed to have been said by Robert Dunstan which were too exaggerated to be founded on fact.

"A man came to see Daddy last night," Elaine announced one morning, "and asked him if he had any jewels. 'This is my jewel,' Daddy answered, pointing to me."

This modern version of an old story which Elaine had learnt in lessons a few days earlier confirmed Sally's suspicions, and she almost wept for the child who must invent evidence of paternal love.

She considered the problem of Elaine for a long time and from every angle and then at last she knew all too clearly where her duty lay.

She made up her mind to seek an interview with Robert Dunstan, but for over a week he eluded her until at last she ran into him as he came hurrying out of the lift into the front hall of the flats.

He was carrying a dispatch-case in his hands and was in the act of putting his soft black hat on his head when she spoke to him.

"Good morning, Mr. Dunstan."

He stared at her for a moment as if he had no idea who she was and then he said:

"Oh, good morning; it is Miss Granville, isn't it? I am sorry, I did not recognise you for the moment."

"I have been hoping to meet you again," Sally said. "I am very anxious to finish our conversation."

"Finish our conversation?" Robert Dunstan was obviously searching his memory. "Oh yes, of course. Well, I hope we shall soon have an opportunity. Now, if you will excuse me, Miss Granville, I am late for an appointment."

He hurried away and Sally had a glimpse of a big black car waiting for him outside. She sighed as she turned towards the lift.

Sally spent the day trying to make Elaine's lessons original and interesting, trying to give some sort of ideals and standards to a child who had been brought up to seek only self-gratification.

She was tired when teatime came, but there was a task to be done when the meal was over. Having given up hope of discussing the matter with Mr. Dunstan herself, Sally had believed Elaine's assurance that he would not mind and had made arrangements for the toys and childish furnishings of the nursery to be sent to a children's hospital.

She had telephoned the Matron, who had promised that a van would call during the evening for them.

When tea was over, she and Elaine started to pack things together.

They wrapped the dolls carefully in paper and searched through the drawers and cupboards in the nursery for all the soft toys, books and childish games which had been accumulating ever since Elaine was a baby.

There was a large number of them, and when five o'clock the van arrived and they were taken away Elaine exclaimed at the bareness of the nursery.

"The room looks bigger, doesn't it, Miss Granville?"

"It gives us more space to move about in," Sally answered. "Did you father say we could buy the desk you wanted?"

"I haven't asked him yet," Elaine answered.

Sally looked at her in surprise.

"But you told him you were sending your toys away?"

"I did say something about it," Elaine answered uneasily, and added honestly—"but I don't think he was listening."

"Oh, Elaine," Sally said reproachfully.

But it was too late to do anything now, for the last bundle of toys was being taken down in the lift to the van.

Sally looked about her. The room certainly did look bare. She wondered if she had exceeded her duties in dispensing with so much.

"Don't look worried, Miss Granville," Elaine said. "Daddy won't care. He doesn't really care what I do as long as I don't worry him."

"You must not say things like that," Sally said automatically.

"But they are true," Elaine persisted. "You have always told me I must tell the truth."

Sally tried to change the subject. It was impossible not to realise that the child was saying what she knew to be a fact.

At that moment the door opened and Robert Dunstan came in.

"Hullo, Daddy," Elaine said with a cry. "You are early tonight."

She ran towards him and Robert Dunstan bent to kiss her perfunctorily as if his attention was elsewhere.

"What is all this about giving away your toys?" he asked. "Bates tells me a children's hospital has called for them."

"That's right," Elaine said, "I am too old for them and I want you to give me a desk, Daddy, a real grown-up desk. This room isn't to be called the nursery any more—it is to be called the schoolroom."

"Indeed!" Robert Dunstan said. "And who has made all these important decisions?"

There was a moment's pause, then Sally spoke:

"I thought Elaine had asked your permission to give away her toys," she said, "but she was really too old for them."

"Too old for them?" Robert Dunstan raised his eyebrows and said, "I think it is time you and I had a talk, Miss Granville. Will you come to the study?"

He turned away without waiting for Sally and walked from the schoolroom across the hall. Sally turned to Elaine.

"Will you do that drawing you promised me?" she said. "I don't expect I shall be long."

Elaine looked at her and at the retreating back of her father with a knowing look of a child who is not deceived by superficial courtesies.

"Don't let him bully you," she said in a whisper.

"I won't," Sally promised.

With her head held high she followed Mr. Dunstan to the study.

He was already seated at his desk; perfunctorily he went through the movements of rising as she entered, sat down again and indicated a chair.

"Sit down, Miss Granville."

Sally did as she was told.

Mr. Dunstan opened the conversation.

"I think you have been here as Elaine's governess for nearly three weeks. I regret that pressure of business has kept me from discussing with you various aspects of Elaine's upbringing, but this has been a very busy time for me and I can only now give my attention to what I know you will agree with me is extremely important—that is the general outline of Elaine's education."

Robert Dunstan picked up a pencil and made a note on the pad beside him.

"When I engaged Miss Harris, I explained to her at some length what I wanted in the upbringing of my child. I do not expect that Miss Harris passed that information on to you. I can only be grateful, Miss Granville, that you took over at a moment's notice and without any instructions from me.

"But I have very definite ideas on how Elaine should be instructed, and as up to now you have been working in the dark, you must forgive me if I do not approve of some of the things you have done.

"First and foremost, Elaine is still a young child. She should not be encouraged to get older ideas or to develop too quickly."

"I don't think Elaine is old for her age," Sally interposed; "in fact in many ways she is very childish."

"That is all to the good," Robert Dunstan said, "but I see no reason why, in those circumstances, she should have been encouraged to give away her toys."

"But, Mr. Dunstan," Sally said, "Elaine is far too old for dolls. I know you brought her a very lovely one

107

from Paris, but surely you do not imagine she plays with it? Elaine is getting on for eleven—she wants far more important things than dolls to occupy her mind."

Mr. Dunstan put down the pencil and thumped his hand on the table.

"I utterly disagree with you, Miss Granville! Elaine is a child and should be allowed to enjoy herself as a child. If you tell her that she is too old for dolls, obviously she will feel ashamed to play with them; but if you encourage her, she will be perfectly happy, as she has always been, with all the toys that little girls enjoy."

"Littls girls—yes," Sally said, "but not girls of Elaine's age. Besides, Elaine is clever, and as far as I can make out her brain has never been allowed to develop. Where ordinary lessons are concerned she knows far less than the average child of her age; but, at the same time, she picks up things very quickly. I think she should be given opportunities to develop her brain on the right lines."

Robert Dunstan made a gesture of impatience.

"I disagree with you most forcibly, Miss Granville, and as Elaine is my child I must insist on my ideas taking precedence over yours!"

Sally stared at him.

"Mr. Dunstan, I do not understand you. Are you suggesting that I should deliberately retard Elaine's development—keep her back?"

Robert Dunstan drummed with his fingers on the table.

"Not exactly, Miss Granville. I am afraid you do not quite see my meaning. I want Elaine to be brought up as an ordinary child, interested in childish things. I do not want her to develop a brilliant brain or any other abnormality, I want her to be just a normal, ordinary child. Is that clear?"

"And that is the one thing she has no chance of being," Sally said decisively.

Robert Dunstan raised his head to stare at her, and taking a deep breath Sally began what she had to say for a long time.

"Have you any idea what Elaine's life is like here? Do you know how she is treated when you are not here? I think, Elaine is the loneliest, most pathetic case of a neglected child I have ever come across!"

"Neglected?"

There was no doubt as to Robert Dunstan's surprise. The word was ejaculated from him sharply.

"Yes, neglected. Nanny is very fond of Elaine, but she is far too old. The servants are lazy and not supervised. Besides, do you consider the companionship of servants really desirable for a child of ten? Elaine has no friends, no interests, nothing to occupy her mind or to make her happy. She is fond of you, but how often does she see you?"

Here Sally paused a moment, then added,

"She misses her mother terribly."

Robert Dunstan got up abruptly from his desk and walked towards the window. Sally was silent for a moment; then, as he did not speak, she went on:

"I wanted to see you, Mr. Dunstan, because I believe the only thing that would be really good for Elaine would be for her to go away to school. She ought to have the companionship of girls of her own age; she ought to grow up in different surroundings from these.

"When I first came to this room I told you I thought she was spoilt. That is not true. She has merely been neglected until to assert herself she gives way to every impulse or emotion which happens to occur to her.

"I am sorry for Elaine, Mr. Dunstan—more sorry for her than for many of the ragged dirty children I have seen playing in the streets."

Sally was speaking quickly. She was driven by her own intensity of feeling.

There was a burning patch of colour in both her

cheeks. She clasped her hands together. She had a feeling that she was battling against almost overwhelmingly powerful currents.

She knew she was in combat with Robert Dunstan and he gave her the impression of so much strength and such imperturbability that she was afraid. Her voice died away and it seemed to her that the room was very silent.

She was conscious of the roar of the traffic outside in Park Lane and of her own heart beating rather quickly. At last, after what seemed a long time, Robert Dunstan turned round from the window.

"Well, you are certainly frank, Miss Granville," he said drily as he walked back to his desk; "but if Elaine goes to school, what about yourself?"

"I shall find another job," Sally said; "it is Elaine of whom I am thinking."

"Although it may be a surprise to you, I have thought of her too," Robert Dunstan said. "You have certainly made out a very good case from your point of view, Miss Granville, yet you have not convinced me."

"I think you will be convinced," Sally said quickly, "if you think it over, if you can spare the time to be with Elaine for a while and realise how lonely she is and what an aimless, empty life she leads."

Robert Dunstan picked up his pencil again. He held it carefully in both hands, turning it slowly. His eyes were on it and Sally watching him thought what a good-looking man he would have been if his face had not been so hard. His expression was set sternly.

Quite suddenly Robert Dunstan said:

"What did you mean when you said Elaine missed her mother?"

"Perhaps I oughtn't to have told you that," Sally said, "but when I came I found that Elaine's mother was never mentioned and then gradually I learnt that the child hated any reference to mothers and children.

Also she would never go to children's houses or have children here and it was because other children have mothers to entertain for them while she has no one."

There was a long silence and then at last Robert Dunstan said:

"I had no idea that Elaine remembered her mother."

"She does," Sally said; "you see, a mother means such a tremendous lot in a child's life."

"Some mothers may do," Robert Dunstan replied. There was a moment's pause and then, looking at Sally, he said: "I have come to a decision, Miss Granville, which may seem harsh to you but which I am certain is the right one.

"I am afraid that you are too young and too impressionable to be the right person to teach Elaine. Before you came I always found her a very contented little girl —now, in the short time you have been here, you seem to have made such drastic changes that I doubt whether it would be possible for her to return to her old contentment. Nevertheless the damage may not be irreparable. I should be greatly obliged therefore, if you would terminate your appointment here as from today. I will, of course, pay you a month's salary in lieu of notice."

Sally stared at him, too surprised for the moment to say anything; then with an effort she rose to her feet.

"I quite understand, Mr. Dunstan," she said quietly. "I am only sorry for Elaine. I am fond of the child and I think she is fond of me."

"I assure you you need not worry about Elaine," Robert Dunstan said with dignity. "Good-bye, Miss Granville."

He held out his hand, but Sally ignored it. She was so angry that as she turned towards the door she realised she was trembling. As she reached it, Robert Dunstan's voice arrested her.

"I may trust to your good sense, Miss Granville, not to distress Elaine about this?"

"I will leave you to break the news to her yourself in your own way," Sally answered. "When I leave in half an hour's time I shall not tell her that I am not returning tomorrow."

"Thank you, Miss Granville."

Sally opened the door. She would have liked to have replied, to have made some bitter and cutting retort, but as she walked across the hall she knew she was perilously near to tears.

Elaine jumped up as she entered the nursery.

"Oh, here you are! You have been a long time. I was so worried in case Daddy was being cross with you."

Sally put her arms round her shoulders.

"Let me look at your drawing," she said, trying to keep her voice steady.

"There it is!" Elaine said proudly.

It seemed to Sally that half an hour had never passed so slowly. When at last it was time for her to go, she put her arms round Elaine and held her very close.

"You have been a very good girl today," she said. "You will try to remember all the things I told you—to be kind to people—never to be rude?"

Elaine nodded.

"Of course I will! You won't forget you promised to take me to the Tower of London, will you? You promised!"

"Yes, I promised," Sally said.

She got to her feet, pulled on her hat and gloves.

"Be a good girl," she said.

"I am so good that I ought to get a prize," Elaine laughed.

Slipping an arm through Sally's she danced light-heartedly with her towards the lift.

"As Daddy is so early he might have time to talk to me tonight."

"Yes, go and talk to your father," Sally said, "I think he would like to speak to you."

"Good-bye, Miss Granville," Elaine called as the porter shut the lift gates behind her. "See you tomorrow!"

She waved as the lift went out of sight.

Sally hurried from the big, luxurious building in which she had found and lost her first job. She went home feeling miserable and depressed. Mrs. Jarvis greeted her as she opened the front door.

"There's a gentleman to see you, dear, that doctor chap who often comes. I told him you were not in, but he's waiting."

"Oh, it's David!" Sally exclaimed.

She hurried up the stairs to find David stretched out in the armchair, his head back and his eyes closed. He awoke with a start as she shut the door behind her.

"Hullo, Sally."

"Sorry to wake you."

"I only closed my eyes for a moment. I was on duty half the night."

"It is lovely to see you," Sally said.

She went behind the curtains to comb her hair and put some powder on her nose and came back to the sitting-room.

"Marigold not back yet?"

David shook his head.

"I telephoned her at lunchtime and she said she would be late. She sounded rather cross and upset so I came here to see if she would come out to dinner with me."

"Oh dear, I do hope nothing has happened," Sally said.

David smiled.

"You take all the family troubles on your shoulders, don't you, Sally?"

"I've got a lot of my own at the moment," Sally answered. "David, I've got the sack."

"The sack?"

Sally told him what had happened.

"The man ought to be shut up!" David exclaimed. "He has no right to behave like that!"

"I suppose he can do as he likes with his own child, but I have improved her so much."

"I am sure you have!" David reached over and patted her hand consolingly. "Poor little Sally, I hate to think you are worried. I can never realise you are grown up enough to have a job—I always think of you as a small, wide-eyed child being scolded by Anne and Marigold because you could not keep up with them."

"But I have grown up, you know, David."

There was something wistful in Sally's voice.

"Have you?" David asked. "That's a mistake. We were much happier when we were children racing each other along the beach and catching crabs."

"Much happier!"

There was deep feeling in Sally's voice.

"You never had to worry then what might happen in the future," David said.

"No," Sally said. "There was always Daddy to look after us."

"Now you have got to fend for yourselves," David said. "Poor Sally, and you are the one who does all the worrying. I wish I could help."

"You do help, David. It is wonderful to have you here."

There was no mistaking the sincerity in her voice. David smiled at the little oval-shaped face turned towards him.

"Dear little Sally! We'll find you something to do, don't you worry. You are too much of a child to look after other children. Why not try another sort of job?"

"I am not a child, David," Sally said firmly, but she did not meet his eyes—instead, she walked across to the window where she could see that one glimpse of silver water.

The door burst open and Marigold came in.

"Goodness, I am tired!" she said. "I wish we had a lift in this place. Hullo, David, what do you want?"

There was something so ungracious in her voice that Sally turned from the window to stare at her in surprise.

"Still cross?" David asked with the familiarity of someone who had known her since babyhood.

"Yes, I am," Marigold snapped, "and I shall be crosser still if you start asking idiotic questions."

She flounced through the curtains into the bedroom just as there was another step on the stairs and Anne came slowly through the door.

"Hullo, darling," she said to Sally, and to David, "Hullo, how's the hospital?"

"Full to bursting!" David answered.

"There are too many ill people in the world." Anne sank down in an empty chair. "The buses were packed! I've had such a day; the Duchess was in one of her moods—nothing was right. I had to arrange the flowers three times before she was satisfied, then the Library must needs give me a book she had read before."

"Poor Anne," Sally sympathised. "It seems to have been a bad day all round."

"Sally's lost her job," David explained.

"Oh, Sally!" Anne exclaimed. "What happened?"

"I will tell you later," Sally answered. "David will not want to hear the whole sad story a second time."

Marigold came through the curtains.

"What is this?" she asked. "Has Sally lost her job? That's a nuisance because I was just going to ask if you would mind if I did not pay my share of the rent for the next three weeks. I have simply got to have a new evening dress."

"That's all right, darling," Sally said quickly, "my late employer has offered me a month's wages and I shall take them. If I had any pride I suppose I would

115

throw the money in his face, but your evening dress is far more important."

"I have been asked to a party next Friday; Ben Barlow is giving it."

Marigold said the name defiantly as if she expected some comment. For a moment there was silence, then David asked:

"The racing motorist?"

"Yes," Marigold replied.

"That's the man who is always in the papers," Anne said. "Didn't he give a pearl necklace or something to a chorus girl and then ask for it back?"

"Yes, that's the man," Marigold said sweetly. "He is very rich and I am going to his party."

Sally said nothing. She realised, as neither of the others did, that something was wrong. She had thought that Marigold seemed upset this morning before she went to work; now she knew that it was something far more important than a burst of bad temper or irritability.

Marigold was unhappy. There was a note in her voice Sally had never heard before and as she watched her moving restlessly and looking defiant she felt perturbed.

Sally took no part in the ensuing conversation. She was watching Marigold and at the same time at the back of her own mind there was an aching misery for Elaine.

Would the child be unhappy, she wondered, when her father told her the new arrangements he had made? She felt sure that Elaine was fond of her, but how fond or how deep that affection went it was difficult to tell.

The clock on the mantelpiece struck the half-hour after seven and Marigold agreed to go out to dinner with David. She was not very enthusiastic about it, but nevertheless David looked pleased and happy.

"I won the hospital sweepstake on the Derby!" he

said. "It wasn't a fortune, but enough to give us a good dinner. We can go anywhere you like."

"I really don't care," Marigold said.

"What about the Berkeley Grill?" David suggested. Marigold stood very still.

"Anywhere but there," she said sharply.

Sally looked at her, but Marigold turned away.

"I will get my hat," she said.

When they had gone Sally sat down in a comfortable chair and looked at Anne.

"We had better go and get something to eat."

"I have been thinking," Anne said. "The Jarvises might let us put an electric cooking stove in that little alcove at the top of the stairs. It has got a window. If we could cook something there it would save us going out every night."

Sally gave an exclamation.

"Anne, that's brilliant of you! I cannot think why it has not occurred to me before."

Anne smiled.

"You do all the thinking, Sally; it is about time one of us should take our turn."

"But it's a splendid idea!" Sally enthused. "It would be much more comfortable and it would save us money, even if we have to have the stove installed ourselves. I will see Mrs. Jarvis in the morning, she will be busy now in the bar."

"Yes, I should see her in the morning."

"Well, let's go and eat our lentil cutlet, or perhaps it will be fish pie! I am awfully tired of restaurant food," Sally said, and added, "Do you remember those lovely steak-and-kidney pies old Hannah used to make us when we were children?"

"I should say I do!" Anne said. "But don't let's think about them, it makes me so hungry!"

They walked out into the sultry streets. It was a hot evening without a breath of air.

117

"Can you imagine what it will be like at St. Chytas tonight?" Sally asked. "Do you miss it, Anne?"

"Sometimes," Anne answered, "but I like London, don't you?"

Sally shook her head.

"I don't like London and I don't think it likes me."

"Don't you worry about losing your job, darling," Anne said consolingly; "you were just unfortunate to meet with such beastly people."

"The funny thing is," Sally said reflectively, "that when you were all warning me how tough Robert Dunstan was likely to be, I kept thinking you were wrong. Even now I feel I must have tackled him the wrong way, misunderstood him or something. There must be some reason for his being so extraordinary."

"He is not worth thinking about," Anne said firmly.

Nevertheless Sally found herself thinking about Robert Dunstan all through dinner. She had always found people so friendly that the mystery of Robert Dunstan was not easily dismissed.

"I shall ask the Duchess if she knows of anything for you," Anne said as they walked back towards the Saracen's Head. "She knows lots of people and there must be one of them who could fit you in somewhere. It seems ridiculous that you should be out of a job while Marigold and I, who were always the improvident ones, should be bread-winners."

"I will find something," Sally said with a confidence which did not go much deeper than the words.

It was growing dusk and at last a faint breeze seemed to come blowing up the street from the river. Sally took a deep breath.

"That's better," she said. "I have been feeling stifled all day."

The streets were nearly empty, but the windows of the Saracen's Head were bright and as they passed by there was the chatter of voices and a sudden burst of laughter.

"The Jarvises are doing good business," Anne said with a smile.

They turned the corner to find their own door and it was then that Sally saw a small figure waiting outside. She stared and gave an exclamation.

"Elaine, whatever are you doing here?"

The child turned round and gave a cry of joy.

"Oh, Miss Granville, I rang and rang and nobody answered! I thought you must have gone away!"

Sally saw that her eyes were red and swollen and there were traces of recent tears still wet on her cheeks.

Eight

Sally took Elaine upstairs and when they had reached the privacy of the little sitting-room she put her arms round her and said:

"Now, darling, tell me all about it."

In reply Elaine burst into floods of tears, flinging her arms round Sally's neck and hugging her close with the desperate, passionate strength of an overwrought child.

Her sobs were heart-rending in their intensity and Sally could do little but murmur over and over again:

"It's all right, darling . . . don't cry! . . . It's all right!"

At last Elaine became somewhat quieter and Sally, sitting down in an armchair, drew her on to her lap while Anne mixed a cooling drink of orange juice with plenty of sugar added to it.

"Drink that up, darling," Sally coaxed Elaine.

In an effort to make her more comfortable she undid her overcoat.

Then she gave an exclamation of surprise, for Elaine

119

was wearing nothing underneath except her nightgown tucked into a pair of elastic-topped knickers. Seeing Sally's astonishment, Elaine explained:

"Daddy sent me to bed."

The tears began to flow afresh.

"Don't cry any more, darling," Sally pleaded. "Drink up your orange juice and when you feel calmer you can talk."

Elaine did as she was told and then with a little sigh laid her head on Sally's shoulder and cuddled close to her.

"I do love you, Miss Granville," she said. "I love you more than anybody else in all the world."

Sally's arm tightened round the child.

"I am glad, darling," she said, "but you ought not to have come here alone."

"I had to," Elaine answered simply, and then with many pathetic little catches in her voice she began to tell her story.

"After you had gone," she said, "I went to see Daddy and he was looking awfully cross and scowly. I thought perhaps he was angry about something and I tried to talk to him about other things and make him in a good temper, but after a moment he said,

'Elaine, I hope you won't mind very much, but I have decided it would be better if Miss Granville did not come here any more.'

"I stared at him. For a moment I could not understand what he was telling me and then, when I asked him why, he said, 'You are too young to understand, but I will find someone else to teach you—someone nice and sensible whom you will like very much.'

"Then I said quickly: 'But I don't want anyone but Miss Granville. I love her, Daddy, I want her and no one else.'

'I am sorry, Elaine,' he said rather crossly, 'but you cannot have Miss Granville.'

120

"When he said that I think I went mad."

Elaine hid her face for a moment, then she went on in a whisper:

"I screamed and screamed and threw things about. I told Daddy I hated him and that the only person I loved was you."

"Oh, Elaine!" Sally said reproachfully.

"I knew you wouldn't be pleased with me, but I couldn't help it, I couldn't really! At last Daddy got perfectly furious and he rang the bell for Nanny and told her to put me to bed. I was still crying and my voice was quite hoarse from screaming and Nanny cried too and kept saying, 'You poor motherless child!' over and over again until I told her to shut up and that I didn't want a mother, I wanted you."

Elaine put her arm round Sally's neck and gave her a convulsive squeeze.

"What happened then?" Sally asked quietly, afraid of her own emotions.

"Nanny brought me some supper and then left me alone. As soon as she had gone I slipped out of bed, put on my shoes and socks and overcoat and crept down the back stairs. I knew no one would see me. I came out by the back door into the mews and I ran as quickly as I could to the bus-stop.

"It was only when I got there that I remembered I had no money with me. I never thought to take my purse. So I've walked here. I had to ask lots of people the way, but they were very kind and told me."

Elaine drew a deep breath and added:

"I'm going to stay with you. I'm never going back to Daddy again!"

Sally smiled.

"But, darling, that is impossible, you know that."

"It isn't and I won't go back!" Elaine cried. "You're not to make me—promise me you won't make me! I hate Daddy, I hate the flat and everyone there! I want to live here with you! Oh, please let me! I won't be any trouble . . . I promise you I won't . . . let me stay, please, please, Miss Granville, let me stay!"

Elaine's voice began to rise hysterically and Sally saw that the child was nearly frantic with fear and unhappiness. Soothingly she tightened both her arms round her and held her very close.

"You are tired out, darling," she said gently. "We won't talk about it now; instead let us just sit quietly for a moment and think about other things."

"You won't take me back again, will you?" Elaine pleaded. "Promise. If you try to do that I will kill myself—I will throw myself under a bus or in the river! I will, I will!"

"Elaine, it isn't like you to talk like that," Sally protested; "but don't let us bother about such things at the moment. You must be awfully tired. It has been a long walk and it is long past your bed-time. Do you know what I am going to do? I am going to tuck you up in my bed."

"But you won't leave me—you won't go and fetch Daddy?"

"No, I won't leave you," Sally said, "I promise."

"Really and truly?"

"Really and truly," Sally said solemnly.

Elaine accepted her promise and allowed herself to be led through the curtains into the other room, while Anne, at a suggestion from Sally, ran downstairs to fill a hot-water bottle.

Sally took off Elaine's coat and removed the dusty shoes from her tired little feet, brushed back the tangled hair from her face and helped her into bed.

"Try and go to sleep, darling," she suggested. "You will feel much better in the morning."

"I like your bed, Miss Granville," Elaine said, "but where are you going to sleep?"

"I'll manage," Sally replied, "don't you worry about anything."

Anne came back with the hot-water bottle.

"Look what my sister has brought you," Sally said. "Would you like to cuddle it?"

She thought warmth might soothe the child, who was still trembling from overwrought nerves.

"That would be lovely!" Elaine said, and looking up at Anne remarked, "She's awfully pretty, isn't she?"

Anne laughed while Sally agreed.

"Yes, isn't she? She is very nice too!"

"She couldn't be as nice as you," Elaine answered loyally; then cuddling the hot-water bottle to her she snuggled down into the pillows.

Sally tucked her in and moved across the room to draw the curtains. Instantly Elaine sat up in bed.

"You're leaving me!" she accused. "You're going away!"

"I'm only drawing the curtains," Sally answered, "and I have promised you, Elaine, that I will not go away. You know I wouldn't break my promise. I am going to sit just the other side of the curtains. If you want me, you have only to call out. I shall be there!"

Elaine's suspicions subsided and she lay down again. She was desperately tired and almost before Sally could reach the other side of the room the child was asleep.

However, to be quite certain, she put her fingers to her lips to warn Anne against saying anything which might be overheard, and they waited in silence for nearly five minutes before they were certain that Elaine was in such a deep slumber and that nothing they could say would disturb her.

"What are you going to do now?" Anne asked in a low voice.

"I shall have to let Mr. Dunstan know," Sally replied. "If they find out the child is missing, he will be desperate with anxiety."

"And a good thing, too, if you ask me!" Anne said. "Poor little thing, I am terrribly sorry for her."

"So am I," Sally answered, "but I feel there must be something behind all this. It is such a strange way to behave!"

"I think he sounds awful."

"I must let him know that Elaine is safe."

"Suppose he comes rushing round demanding that she should go back at once?"

"He couldn't do that, could he?" Sally asked, but there was a note of uncertainty in her voice.

"You know him better than I do," Anne answered, "and from all accounts he does not seem to have much sense where his own child is concerned."

Sally sighed.

"All the same, we must do the right thing," she said. "Will you be an angel and telephone him for me from the call box? I must keep my promise to Elaine and not leave her."

"What on earth shall I say?" Anne asked.

"Just tell him the truth," Sally replied. "Say that Elaine has walked here and arrived in a very hysterical, unhappy state. Tell him I have put her to bed and that really it would be best if he would leave everything until the morning."

"I will tell him all that," Anne promised, "but I feel terrified of him myself." She picked up her bag. "Let me see if I have any pennies. Yes, I have. If he is out, what shall I do?"

"Speak to Nanny and tell her that it would be much better for Mr. Dunstan not to come here tonight."

"All right," Anne said. "But I hope when you get your next job, Sally, you will choose more or less normal people to deal with!"

She left the room and Sally, sitting alone, thought over the implication in her last remark.

It was true. Robert Dunstan could hardly be described as normal, and Elaine was certainly having abnormal difficulties to cope with, poor little girl.

Sally sighed and peeped through the curtains to see if she was still asleep. Elaine was lying relaxed with one arm thrown out in the utter abandon of childish slumber.

Every now and then her breath came in a little sob through her parted lips and her long eyelashes were still wet with tears. She looked very young and defenceless hardly more than a baby, and Sally felt her heart contract.

How she hated to see a child suffer! She felt angry and resentful that Robert Dunstan should have caused all this.

However, back again in the sitting-room she questioned herself as to whether she had done the right thing. Had she handled things tactlessly? Had she been too frank in her dealings with Elaine's father?

Silently and wordlessly she sent up a little prayer to her own father for his help and guidance.

"If only he was alive," she thought, "how easy it would be to ask him what he thought!"

He never failed to know the remedy for everything, it seemed to Sally, especially in one's dealings with human beings. Now she thought that gently he rebuked her.

"Human beings are strange cattle," she almost heard him say. "Drive them and they want to go in the opposite direction. Lead them and they follow!"

"Yes, that is what I tried to do," Sally admitted to herself. "I tried to drive Robert Dunstan and it was a mistake."

Suddenly she realised that one of the reasons for her talking to Mr. Dunstan quite so forcibly was because she was afraid of him. How often had her father said to her,

"Never be afraid of a horse or a man—they know it instinctively and they will always get the better of you."

"And why am I afraid of him?" she questioned herself, and knew the answer.

"Because he is so rich! How despicable!"

She whispered the words out loud and getting up moved restlessly about the room.

Now she knew where things had gone wrong from the very beginning. She had felt antagonistic towards Robert Dunstan even before she met him, antagonistic because within herself she had been afraid of a man who controlled so much money, who was spoken of in awe by so many people.

Had she found herself in the same situation with one of the people in the village she would never have rushed her fence, she would have approached her employer gently and tactfully and eventually coaxed him round to her way of thinking.

"Money! Money!" Sally muttered. "How I loathe it and what it does to people! Yes, even to me!"

She was as bad as Marigold, if not worse. Money had altered her normal course of behaviour and in this case swift retribution had followed her initial mistake, bringing suffering not to herself but to Elaine.

Alone, Sally suddenly put her hands in front of her face and prayed with all her strength for simplicity. It was only simplicity, she knew, which could help her in the strange, new, unexpected life where she was confronted on every side by different values, strange standards.

She must be strong enough to resist the encroachment of worldly things and to remember only the teaching she had received from her father which had guided her so securely and safely all through her childish years.

Then she had made friends—never enemies. She had been helped in all she had undertaken, never frustrated.

126

"Oh, help me, God, help me now," she prayed, "for Elaine's sake!"

It was some time before she heard footsteps on the stairs. Anne had come back.

"What happened?" Sally asked quickly.

"I could not get through at first," Anne answered, "the telephone was engaged for simply ages. That is why I have been so long. And I gathered when I did speak to Mr. Dunstan that he had been telephoning wildly to the police and anyone else he could think of. The joke was that he had not got your address and, of course, he could not get Mrs. Bellows at this time of night."

"He hadn't my address? No, I suppose he hadn't. How awful! I never thought to leave it at the flat. Elaine knew it because she wanted to send Marigold a card on her birthday, and I wrote it down for her."

"Well, I told him who I was," Anne went on, "and that Elaine was safe and he ejaculated 'Thank God', which I thought was a good sign. At least he has been anxious about the child."

"I am sure he has been anxious," Sally said. "What happened then?"

"I told him she was here and said that you thought it was best to leave everything until the morning, but he insisted that he wanted to see you now, at once. So he wrote down the address and is coming along right away."

"Coming here?"

"Yes," Anne replied. "I couldn't stop him. I tried, but he insisted."

"Oh well, it cannot be helped," Sally sighed. "Thank you, darling, for doing all that."

"There is no reason to thank me," Anne replied, "I am only so sorry for you. It is all upsetting and rather unpleasant. Do you want me to go out when he comes?"

"Oh no!" Sally said quickly. "Please stay with me. Between ourselves, I am terrified of seeing him again. I am sure he will think it is all my fault Elaine ran away."

"He had better not be rude to you." Anne bridled. "I shall hit him or something!"

Sally laughed spontaneously. It was so impossible to think of the calm, sweet-tempered Anne hitting anyone.

She got up and began to tidy the room.

"So long as he does not take the child away tonight," she said at length, but Anne knew the idea of Elaine being upset was worrying her.

"We can't stop him legally," she answered.

"I won't let him," Sally said, her chin set firmly as it always did when she was obstinately determined about something.

"Do you think it would be a good idea," Anne suggested, "if I went downstairs and waited at the door? If he rings, the Jarvises will answer it. They might think it a bit strange our having a man here at this time of night."

"Yes, do that," Sally agreed. "How clever of you to think of it! I would hate the Jarvises to be shocked, and it is such a long and complicated story to have to explain to anyone."

"I will stand just inside the door," Anne said, "and then when I hear his car draw up I will go out and bring him in. I will take my coat, too, it is getting chilly."

She picked up her coat which she wore over her blue-and-white-patterned summer dress, then she bent to kiss Sally as she passed her.

"Cheer up, darling! I expect you will get your own way, but if you don't there are millions of other children in the world you can weep over."

Sally smiled.

"It would give me less of a heart-ache if I got my own way where Elaine is concerned."

"Then get it," Anne advised. "I have seldom known you to fail when you really want a thing."

She went quietly down the stairs while Sally sat on alone. After what seemed a long time she heard Anne coming back and someone else accompanying her.

She got to her feet and realised that her hands were trembling, so she put them behind her back and stood very straight and defiant in the centre of the room awaiting Robert Dunstan.

The door opened.

"Here is Mr. Dunstan, Sally."

He came into the room looking very big and overpowering. The thought came swiftly to Sally:

"How strange this must seem to him, this shabby, tiny room beneath the eaves, after the luxury of his Park Lane flat!"

Because she was perturbed she plunged quickly into speech without waiting for him to greet her.

"You will have to talk rather quietly, Mr. Dunstan; Elaine is sleeping on the other side of those curtains."

She looked at him and something in his face encouraged her to say:

"Would you like to see her?"

She drew aside one of the curtains and the light streaming through rested on Elaine's face. Robert Dunstan stood for a moment looking at his only child. Sally wondered if he noticed how young and vulnerable Elaine looked in sleep and if he saw the traces of tears on her cheeks.

For a moment he did not move; then he turned to Sally.

"Thank you, Miss Granville."

He walked back into the sitting-room and Sally drew the curtains.

"Won't you sit down?"

She indicated the most comfortable armchair. She sat down in another while Anne stood at the uncurtained window, her golden head silhouetted against the darkness.

For a moment Robert Dunstan's eyes rested on her; then he turned to Sally.

"Your sister was kind enough to telephone me, Miss Granville. I understand you found Elaine about nine o'clock."

"Yes," Sally replied. "She was very tired and exhausted, having walked all the way here from Park Lane. When she tried to tell me what had happened she became quite hysterical, and I thought it wiser to put her to bed and let her sleep."

"That was kind of you."

It seemed to Sally as though the words had to be dragged from between his lips.

It struck her that, sitting in the armchair, he looked less formidable and more human. It seemed to her, too, that he was very tired and his expression instead of holding its usual sternness was sad. Impulsively Sally dropped her defiance.

"I am sorry about all this, Mr. Dunstan. I am afraid that you will think it is my fault."

"Elaine loves you," Robert Dunstan said slowly.

"Yes, I know," Sally answered, and her voice was soft as if she pleaded for understanding. "I did not try to make her love me, Mr. Dunstan; it just happened because she is such a lonely little girl and her emotions had been pent up for so long."

There was silence for a moment and then Robert Dunstan said:

"I acted impulsively and perhaps stupidly this afternoon, Miss Granville. I ought to have understood that one cannot dismiss someone a child loves as one can . . ."

He searched for a simile.

". . . an office boy," Sally supplied.

130

He looked at her and there was a faint shadow of a smile at the corners of his lips.

"I was going to compare yours with a much more responsible post, Miss Granville; but the point I am trying to make is that I was forgetting in my plans for Elaine the human element."

"Poor Elaine!"

Sally could not help the exclamation.

"Are you really sorry for her?"

Sally nodded.

"I am not just saying 'yes' to that because I want to make myself unpleasant, Mr. Dunstan. I am afraid I have said far too many thing about Elaine to you on the few occasions we have met, but I am sorry for her. She is a dear little girl and she wants to love people, to give them the normal affections of a normal child. Children are very loving and they cannot hide their emotions."

"So I learned from Elaine this evening," Robert Dunstan said.

Again there was a faint smile on his mouth.

"She told me she had been very naughty!"

"I had no idea that one small girl could make so much noise." He looked at Sally for a long moment and then he really smiled. "I think I have a lot to learn from both of you, Miss Granville. Will you forgive me?"

"For what?" Sally asked.

"For making the very ineffective effort to dispense with your services. Please stay on!"

There was a light in Sally's eyes, but she forced herself to prevaricate, to go slowly.

"You are quite certain that you want me to? I am afraid I can only teach Elaine in my own way."

"I am content with that," Robert Dunstan said. He hesitated for a moment. "One day I will try and explain to you, if I may, the reasons for the attitude I have taken up in the past . . . but not now."

His voice was deep and grave and somehow Sally

knew instinctively that there was a great deal to be told. He got to his feet.

"I had better be going home. Perhaps you will tell Elaine before I see her tomorrow that everything is settled as she wanted."

"I shall not put it quite like that," Sally replied. "Elaine has had far too many things her own way in the past. I will tell her that if she is very good and sorry for her behaviour today, it might be arranged for me to stay a little longer."

Robert Dunstan raised his eyebrows.

"Are you putting a time limit to it?"

"I don't want to talk about that now," Sally said, "but I do want Elaine to go to school."

"We'll have to see about that, Miss Granville." He looked towards the curtains and a sudden thought struck him. "You will forgive me for mentioning it, but I think Elaine told me once that you lived with your two sisters, in which case won't one of you be without a bed tonight?"

"Please do not worry," Sally replied. "We shall manage somehow."

"But I will not hear of such a thing. Let me wake Elaine and take her home. I can explain to her that you are coming in the morning."

"No, please!" Sally pleaded.

Unexpectedly Anne spoke from the window.

"It will be all right, Mr. Dunstan," she said; "we have our eiderdowns which we brought up from the country. Three of them can make a very comfortable mattress on the floor and we have plenty of extra blankets."

"You are sure?"

"Quite sure!" Anne answered.

"Then I can only thank you once again."

Robert Dunstan held out his hand to Anne. He shook it as Sally turned towards the door.

"I will take you down," she said.

She preceded him down the dark, narrow stairs. When they reached the hall she switched on the light and opened the door.

"Good night, Miss Granville. I am more grateful to you than I can express in words."

He shook her hand and stepped out on to the pavement. Outside, Sally could see that his chauffeur was waiting at the door of his big black car. She was about to shut the door when surprisingly Robert Dunstan turned.

"Your sister is a very beautiful girl."

"Yes, isn't she?" Sally smiled.

She thought Robert Dunstan was about to say something else, but he raised his hat in silence and walking across the pavement got into the car. Sally closed the front door and rushed up the stairs.

"What do you think of him?" she asked Anne, breathless from her haste.

"He is much nicer than I thought he would be," Anne answered.

"I know," Sally replied. "It was my fault. When you were away telephoning to him, I realised that I had deliberately antagonised him by being on the offensive from the very beginning of our acquaintance. All the same, you must admit that he is rather terrifying."

"Yes, I suppose he is," Anne said reflectively. "At the same time, he is distinguished. I did not imagine him a bit like that. I thought he would be ugly, shrewd and grasping."

"I have been so busy thinking he was all those things," Sally said, "that I don't think I have ever looked at him properly."

"He is good-looking."

"And he thinks you are beautiful," Sally said, and added, "He said so just now as he was leaving."

Anne made no reply and Sally could not tell whether

133

she was pleased or not. At that moment the door was opened and Marigold came into the room.

She was looking very tired and as she entered she pulled her hat from her head and threw it with her bag with a clatter on to the table.

"Sssh!" Sally said. "We have got a visitor!"

"A visitor?"

Sally explained briefly what had happened during the evening.

"And Robert Dunstan has been here?" Marigold asked.

Sally nodded.

"You have just missed him."

"Just my luck!" Marigold exclaimed. "You know I am dying to meet him."

"It was not exactly what I would call a social occasion," Sally smiled.

"All the same, I wanted to meet him," Marigold replied. She stretched her arms above her head. "Heavens, I'm tired!"

"Have you had a good evening?"

"No, beastly!" Marigold replied.

"Oh Marigold, you didn't quarrel with David?"

"Of course!"

"But what about?"

"Need you ask?" Marigold enquired. "Same old subject of course! Whether money was important enough or not . . . and to think that I should have spent the evening fighting with David when I might have been sitting here meeting Robert Dunstan!"

Sally's eyes were troubled.

"Poor David. Were you unkind to him?"

"I hope so! He bores me horribly. He is so frightfully intense. Who but a fool would do all that work with such a potty little salary?"

"Doctors don't work for salaries," Sally said quietly.

"They work to alleviate suffering, to help others. A doctor undertakes a mission, not a career."

"So David tried to explain to me," Marigold said, "but he did not put it so eloquently as you have. What fools men are!"

There was so much bitterness and suffering in her voice that instinctively Sally turned towards her.

"Marigold, darling, what is the matter?"

"Nothing!" Marigold snapped; "and for goodness sake leave me alone!"

She went through the curtains. Anne and Sally looked at each other in bewilderment.

There was very little more said between the girls that night.

Sally made up her bed with eiderdowns and extra blankets on the floor, and pulled back the dividing curtains so that there should be plenty of air for them all. She was tired and was just dropping off to sleep when she heard a little sound.

For a moment she thought it was Elaine, and then with a throb of unhappiness she knew that Marigold was weeping bitterly into her pillow.

Nine

"His Grace would like to see you in the library, miss."

Dalton, the butler, spoke in his usual stentorian, pompous voice which made him sound like an archbishop in a cathedral with bad acoustics.

Anne looked surprised.

"His Grace? I didn't know he was in London."

"He came up last night, miss, and he would like to see you."

Anne put down her shopping-bag on the table in the hall. She had spent her luncheon-hour buying a new blouse and had run the last few yards to the house feeling that she might be late.

The idea that the Duke had been waiting for her flustered her and her cheeks were pink as she drew off her gloves and followed the butler to the library.

"Miss Granville, Your Grace!"

The Duke was sitting by the fireside. He looked up as she entered.

"Good afternoon, Miss Granville. Isn't it a lovely day?"

"Yes, lovely!" Anne replied rather breathlessly.

"Won't you sit down?"

The Duke indicated a chair on the other side of the fireplace opposite him. Anne sat down and was suddenly conscious of the hat she was wearing, made from a bunch of flowers and a yard of ribbon she had bought in Chelsea.

She wished she had taken it off. Somehow she felt that its frivolity was out of keeping with the solemnity of the library. However, the Duke's pain-lined, attractive face was somewhat reassuring.

There was nothing pompous about him. He was just a man who had suffered and had come through his suffering into a calm haven of his own making.

"I wanted to talk to you, Miss Granville."

"Yes?"

"It is about my mother, of course. I am a little worried about her."

"Worried about her?" Anne repeated.

She felt she was being stupid but at the same time wondering what could possibly worry the Duke. The Duchess was well, extremely well . . . in fact she had shown her good health by being more difficult and more exhausting than usual!

"Yes," the Duke went on. "It may sound stupid to you, but I am anxious for my mother to have a calm and peaceful old age. She is getting on now, we all realise that, but at the same time her extraordinary vitality makes her inclined to create situations and to cause disturbances even as she did when she was young."

He smiled and his eyes twinkled.

"There were quite a lot of incidents then, I don't mind telling you!"

"She is wonderful for her age," Anne said.

"She has always been wonderful," the Duke corrected. "I can remember her when I was a little boy organising and running our big house, arranging parties for the girls, fetes and sports for the village and the county, and having a finger in every possible pie which concerned the well-being or the happiness of everyone on our estates.

"She never seemed to be tired and I should think she got through as much work as any Cabinet Minister, but she always had time for us and for anyone else who needed her. She was an amazing woman. They don't make them like that in these days."

"But why are you worrying about her?" Anne asked.

"I am speaking to you in confidence at the moment," the Duke answered, "and I know you will respect that confidence. Has my mother ever talked to you about her second son Adrian?"

"Yes, of course. He was killed in a motoring accident, wasn't he?"

The Duke nodded.

"He was always a careless driver. He loved speed. We were for ever warning him. I think he had his licence endorsed more times than one would think possible and one day retribution overcame him. He was driving home from a party along the Great North Road. He loved driving at night.

"He must have been going very fast—about seventy the police estimated it. He hit a stationary lorry—they are dangerous at any time because one can often miss seeing their rear lights. He hit it and neither he nor his wife ever regained consciousness."

The Duke sighed and looked into the empty fireplace. It was a silence Anne did not like to interrupt.

She knew he was remembering his brother, seeing him as a little boy running about the garden, climbing haystacks, fishing in the lake. It must have been fun when all the children were at home together—they must have been happy and united like other families before the responsibility of their position fell heavily upon them.

"They both died without knowing what had happened," the Duke went on after a moment, "and they left behind a son. It is about his son—his name is Montague—that I am going to speak to you. My mother was very unhappy at Adrian's death. She loved him perhaps more than any of us.

"I don't know why exactly except that as a boy he was rather a weakling and I am told mothers always give more affection to an ailing member of the family, in which case I am due for all her love now!"

He smiled at the reference to himself, but without bitterness. Anne had learned by now that the Duke could always talk of himself without being the least self-conscious or awkward about his affliction.

"But . . . he went on, "my mother, made as she is, had to show her affection for Adrian in a practical manner. She wanted to run his son's life; she interfered, she planned, she schemed, all for a boy who I think was at first knocked sideways by his bereavement and wanted only to be left alone to recover.

"Anyway, there was a row—one of those absurd, nonsensical family rows which tear everyone to pieces emotionally but which do no good and in which eventually no one is the victor. Montague defied his grandmother. None of us blame him for it. He told her that he intended to lead his own life and wanted no interference.

"Of course my mother was bitterly hurt, but instead of saying so she merely made things worse by informing Montague that she was cutting him off without a penny! I think I must explain to you that any money there is in our family belongs to my mother.

"She was an heiress and my father when he married her was practically penniless. He had big estates and the house, but they were heavily mortgaged. Luckily, he fell in love; and I say this in all sincerity—he fell in love with a very beautiful and rich young woman and she fell in love with him.

"Everyone looked on it of course as a marriage of convenience, but it was nothing of the sort. They loved each other devotedly until the day that my father died. My mother paid off the mortgages on the estates while my father was alive; but as most of her money was in trust and she could not touch the capital, land had to be sold when my father died to meet the death duties.

"The position now, and as far as I am concerned it is no secret, is that on my mother's death, what remains of her fortune is to be divided amongst her children—the son who holds the title having the major share.

"Unfortunately, as the present holder of the dukedom, I have no children, and I consider it only fair that Adrian's son should receive what would have been his inheritance. My mother, however, is determined to disinherit Montague unless we can somehow effect a reconciliation."

The Duke paused.

"I want you to help us, Miss Granville."

"Of course I will," Anne answered, "but you know how difficult the Duchess is!"

"I do indeed!" the Duke sighed. "However, she is very fond of you, and when she is talking to you, as I know she does talk to you about the old days, if you could encourage her to remember how much she loved Adrian and what a sweet little boy he was, perhaps it would help."

"Couldn't her grandson say he was sorry?" Anne suggested tentatively.

The Duke made a gesture with his hands.

"I wish he would," he said, "but he is a very pig-headed young man. You see, he too has some of my mother's blood in him. She has threatened him and he has wiped the dust of the family from off his feet. That is how the position stands at the moment."

"How sad," Anne said.

"Yes, it is," the Duke agreed, "especially when I remember how much my mother loved Adrian—and his wife. She was a very beautiful and very sweet woman."

"I will certainly do my best," Anne promised, "but if I say too much I might do more harm than good. The Duchess always prefers to take up a contrary attitude."

The Duke laughed.

"How well you know her! You must be a very shrewed person, Miss Granville."

"I wish I were," Anne answered. "But I do love being here, and I am terribly grateful to the Duchess for giving me the opportunity."

"Don't tell her that," the Duke admonished. "She will bully you and make you her slave for life. My mother only respects what she is not quite certain she possesses."

Anne smiled and got to her feet.

"I will do my best," she repeated.

"Thank you, Miss Granville."

The Duke's eyes followed her appreciatively as she walked towards the door.

When Anne got upstairs, the Duchess was in a bad temper.

"You are late, Miss Granville; it is nearly twenty

minutes past two! You went to luncheon at one . . . what have you been doing?"

"I am sorry," Anne said. "I went to buy something and they kept me ages in the shop."

"Haven't you had anything to eat?" the Duchess asked.

"Yes, thank you, I had a sandwich and a cup of coffee."

"Ridiculous!" the Duchess snorted. "Why don't you have something substantial to eat? You girls think it is attractive to have a figure like a lamp-post, but I am sure the men don't like it! When we were young, we had figures that were figures, curves everywhere and round faces with beautiful complexions.

"No wonder we were successes! I can promise you one thing: having a husband and a home is far more comfortable in the long run than striving for a career."

Anne had heard this argument often enough before.

"I am sure it is," she said quietly; "but until one meets the right man, one has to provide for oneself."

"Right man?" the Duchess ejaculated. "Stuff and nonsense! You don't want to marry for money, but to love where money is. I can tell you another thing. It is better to be married and unhappy than never to be married at all."

"Yet you married the right man," Anne said softly.

The Duchess started.

"Who has been telling you stories?"

Anne laughed.

"One of your children told me. It might not have been true, of course, but they think of you as being ideally happy."

"Not true?" the Duchess exclaimed. "Of course it's true! My husband was the most wonderful man who ever lived. My dear, I wish you could have seen him—tall, handsome, good looking . . . he stood out in any gathering, even at the opening of Parliament."

"I am waiting for someone just like him," Anne smiled.

"Then you will have to wait," the Duchess retorted, but her tone was mild. As she watched Anne tidying the things on her bed she added: "You are pretty enough. I would like to see you married to someone really nice. Do you ever meet any men?"

"Not many," Anne admitted.

Then, because she wanted to keep the Duchess amused and she knew it would be of interest to her, she told her what had happened last night. The Duchess listened enthralled.

"It must have been a very essential part of her charm all through her life," Anne thought, "that she can absorb herself completely in other people's interests."

No incident was so small, none so unimportant, that the Duchess was not prepared to hear about it and comment upon it.

"So Sally has gone back?" she said when Anne ended her story.

"Yes," Anne answered. "She loves the child. Besides, Mr. Dunstan was quite sincere in his apology."

"So he ought to be," the Duchess said. "Ridiculous man! But men never have any sense where children are concerned. I remember my husband always had the most absurd ideas about the children. I used to agree with him at the time and then did the exact opposite of what he had suggested. He never noticed. He was always satisfied that he was bringing up his children himself quite perfectly."

"I wish we knew what Mr. Dunstan's wife was like."

The Duchess puckered her brow.

"I seem to remember him getting married; a big, splashy wedding in the *Tatler* and the usual impertinent Press comments about his income, but I cannot remember who she was. Tell your sister to find out what the woman's name was before she married."

"That might be difficult," Anne said. "She cannot ask Mr. Dunstan and she can hardly talk about it to the servants."

The Duchess sighed impatiently.

"Who has suggested that she should talk to the servants? She will find out one way or another if she has any gumption. Tell her to say to that old Nanny:

'Wasn't Mrs. Dunstan a Miss Blake? I think I met some of her relations the other day.'

"Then old Nanny will reply:

'Oh, dear me no, her name was Jones!'

"That is not talking to the servants, my girl, but it is getting the information you want!"

Anne laughed.

"Oh, Duchess, you are funny! I cannot help feeling that you have always got what you wanted in your life."

"Pretty nearly everything," the Duchess replied. "When one gets old, one looks back on life and the only things one regrets are the things one did not do. Old age has its compensations; if things go wrong you may find out later, perhaps years later, that it was all for the best. It is just the way life is. If you have got courage to do what you want, you are nearly always rewarded."

"Courage!" Anne said reflectively. "I am afraid that is what I haven't got."

"What do you mean?" the Duchess asked.

"I am afraid of so many things," Anne answered, ". . . people, ill-health, having to struggle. I am not brave. Sally is and so is Marigold. I am the faint-hearted one of the family."

"Nonsense!" the Duchess said. "I don't believe a word of it! Why, you are not even afraid of me!"

"I am terrified," Anne answered.

The Duchess chuckled.

"Then you don't show it, and that is half the battle. You are not a bit like my previous companions. Now, I wonder why I put up with them so long. How they used to annoy me—peeping at me with scared eyes and giving little squeals of horror when I said something outrageous! I used to lie awake at night thinking out things to shock them."

"Oh dear," Anne exclaimed; "and now I have deprived you of that pleasure."

"You are a good girl," the Duchess said fondly. "What are we going to do now?"

"I will read to you if you would like me to," Anne suggested, "or would you prefer a game of bezique?"

"Bezique!" the Duchess answered. "And don't you have the impertinence to beat me. You ought to let me win out of respect."

"You would hate it if I did.

The Duchess chuckled.

"I have a nasty suspicion you are really to good for me. Who taught you?"

"My father," Anne replied. "He was ill one winter and he was not allowed to read. It drove him nearly crazy to lie in bed all day with nothing to do, so we took it in turns to play games with him. In consequence we all became experts, especially at bezique, and chess which were his favourites."

"I would like to have known your father," the Duchess said unexpectedly.

"He was a darling."

"You are like him?"

"Not a bit" Anne answered. "But Sally is, in character and temperament as well. My father was a saint and Sally is halfway to becoming one."

"She sounds a little prig," the Duchesss said.

She spoke provocatively just to see the colour come into Anne's cheeks and her eyes flash.

"She can easily come round here when she is taking that child of Robert Dunstan's for a walk."

"She would love to meet you," Anne said.

"Then tell her to look in one afternoon," the Duchess commanded.

Anne went home ready to relate the invitation to Sally, only to find that she had already come in and gone out again.

"Where has she gone to?" she asked Marigold.

"I have not the slightest idea," Marigold answered. "She changed her dress, powdered her nose and was gone before I had time to ask her a question of any sort."

"You were too busy talking about yourself I suppose," Anne said, making it not a spiteful retort but a mere statement of fact.

"Well, I was as a matter of fact," Marigold replied. "I had quite a show-down with Nadine Sloe today. She accused me of wearing one of their dresses the wrong way. It was ridiculous of course! She was just trying to find fault. I had made the dress look wonderful and not less than three people had ordered from it during the afternoon, so I know that if there was a fault it wasn't mine."

"What happened?" Anne asked, sitting down on another bed and watching Marigold as she pulled on her stockings.

"I wasn't rude, of course," Marigold went on; "I was far too clever for that. I listened to what she had to say, then I said:

'I am terribly sorry if I am in the wrong, Miss Sloe. Do you think it would be a good idea if I put the dress on again and went and asked Mr. Sorrell how he would like it to be worn?'

"She was furious at that, of course! She looked at me to see if I was being impertinent, so I put on a very innocent expression—wide, baby-blue eyes—and waited. After a moment she said gruffly,

'There is no need to do that—just be more careful in the future!'

"The girls and I had a good laugh about her when she had gone, as you can imagine."

Anne looked serious.

"Don't you hate working under those circumstances? I should be unhappy to be in the same building with someone who disliked me."

Marigold shrugged her shoulders.

"I couldn't care less!"

"Do you think she is really in love with Peter?"

"If she is, she can have him," Marigold said sharply.

"That reminds me," Anne went on, "what has happened to Peter? We haven't seen him for days and days! I asked Sally last night and she said she thought he had gone away but that you would know."

"Well, I don't!" Marigold replied. "For goodness' sake don't worry me with idiotic questions at this moment. I have got to get dressed. Ben Barlow is sending a car for me at half past seven."

"Oh, is the party tonight?" Anne asked.

Marigold nodded.

"Do you like my dress?"

She took if from the wardrobe and held it up. Anne gave a cry of admiration.

It was certainly lovely—fold upon fold of pale green tulle made the skirt while a soft fichu of ruched tulle was curved to reveal the shoulders of the wearer. It was caught at the breast with a big bunch of half-opened rosebuds.

"It is lovely!" Anne approved. "But it must have been terribly expensive!"

"It was," Marigold agreed. "Don't tell Sally, but I had to pawn my wrist-watch."

"But she gave you fifteen pounds."

"Yes, I know," Marigold answered, "but you don't suppose a dress like that can be bought for fifteen pounds, even though we mannequins do get a special price."

"Do be careful of it," Anne begged, "I shall want another pair of shoes and some new nightgowns this month. I have already spent half my salary on a new blouse."

She took it out of a paper bag and showed it to Marigold.

"It's pretty," Marigold said carelessly, "but rather dull; you don't want to look stuffy! We were all so fearfully unsophisticated when we came to London. We have got to drop our country airs and become really up-to-date and smart."

"Why should we?" Anne asked. "Really smart people like the Duchess's daughters are not a bit sophisticated. Lady Catherine has very nice clothes, but they are very plain and simple—nothing much to them."

"They are not smart people, stupid!" Marigold said. "They are just the old aristocracy and they are completely out-of-date in these days."

"Well, who are the smart people?"

"It is rather difficult to say; Hetty Lelong for one."

"But she's an actress!"

"It doesn't stop her being smart and going to all the most wonderful parties and being asked everywhere," Marigold answered.

"And who else?"

"You wouldn't be any wiser if I told you their names; I see them come into Michael Sorrell's and they are not all lords and ladies by any means! They are actresses, financiers' wives, dress designers and people who have lots of money and go to the best restaurants night after night. There is nothing particular about them except that they are smart and everyone acknowledges they are the 'right people'."

"The Duchess wouldn't know them."

"Oh, you and your Duchess!" Marigold said. "She just doesn't count any more. She is out of date. Now Ben Barlow's mother was a barmaid. She would still be

147

serving behind the bar if her husband had not invented a quicker sparking-plug than anyone else. It has made young Ben one of the smartest and richest young men in London."

"I should hate that sort of smartness," Anne said disdainfully.

"You might," Marigold said cheerfully, "but as far as I am concerned it is exactly what the doctor ordered."

She put her dress over her head and slipped through it. Her shoulders were dazzlingly white against the green material, her eyes dancing excitedly beneath the flaming beauty of her hair.

She looked lovely when she was ready and waiting for the car to call for her, but if Sally had been at home she would have been anxious.

There was a false gaiety about Marigold, an un-natural note in her voice as if she was forcing herself to be excited and amused while underneath she was nervous and on edge.

But Sally was sitting in a little restaurant in Soho talking to David.

He had asked her to meet him there. It was near the hospital so that he could slip away for dinner without taking an undue amount of time for it.

"I am worried, Sally," David said. "What is the matter with Marigold?"

"I don't know," Sally answered truthfully.

"She is different since she came to London," David went on. "At first I thought it was just excitement and the natural thrill of finding herself in such different surroundings, amongst so many different people, but she isn't happy, Sally—that's what gets me, she isn't happy!"

Sally agreed with him, but she did not think it policy to admit too much to David.

"Are you quite sure you are not exaggerating Marigold's feelings?" she asked. "She is having a lovely time!"

"Yes, I know she is," David's hands clenched suddenly so that his knuckles went white. "And I can't give it to her!"

Sally said nothing, but her eyes were soft and sympathetic.

"Sometimes I think," David said, "I ought to throw up this and go into business—make money! I daresay I could get a job at the bottom and work my way up to the top. I am not really such a fool, you know."

"You are clever, David," Sally answered softly; "we all know that. But do you think any good would come of such a plan? You would not be happy, and if you were not happy yourself you certainly could not make Marigold happy."

David looked down at the table, then he said:

"I have got the chance, Sally, of going in for some research work with Sir Hubert Haydn. Have you heard of him?"

"Of course I have heard of him," Sally replied with a little laugh. "You and your father seldom talk of anyone else."

David smiled in response.

"Well, he is a wizard, you know!"

"So I believe."

"Well, he has asked me if I would do some work with him in his laboratory. It is a compliment, Sally, a tremendous compliment, but at the same time he will keep my nose to the grindstone. That means I shall not see so much of Marigold."

Sally chose her words carefully.

"Don't you think, David, that might be a good thing? Marigold is going through a difficult time in her life. She is adjusting herself to new circumstances, new friends. I think that she . . ." Sally paused for words.

". . . is fed up with the old ones," David supplied.

Sally nodded.

"Something like that, but don't be too hurt about it. It is only a passing phase and Marigold is awfully adolescent in lots of ways."

"And how old are you, I would like to know?" David asked.

Sally did not miss the pain in his eyes.

"I feel like the mother of you all."

"And that's what you are," David answered. "You mother us and look after us, Sally, and half the time we do not even remember to say 'thank you'. We are an ungrateful collection of brats. I cannot think why you worry with us."

"Perhaps because I love you all so much," Sally said.

There was a suspicion of moisture in her eyes because his words were very sweet.

"Sometimes I feel as though you were about five years old snatching the flag from my sand-castle and throwing it into the sea just to annoy me, and at other times I feel you are at least one hundred and eighty and I can't get along without your advice."

"Well, my advice now," Sally said, "is to go into Sir Hubert's laboratory and do something really wonderful. We should all be very proud of you, David, and so would your father."

"Dear old Dad! I didn't really mean what I said just now about chucking up my job. It would break his heart. He has dreamed of my being a doctor like himself ever since I was a little boy; but oh, Sally, I wish I could give Marigold all the things she wants!"

"Don't you think that is rather selfish of you?"

"Selfish?"

"Yes, selfish! Things we get too easily—things we don't have to fight for—we don't appreciate. Marigold will always get such a lot because she is so lovely, but don't let it be too easy or she will begin to want something else."

"Perhaps you are right." David spoke despondently.

"Like so many doctors," Sally said sadly, "when it comes to the people you love you want to prescribe with your heart and not with your head."

"That's true enough."

"Daddy used to say," Sally went on, in the hope that she might ease the cloud of depression which seemed to encompass David at the moment, "that we could never really help the people we loved unless we could look on them quite impersonally and that our own feelings and inclinations must never intrude on their problems."

"Your father was a wonderful man," David said, "but he did not happen to fall in love with anyone like Marigold."

"I don't know," Sally replied, "my mother kept him waiting for five years before she married him."

"Five years? Did she really?"

"Yes, five years! It was a long time, wasn't it? I think she must have been rather like Marigold. She wanted to have a good time and also to marry somebody rich and important. A curate of an obscure Cornish village wasn't much of a catch."

"Sally, you have given me hope."

David reached out both his hands towards her across the table.

"I don't want particularly to give you that," Sally answered. "I want to give you ambition to be a success at your own job."

"That goes with it; I cannot work if I am miserable, wondering what Marigold is doing, anxious in case she is falling in love with someone else. Now, after what you have said, I can work like a Trojan! 'The years for Rachel!' Why don't we always remember our Bible stories? And perhaps it need not be as long as five years."

"I hope not, David," Sally said.

Her tone was hesitant and her lips were dry.

Somehow she knew at that moment that David would

never marry Marigold. At times Sally had an intuition which was almost fey.

She would know things so clearly, so positively, that nothing in heaven or on earth could shake her conviction that what she knew was the truth.

She knew now that David would never win Marigold and that Marigold would never come to love David, and her heart ached for him while she was wise enough to say nothing.

Ten

Marigold was putting the finishing touches to her hair when Ben Barlow arrived in his big Mercedes.

Mr. Jarvis shouted up the stairs that he was there and Marigold ran down wondering what Ben would think of the rather sordid and unattractive appearance of the Jarvises' front hall.

At the same time she had no intention of asking him upstairs. She did not wish him to meet Anne and Sally, for, deep in her heart, although she would not yet admit it to herself, Marigold was ashamed of Ben.

He was a tall, rather swarthy young man with too low a forehead and eyes that were slightly close together.

He had, however, a genuine *joie de vivre* which made him enjoy everything and everybody and which prevented him, despite all his excesses where women, horses and money were concerned, from being an out-and-out bounder.

There was something disarming and ingenuous about him, and he had among a crowd of riff-raff acquaintances many genuine friends.

At the same time there was no disguising Ben's reputation, and despite her championship Marigold was aware that she would have been afraid to introduce him to her father.

"Hullo, Sweetie, you look like a million dollars!" was Ben's greeting as she came down the stairs and into the hall.

"Thank you, Ben. I have got a new dress and I hope the party is going to be worthy of it."

"You bet your life it will be! We're going places tonight!"

He helped her into the car with a deftness which bespoke long practice and they roared away down the less frequented streets.

"Glad to see me?" he asked after a moment.

"Don't expect me to say the obvious," Marigold retorted.

"Why not, when it is true?"

Marigold laughed. She could not help it. Ben was so confident and cocksure of himself that it had an attraction all its own.

"Who is coming tonight?" she asked.

"Just my best friends," Ben assured her solemnly.

But Marigold, used to remarks of that sort and taking them at their true value, was not surprised when they arrived at the restaurant to find that dinner was arranged for thirty people and that more were expected later.

There were orchids on the table and big Jeroboams of champagne in silver ice-buckets and a number of Ben's guests were already waiting for him in the cocktail bar.

Marigold looked them over quickly and somehow in spite of her resolution to be worldly-wise and sophisticated her heart shrank.

The men were all right up to a point. They were racing men, stock-brokers, celebrities in the world of sport, in fact the usual crowd of acquaintances and hangers-on who were always prepared to enjoy a good meal at Ben's expense.

The women were different; Marigold had lunched with Ben on two or three occasions and she thought that his taste in women was hardly to be admired, but the ones he had invited tonight were worse than anything she had imagined.

Hard-faced and elaborately-dressed, there was something synthetic about each one of them, something which was betrayed by their glittering jewels, the expensive orchids pinned on their shoulders and the long, blood-red nails which ornamented their fingers.

Marigold was conscious, too, that they stared at her in what amounted to open hostility. She was new, unknown and lovely—all these things being to them a potential danger.

Ben introduced her and Marigold could not help being amused by their names.

They were so pretentious and high-sounding; Gloria de Vere—Cynthia Claremont—Desiree Doncaster. It was all too obviously calculated and dramatic and revealed the owner's taste.

"Well, let's go in to dinner," Ben said at last.

There had been several rounds of cocktails of which Marigold had only one, sipping it deliberately and hiding the glass half full behind a vase of flowers.

They trooped into the restaurant. The band was playing a rhumba and one of Ben's guests, already exhilarated, danced a few steps alone.

Every eye was on them, everyone in the room seemed to Marigold to stop eating and talking as they watched this ornate, over-colourful party arrive.

"At least nobody knows me," she thought.

She had no idea how different she looked in her leaf-green dress with her clear, natural complexion and shining hair.

"Come and sit on my right, Marigold," Ben commanded.

Marigold felt a wave of antagonism sweep through the other women in the party.

Opposite her on Ben's left there was a very expensive-looking blonde, with her hair swept up from a long neck into a thick artificial coil on top of her head. Her arms were weighed down with diamond and ruby bracelets and there were rubies in her ears and at the opening of her very low-cut dress.

"You've met Laura, of course," was Ben's casual introduction.

The blonde inclined her head stiffly and was apparently unaware of Marigold's friendly, outstretched hand. She bent forward as Ben sat down and whispered in his ear.

Marigold had no idea what Laura said but her intuition told her it was something personal and she felt the colour rising in her cheeks.

She turned to the man on her other side and to her relief found he was a rather nice-looking, older man she had noticed earlier in the evening. He smiled at her.

"Shall we introduce ourselves?" he asked. "I am Toby Dawson."

"And I am Marigold Granville."

"I have heard about you," he said.

Before she had time to ask him what he had heard Ben claimed her attention.

"I've bought you a present, Marigold. I had a good day's racing and thought as you are my most important guest tonight we ought to celebrate."

He passed a little box across the table to her. Marigold took it—embarrassed and not quite knowing what to do. She was well aware that Laura on the other side of the table was gazing at her in undisguised fury.

She opened the box and there, lying against a background of black velvet, was a lipstick set with what appeared to be brilliants. Marigold stared at it unable to make up her mind what to say or do.

Had it been anything but a lipstick she could have refused it gracefully on the ground of its being jewelry, but she was not certain in her own mind whether it was real or imitation.

If the stones were real it must have cost a lot of money and she would be perfectly justified in saying "no"; if on the other hand they were false, she would make a fool of herself by returning it and letting the others see that she thought Ben, a comparative stranger, might be giving her something of value.

Coolly, without betraying the anguished indecision within herself, she glanced at it and then at the woman opposite.

"How sweet of you," she said at last to Ben. "Thank you very much indeed, but, as it happens, I already have one."

She turned to Laura.

"I noticed your lipstick was rather worn just now—wouldn't you like this one? I would love you to have it."

There was a moment's stupefied pause and then Laura with an indescribably note of insolence in her voice said:

"All right, if you don't want it."

She reached over, took the case from Marigold and slipped it into her bag, then looked up at Ben with something glittering and unpleasant in her dark-fringed eyes.

For a moment Marigold thought Ben was going to lose his temper, but instead he threw back his head and laughed.

"You are a cool one and no mistake!" he said to Marigold. "I suppose you think you have put me in my place? All right then, let's see how long I stay in it."

"Tell me about your racing today," Marigold suggested.

She was anxious to change the subject and feeling that this at any rate was a safe topic, for she knew that Ben spent most of his life on race-courses of one sort or another.

He had distinguished himself as a racing motorist, but he also had a stable and had managed to win two or three flat races during the season. Ben was not loath to launch out on his favourite topic.

Too often the women with whom he spent the evening wanted to talk only about themselves, and they had nearly finished dinner before Laura managed to recapture his attention.

The food was superlatively good, the champagne of a notable vintage, and by now the restaurant was filled with people.

"I ought to be enjoying myself," Marigold thought, and knew that she was not doing so.

She felt suddenly ashamed of the money she had spent on her dress, money which could be ill afforded from the family exchequer and which, expended extravagantly on her, meant that Anne and Sally would go without something essential.

What did all this frivolity, excitement and expenditure amount to, she asked herself, not only for herself but for all the people packed into this comparatively small low-ceilinged room?

For the men perhaps it was relaxation, for the women something more important—the eternal search for security, marriage and a husband? But was this the right way to pursue a state which should be, if it were to be successful, fundamentally sacred?

"A penny for your thoughts," Toby Dawson's voice said suddenly.

Marigold realised she had beeen staring at her plate oblivious of her surroundings.

With an effort she tried to force herself to be gay and bright.

"They are worth more than a penny."

"How much then? The price of a diamond bracelet?" Marigold smiled.

"More than that, perhaps even the price of a plain gold wedding-ring."

Toby laughed.

"Aren't you being over-optimistic?"

Marigold looked at him in surprise and then realised to her horror that he thought she was referring to Ben. She could think of nothing to say and the colour flooded into her cheeks. Toby Dawson did not seem to notice.

"As an old friend of Ben," he said, "let me warn you. He isn't the marrying sort. They have all tried, every one of them." He looked round the table. "But it has got to be a very special sort of sprat to catch that mackerel."

Marigold felt as if words choked her. To think that he thought she was trying to capture Ben Barlow! How dare he!

Then even as her rage surged within her, she realised it was true. Had she not bought the dress she was wearing for that very reason, dressed herself up and defied the warning of her own conscience for just that very purpose?

"I don't know Ben at all well," she said lamely because she felt it was impossible to say anything to defend herself against the suggestion which Toby Dawson implied and took so easily for granted.

"He will be a good lad when he can stop sowing his wild oats," Toby remarked. "He has a shrewd cleverness in him which one cannot help admiring, but . . . isn't there something in the Bible about it being easier to go through the eye of a needle than for a rich man to find happiness?"

"Is he so very rich?" Marigold asked. "I thought no one had any income in these days with taxation what it is."

"Taxation does not worry Ben all that amount," Toby Dawson replied. "He has the luck of the devil and what he makes on the markets is not taxable anyway!"

He saw Marigold's puzzled look.

"I am referring to stock markets; I am Ben's stockbroker so I know what I am talking about. Besides, old man Barlow collected some very pretty treasures with his money before he died. It is extraordinary how a man of his origin should have had such good taste. He was never ostentatious.

"He settled down in a nice little house in the country and filled it with treasures from all over the world—pictures, china, books and furniture. He liked buying—he liked collecting. Ben is reaping the benefit of that now.

"When he wants to give a party of this sort he has only to sell a picture or send a van-load of the old man's treasures to Christies."

Marigold suddenly felt sick.

She thought of Ben's father collecting his treasures, as Toby Dawson called them, thought of his pride and pleasure in obtaining a bargain, thought of him touching it gently, reverencing it for the beautiful thing it was, perhaps feeling, even as her father had done, a real protective love for his personal possessions.

And now they were being sold to provide champagne and orchids for greedy, worthless people, to buy rubies and diamond bracelets which would only intensify and never dispel the look of greed in mascara-fringed eyes.

"I ought never to have come," she told herself.

She longed to run home to Sally and Anne and to the sweet, clean sanity of their affection.

At that moment Ben touched her arm and asked her to dance. She rose automatically and preceded him to the dance-floor. He swept her into his arms and she knew in that moment that he was a beautiful dancer.

Their steps matched and they danced in silence. It

was only after they had been moving round the room for some time that Ben spoke.

"You are not cross with me, are you?"

"Of course not," Marigold answered; "why should I be?"

"I don't know—I just felt I had put my foot in it somewhere. Perhaps I oughtn't to have asked Laura here tonight."

"Why not?" Marigold queried.

"Oh well . . . I never was good at explanations, but I am sorry about the lipstick. It was like her to snatch it from you. When she was a baby she had three bottles to all the other children's one!"

Marigold laughed at his joke, but at the same time she began to realise that Laura was something rather special in Ben's life. If that was true she was sorry for Ben.

With all his faults he was frank, unpretentious and generous. Laura was all too obviously the opposite.

"I will tell you what," Ben said, "we will enjoy ourselves tonight with the crowd but you must come out and dine with me alone and then we can talk. There are lots of things I want to talk to you about."

"Such as?"

"You, of course!" Ben answered. He held her eyes for a brief moment. "You're very lovely."

"So are lots of other women."

"But you've got something different—I wonder what it is?"

"Oughtn't we to go back to your party?" Marigold suggested, somewhat afraid of the conversation.

"There is plenty of time for that. I saw you getting on well with Toby. He's a grand chap! The rest of them are not really up your street, I can see that now. I must have been rather stupid when I asked the crowd to dine."

For a moment Ben looked puzzled, like a small boy

who has come up against something too big for his comprehension. Then he smiled.

"You're a good sport, aren't you, Marigold? I am looking forward to that evening of ours alone!"

He slipped his hand under her elbow as he took her back to the table, and despite the feeling that she must make an effort to be a good sport Marigold wanted to shake herself free.

"What is the matter with me?" she asked herself. "I have been wanting to go to expensive parties, I have been wanting to meet rich people, and now, when I am here, I don't like it!"

She looked round the restaurant. The men and women at the other tables seemed little different from those at her own table. The women were all smart and beautifully jewelled, their faces curiously doll-like under an excess of make-up.

Marigold found herself wishing that Anne would come in. If Anne was well dressed she would knock all these women sideways. She was beautiful, really beautiful, with a beauty that owed nothing to artificiality.

At the same time Marigold wondered if the men in the room would really appreciate Anne. She was not vivacious, she did not know how to be amusing, to make men laugh and compliment a woman so that there was a sting lying beneath the flattery.

"Oh dear," sighed Marigold, torn and bewildered within herself, "what do I want, what is the matter with me?"

Because she was flying from her own thoughts she was glad when Ben suddenly cried out:

"This place is getting dull. Come on, let's go somewhere else!"

The party piled into cars and taxis and rushed off to a night club. Here there were low lights, tables in discreet alcoves and a band which seemed to command one's feet to move as if hypnotised by their rhythm.

Marigold danced with one after another of the party. She grew used to their compliments.

"Where have you been all my life?"

"The moment I set eyes on you I thought to myself . . ."

"Never have I seen a lovelier . . ."

"Are you as sweet as you look?"

Somehow their voices ceased to have any meaning. She danced and danced, the full skirt of her green dress billowing out around her, her feet untiring on the highly-polished floor. At last the party began to break up.

"I have got some work to do tomorrow, Ben," Toby Dawson said, "and I am taking Rosa home—she is tired."

"Never too tired for you, darling," Rosa pouted by his side.

"I have got a directors' meeting at ten o'clock," Toby went on, "and I cannot go to it looking like a New Year's Eve hang-over."

"That's all right," Ben said, "tell them I kept you. I don't fancy they are going to fight with my account this year."

"I don't fancy they will," Toby Dawson smiled, "but at the same time, old boy, I am going home."

"He's bored, that's what's wrong with him," Ben cried, "and who shall blame him? This place is a morgue. Let's go back to my flat—we'll drink there."

"Oh yes, let's!" everyone exclaimed except Marigold.

She was wondering how she, too, could get away. She knew that Ben would protest if she made the slightest effort to go and that she could not be firm with him as Toby Dawson was being.

"Good night, Miss Granville."

She put her hand into Toby's. The words were formulating on her lips, "Please take me too!" but it was too late . . . from the doorway came Rosa's shrill tones:

"Come on, Toby, they've got a taxi for us!"

"I hope we shall meet again," Toby Dawson said politely and was gone.

Once again what remained of the party piled into cars and taxis. It had increased in size since the evening started. Several people had come on when the theatres had closed, some of them, as Marigold gathered, being show girls in a very spectacular high-kicking revue which was the talk of the West End.

When she went to the cloak-room to pick up her wrap the other women chattering in high-pitched voices around her seemed cheap and rather squalid.

They were smart enough, they were all draped in capes of fox or sable and nearly every one of them was wearing glittering, spectacular jewelry.

"I am a snob," Marigold thought. "But they are not my sort."

One of the girls with long, bleached hair which hung below her shoulders stopped her as she turned towards the door.

"You are new on Ben's parties, aren't you?" she asked.

"This is the first time I have been to one," Marigold confessed.

"I thought I had never seen you before. How do you like Ben?"

"Very much," Marigold answered politely. "But I do not know him very well."

"That needn't stop you," the girl said pointedly. "You have to be a fast worker where our Ben's concerned."

There were shrieks of laughter from the others and Marigold knew that her cheeks were flaming. She was spared a reply, however, by Laura's voice from the doorway.

"Come on, girls, we can't stay here all night!"

The party surged out, their strong, exotic perfumes mingling almost overpoweringly.

"If only I could slip away!" Marigold thought dismally.

It was impossible. She found herself sandwiched in the back of Ben's car with two girls to whom she had not previously spoken and two men. It was uncomfortable and the girls were giggling at being crowded.

Fortunately it was for only a short distance. Ben's flat was just round the corner and once again they struggled out on to the pavement.

"Come on, chaps," Ben called and they shot upwards in a fast lift which took them to the sixth floor.

Ben's flat was everything Marigold had expected it to be; super-luxurious and chromium-plated, mirrors reflecting and re-reflecting, cocktail bars concealed in walls, a trans-atlantic radio which played incessantly and great vases of hot-house flowers everywhere.

"I have them sent up from the country," Ben said when somebody exclaimed at their fragrance. "I don't know much about flowers myself but I like to see them about the place."

"That's a typical trait in his character," Marigold thought. "He doesn't know much about anything, including women, but he likes to see them about—he is afraid of missing anything. He is very young."

She glanced at the clock over the mantelpiece and to her horror she saw it was after three o'clock.

The others had already paired themselves off and were sitting intimately close on the sofas while Laura and the young man with whom she had been dancing had disappeared into another room.

Ben was getting out the drinks and was for the moment approachable. Marigold went to his side.

"Ben, I want to go home."

"Go home?" he laughed at her. "You can't go home yet!"

"I'm tired, Ben. I have got to work tomorrow. It's pretty hard work too."

"What? Putting on pretty dresses? You can't call that hard work—it's what every woman likes!"

Marigold thought of the innumerable changes she made during the day, the careful lifting of the dresses over her head, the rearranging of her hair, the change of make-up for different dresses, the accessories that must not be forgotten, customers who asked to see the same dress over and over again. Not hard work?

Oh well, there was no point in trying to explain.

"I must go home, Ben," she said urgently, "I really am tired. Could someone get me a taxi? If not, perhaps I will be able to pick one up."

"I don't want you to go!" Ben's jaw was set defiantly.

There was a shriek of laughter from the other end of the room. A man and girl were struggling together.

They had obviously both had too much to drink and as the woman got to her feet she knocked over a small table. Ben looked at both of them, then at Marigold.

"Perhaps you are right," he said quietly. "I will take you home."

"Oh, I don't want to bother you to do that," Marigold expostulated.

But already he had slipped her coat round her shoulders and was leading her out of the flat towards the lift.

"Please, Ben, you ought to look after your guests."

"They will look after themselves," he replied. "I fetched you and I am taking you back. That is understood."

They got into his car and he drove off.

"Enjoyed yourself?" he asked, then before she could answer, added: "No, of course you haven't! I will give another party for you one night with the sort of people you would really like."

"How do you know the sort of people I would like?" Marigold asked.

"I don't," Ben answered, "but I want you to like me."

"I do. You are very kind."

They reached the Saracen's Head and Ben stopped the car.

"I'd like to be kind to you, Marigold." He turned sideways in the driving-seat to look at her. "You are awfully pretty—the prettiest girl I have seen in years."

"Thank you, Ben. Now I had better get out."

Marigold spoke quickly. There was something in Ben's voice and in the bold appraisal of his eyes which frightened her.

"Don't go in yet," he begged, putting his hand on hers. "I want to talk to you. I want you to talk to me. There are a lot of things we've got to say to each other. You are different from anyone I have ever met before."

"One day we will talk," Marigold said, "but not to-night."

"Why not tonight?" Ben pleaded. "You are here, I am here . . . what the hell does anything else matter? Tomorrow other things, other people, may come between us or may interfere, but at the moment we are together."

"I am sorry, Ben," Marigold began and then his arms were round her shoulders.

"Be nice to me, Marigold," he whispered, "you fascinate me!"

His lips were almost on hers but she wrenched herself free.

"No, Ben, no!"

She was surprised at her own strength as she pushed him away from her, and finding the handle of the car door she opened it and got out into the street.

He jumped out after her, but by the time he reached her she had her key in the lock.

"Good night, Ben, and thank you."

"Marigold, don't go, I must talk to you! You can't leave me like this!"

"I can," Marigold said cheerfully, and did so, slipping throught the door and closing it firmly in his face.

She had reached the top of the stairs and stood for several minutes listening in the darkness of the bedroom before the car drove away.

Now she was safe she could smile at the astonishment on his face. Ben Barlow was not used to such treatment.

Sally and Anne were sleeping peacefully and to avoid disturbing them Marigold did not put on the light.

The moon was shining through the windows for the curtains had not been drawn, and she undressed in the silver pool of light, unfastening her dress and letting it slip in a tumbled heap to the floor.

It looked sad and lifeless lying there and she thought to herself whimsically that it was like her evening—she had expected too much of it and had come home tired and disappointed.

"What is the matter with me?" she asked herself once again. "What is it I want? What is it that makes me so dissatisfied?"

She knew the answer, it was spoken only too clearly in her own heart, and defiantly, because the truth hurt her so desperately, she threw back her head and stared through the window.

"I am only crying for . . . the moon," she whispered, but the words ended with a sob.

Eleven

Anne stood in Piccadilly and watched yet another bus full to capacity pass without stopping.

It was teeming with rain and she was conscious that her umbrella, small and attractive enough to do service as a sunshade, was pitiably inadequate in a real downpour. What was more, both her feet were soaking wet as her shoes needed repairing.

She had been intending to see about them for over a week, but there was not only the expense of the repairs, there was also the cost of buying others to replace them, and she had put off doing this simply from lack of money.

The electric stove which the Jarvises had agreed to allow them to erect on the landing had cost more than they had anticipated; and while it was a joy to think that they need not go out night after night, the bill had somehow to be met and out of current expenses.

They had so very little capital in the bank that Sally had made them promise that they would draw no further upon it but would try to make do out of their wages.

"Suppose one of us were ill," she said, "or had to have an operation. We have no one to turn to and this must be our nest-egg to be touched only in a real emergency."

Anne and Marigold had both agreed, but Anne knew secretly that Sally's words were more for Marigold than for herself.

Marigold had been extravagant. She was always buying things—dresses, hats, underclothes, shoes. Although she was earning good money, she was as often as not down to her last shilling at the end of the week, having to borrow from her sisters for bus fares and not contributing her fair share towards the meals.

Not that she was in for many of them—she was out night after night, although it seemed to Anne that she derived little pleasure from such gaiety. In fact it was difficult to know what was the matter with Marigold during the last three weeks.

She seemed out of sorts, irritable, cross, and at times perilously near tears. She gave her confidence to neither of her sisters, only whisking back to Saracen's Head when Sorrell's closed to change into evening dress, waiting impatiently once she was ready to be fetched by high-powered and expensive cars.

She returned long after they were asleep and got up in the morning, usually in sleepy silence, more often than not refusing to eat any breakfast as if the mere sight of food made her feel ill.

When dressed she would rush for her bus with perhaps only half a dozen sentences exchanged between her and her sisters.

"What is the matter with her?" Anne asked Sally more than once.

Sally was no wiser. She could only sigh and look anxious and Anne knew that she worried incessantly about Marigold.

"She is selfish," Anne said once and then rebuked herself for condemning her younger sister.

Marigold was so pretty, so naturally gay, that it was impossible to want her to be anything but a lovely, frivolous butterfly.

"I'm the dull one," Anne thought to herself as she plodded through the quiet Mayfair streets towards Berkeley Square. "I don't expect anything to happen in my life and I don't suppose it ever will."

Somehow after the first few weeks of looking after the Duchess the glamour and excitement had palled into a dull monotony. The house itself seemed as quiet, dim and decrepit as its owner. Nothing seemed to happen.

Day after day things went on with a heart-breaking regularity. The old servants pottered about the place, cleaning away the surface dirt, leaving cobwebs and dust in the corners.

The Duchess grumbled and complained about high taxation, the vagaries of her family and the discomfort of the modern age. There were library books to be changed, letters to be written, newspapers to be read, telephone calls to be made—with nothing unusual or sensational about any of them—it was just the same from Monday to Saturday.

However, even apart from the monotony of her job Anne found her spirits drooping and she realised that what she was learning first hand of the aristocracy was gradually infringing upon and spoiling her own secret dreams.

She found, contrary to her most treasured convictions, that there was no security even for dukes and duchesses in this hustling, progressive world where nothing seemed to matter but money and where even money could lose its value overnight.

As she stood waiting in the rain Anne thought of what had happened that very day, something which she had never woven into those rosy, romantic day-dreams where everything ran smoothly and magically as a fairy tale.

The Duke had come up to London and had been closeted with his mother for nearly two hours during the morning.

It was nearing the time for the Duchess's mid-day cup of coffee and Anne was just wondering whether it would be wise to go in and interrupt them when the bell rang sharply. She hurried into the Duchess's bedroom. She was sitting up in bed looking old, tired and exhausted.

The Duke in an armchair near by gave Anne a welcoming smile.

"Good morning, Miss Granville, I hope you are well."

"Yes, thank you," Anne replied.

"Miss Granville," the Duchess said sharply, "go down and tell Dalton to give you the family jewels from the safe."

Anne turned to obey and as she left the room she heard the Duchess say:

170

"Well, I suppose it must be the emeralds; they will fetch much more than the others."

Wondering what all this was about, Anne hurried down the stairs, found Dalton and helped him to open the big, old-fashioned safe which had been built into the pantry.

"I suppose this means more to be sold," Dalton said in the grumbling, familiar voice of a privileged family servant. "First the Charles the Second silver, then the pictures—now the jewels! It will all be gone soon and there will be nothing for the next generation. Not that they cares—all they thinks about is motor-cars, aeroplanes and such-like. The old days are gone, miss, and gone for good."

"Oh, I hope not!" Anne exclaimed impulsively.

The old man straightened his back and peered at her.

"It's no use wishing, miss; besides, we're in the minority—who cares what we wish these days?"

He looked at her for a moment and then he added: "We'll never see it come again in our lifetimes."

"See what?" Anne asked.

"The elegance!" the old man muttered. "The elegance of England. That's what it was when I was a boy. I'd like you to have seen parties at Cheyn, miss, and here. You could see your face in the silver—great table-loads of it!

"The flowers were a picture and the dozens of footmen in their livery and the ladies with diamonds sparkling in their hair and on their long dresses. Long gloves and programmes, too, and a nice quiet way of speaking.

"None of this 'slap-you-on-the-back' and 'hail-fellow-well-met' attitude. Ladies and gentlemen were ladies and gentlemen in those days, but now . . ." His old face twisted in disgust. "But there, the Duchess will be waiting. This is what she wants, miss."

He picked up a great pile of pink leather cases embossed with gold and put them into Anne's arms. As she turned away she heard him muttering to himself once again about the "lost elegance of England."

"I have been born too late," Anne admitted to herself sadly. "That is the world I would have liked to know."

As she walked up the wide staircase she tried to imagine it thronged with women in evening dress, men wearing tail-coats and big moustaches.

Faintly it seemed to her that she heard the ghost of a waltz coming from behind the doors of the big drawing-room.

"How lovely it must have been!" she sighed.

Then she quickened her pace as she realised she had been loitering, lost in her dreams of the past.

It was with difficulty that she managed to open the door of the Duchess's bedroom and carry the pile of cases across to the bed.

"Have you brought them all?" the Duchess asked.

"These are all that Dalton gave me," Anne replied.

"Well, he knows," the Duchess said. "Oh yes, here are the emeralds."

She pressed open a case and Ann gasped at the shining splendour of what was revealed. Against a background of velvet there lay a tiara, a necklace, bracelet, rings and earrings of emeralds and diamonds.

Their setting was old-fashioned, but nothing could dim the fire and brilliance of the stones themselves. They glittered and shone and soon, as the Duchess opened the other cases, the whole bed looked as though it had been transformed.

There were necklaces of pearls and diamonds, some set as old-fashioned dog-collars; there were crescent moons of rubies and sapphire stars; there were hard, chunky bracelets with strange stones from Eastern lands, and Victorian lockets, brooches and hair orna-

172

ments out of date in shape but all inset with beautiful and valuable jewels.

Anne had never dreamed that anything could be so magnificent.

She exclaimed again and again at the wonder of the gems, aware from the way the Duchess handled them that she loved each one and that every piece had a history and a sentimental value for her.

There were various tiaras of different shapes and of different stones and with them went the attendant necklaces, bracelets, earrings and rings to match, but the emerald set was undoubtedly the finest.

At last the Duchess, having opened every case, announced:

"Yes, I am afraid the emeralds will have to go."

Anne exclaimed impulsively:

"Oh, you don't mean to sell them! You can't sell anything so lovely!"

The Duchess looked at her.

"Everything will have to be sold eventually and it is better to sell jewelry than land."

"Oh, but you can't," Anne protested, "they are so unique, so . . ."

She struggled for words and failed. She wanted to say that they seemed to her part of the family history of Cheyn, part of the family itself, one of the last links with the tradition and power which had once been so important.

It was the Duke who answered her.

"I know what Miss Granville means," he said. "I, too, shall hate to see them sold. I always remember you, Mother, wearing these emeralds when you were going to a State Ball at Buckingham Palace. I could not have been very old at the time but you came into my bedroom to kiss me good night. You looked very beautiful and wore a dress of silver—I can see you now."

"Of course I remember that dress," the Duchess exclaimed, "and the Ball! I was a great success!" She sighed. "Those days are over, Stebby. You have no wife to wear the emeralds and Eleanor would look a freak in them anyway."

Anne remembered that Eleanor was the wife of Lord Henry—the Duchess's second son. She had seen her once, a small, plump woman with a sense of humour but certainly not the presence to carry the Cheyn jewels.

After a short pause the Duchess added:

"Those silly daughters of Eleanor's have no right to wear them either."

The Duke looked across at her.

"No," he said distinctly, "they will not be wanted until Adrian's son comes into the title."

There was moment's silence, pregnant with unexpressed feelings, then the Duchess's mouth tightened and she slammed down the lid of the case.

"We will sell the emeralds!" she said. "That ought to pay both the taxes for this year and the repairs to the farms." She turned to Anne. "Take the other boxes back to Dalton."

Anne longed to protest, somehow to make the Duchess change her mind, but she knew it was no good. Quietly she collected together the other boxes.

Beautiful though they were, the other jewels had not the majesty nor the almost imperial splendour of the emeralds and diamonds.

No one spoke until she had left the room and as she went downstairs she guessed that the Duke had mentioned this nephew intentionally. She wondered what Montague was like.

"It would be interesting to meet him," she thought.

The rest of the family were another generation and, although they were good-mannered and charming enough in themselves, they seemed to her to lack the personality and strength of purpose of the Duchess.

Certainly there was not much to be said for the grand-daughters' looks. The three daughters of Lord Henry had come to see their grandmother the previous week.

They were nice-looking country girls who might, if they were lucky, make happy marriages: but Anne felt that there was no possibility of their ever doing anything original, adventurous or even interesting in their lives.

The Duchess herself was so different.

Somehow she would have been outstanding in any generation and Anne could well understand now why she ruled her family with a rod of iron and why they dared not make any major decision without her approval and advice.

When the Duke had gone Anne had seen the big case containing the diamonds and emeralds lying at the Duchess's side and had ventured to ask if she might look at it again. The Duchess had smiled at her eagerness.

"Of course, dear!"

Anne opened the case and as she stood looking down at the glittering gems the Duchess added:

"Put the tiara on your own head. I want to see how you look."

"Oh, may I?" Anne said breathlessly, like a small child who has been told she may dress up.

She took the tiara from its velvet setting and raised it on to the correct position on her golden hair.

"Is that right?" she asked.

The Duchess looked at her—at the lovely flushed face and the wide and shining eyes.

"Put on the earrings," she commanded.

Anne did as she was told, finding them unaccountably heavy as they swung against her cheeks.

"Now look at yourself!"

Anne turned to the glass. Even allowing for the incongruity of the summer dress she wore, there was no mistaking that the jewels became her.

She looked magnificent; not so much the young girl masquerading but someone who might have been born to wear such things without embarrassment. For a moment she stood staring at herself, then she turned round to face the Duchess.

"They are lovely," she said.

"Let's hope we get a good price for them," the Duchess said sharply. "Put them back!"

There was almost an expression of pain in her voice as if Anne recalled too many memories from the past.

Anne did as she was told. When the jewels were secure again, each in its own particular velvet groove, the Duchess closed the case with precision.

"That is the end of a chapter in my life," she said. "When these go it is time for me to go too."

"Don't say that," Anne pleaded.

"It is true," the Duchess said heavily. "My husband had them specially arranged and set for me when I married him. The jewels belong to the family, of course. They have been handed down for four centuries. I believe Charles II gave the first emeralds to one of the Duchesses. She must have been very beautiful. Every generation collected one or two more and then eventually my husband had them arranged together. It was his wedding present to me."

The Duchess's voice was low. It was almost as if she were talking to herself, forgetting that Anne was beside her.

"I can see him now coming into my fathers library. It was a wet afternoon. I had washed my hair and it was hanging over my shoulders as I dried it by the fire. I had lovely hair in those days, everyone told me so. I could sit on it, which was considered as much an achievement as having an eighteen-inch waist. I managed to have both.

"My hair was not such a beautiful colour as yours. But it was fair and was inordinately admired in the days when women, not having easy access to the dye-pots, were in the majority content with mouse-coloured, rather lifeless tresses. My hair was fair and full of electricity.

"I remember when the Duke was announced I jumped to my feet and pressed my hands to my head as if to calm the exuberance of my hair. The footman should never have admitted him, of course, but he had no idea I was in the library.

"We were supposed to dry our hair in my mother's boudoir, but the chimney had been smoking and as everyone was out I thought I was safe in venturing downstairs.

"Having shown him into the room, the footman looked at me in astonishment and when he realised what he had done he thought the best thing to do was to disappear; so he closed the door and left us alone."

The Duchess paused and looked at Anne.

"It was a very unconventional meeting for those days. I remember standing very still, aware that my heart was beating. My fiancé came across the room towards me.

"He came nearer and nearer. Still I waited, half shy, yet thrilled in a way I had never been thrilled before, and only when he stood looking at me, just saying nothing, did I look up at him. I saw then in his face what I had always wanted to see and had prayed that one day I might find there.

"You see, my dear, I was a very rich woman and I knew there were many men who were interested in me because of my money. Deep down in my heart I had been afraid that was the reason the young Duke wanted to marry me. But when I saw his face that afternoon in the library I knew he loved me.

177

"I looked into his eyes and he looked into mine; then at last he said in a very low voice.

'Oh, my darling, how beautiful you are!'

"Still he did not touch me and I didn't want him to. We belonged in that moment, belonged so closely, so perfectly, that nothing which happened afterwards, no ceremony or love-making, could ever make us closer. It was at that moment, with my hair tumbling over my shoulders, that I learned I was the luckiest woman in all the world."

There was a throb in the Duchess's voice as if after all these years a faint reflection of her passionate awakening stirred within her—then she went on:

"It was some time later before he gave me the present he had brought for me. Before that we sat in front of the fire talking of ourselves, of the future, of things we meant to do, even of the children we meant to have.

"We had never had a proper opportunity of being alone before; always we had been chaperoned, always paraded in public with critical eyes watching us and busy tongues speculating about us. It was growing dusk when at last he opened the case you see here and took out the tiara as you took it out just now.

"The firelight glittered on the stones and I think they dazzled my eyes for the moment, but perhaps it was that tears were not so very far away. I was so ridiculously happy! He lifted the tiara high in his hands. I can see him now.

'I am going to crown you my queen!' he said, and put in on my head.

"The other jewelry followed; he clasped the necklace round my throat, the bracelet round my wrist; then at last he was kissing me as if he would never let me go.

"I remember laying my head against his shoulder and thinking how crazy it was and how wonderful, me in my old dress, my hair wild and untrammelled, the diamonds and emeralds sparkling in the fire-light."

There was a long silence, then the Duchess repeated:
"To sell them now means it is the end of a chapter —my chapter!"

"Oh, I wish you hadn't got to!" Anne exclaimed. "If I had the money I would give it to you rather than that they should go!"

She spoke with so much feeling in her voice that the Duchess looked at her in surprise.

"I believe you would, child. But there is no room for sentiment in this world. Hurry up now and get the newspapers, we can't waste the whole afternoon in unprofitable memorising."

Anne guessed that the Duchess was regretting having revealed such an intimate moment of her life. Anyway, as if upset by the wounds which had been opened that day, she was unremittingly cross and difficult for the rest of the afternoon.

Anne had had to run hither and thither and nothing she did, however hard she tried, was right. She was thankful when it was time to leave.

When she opened the door into the square to see the teeming rain she felt sad and disillusioned. Dalton was right, the elegance of England was past.

She wondered what sort of life the Duchess would lead if she were young now instead of being too old for the hardships of everyday modern life.

Was it worse, Anne questioned, to have to sell one's jewels and have only memories to comfort one or to grapple every day with buses and tubes, with shoving, hustling crowds, with rudeness and incivility, with shortages and lack of ordinary necessities?

Life had been leisurely and in a greater degree more comfortable even for the ordinary people when the Duchess was young. There was not that breathless rush from day to day, there was not the hard, unmerciful spur of competition, to drive people on whether they wished or not in a grasping, commercial world.

"Now there seems to be no time for anything," Anne thought; "no time to sew, to read, to paint, be musical or even to make oneself charming and attractive to acquaintances."

Conscious of the dampness of her feet chilling her whole body, she thought how little real pleasure she had had since she came to London.

In Cornwall she had believed that in London she would enjoy theatres, exhibitions, concerts and improve her mind in a thousand and one different ways.

But she had done none of the things she had planned, firstly because everything was so expensive and secondly because when the evening came she was so tired.

It was easy to get into the way of eating at home, of sitting after they had washed up talking to Sally, and then at about ten o'clock of going to bed, sometimes to read, sometimes to fall asleep from sheer exhaustion.

Marigold went out, but Anne stayed at home with Sally content not to have to make an effort and wanting from sheer weariness nothing but the relaxation of her own tired limbs.

"I'm tired now," Anne told herself, and was conscious of a tightening throat and an aching head.

"Here it comes at last!" a woman said wearily.

She shut her umbrella with a snap, spilling a miniature waterfall over Anne's shoulder. A wild rush and scramble and at last Anne found herself on the bus.

There was the stuffy smell of damp mackintoshes and of hot humanity, and although she was fortunate enough to get a seat it was on the outside and people standing swayed and bumped against her all the way to her destination.

At last they reached the Chelsea Town Hall and Anne had to push her way out, getting wetter than ever from the other sodden passengers.

It was still raining and she hurried homewards think-

180

ing that if possible she would have a warm bath as soon as she got in. She opened the front door and putting her umbrella in the stand when Marigold's voice reached her from the top of the stairs.

"Is that you, Anne?"

"Yes, I have just come in."

"Oh, Anne, be an angel and get some milk. Sally told me particularly not to forget it, but, of course, I have! I am going out tonight and there is not a drop in the place and I know Sally will want a cup of tea as soon as she gets in."

Wearily Anne picked up her umbrella again.

"All right," she called.

"Thanks, darling," Marigold replied carelessly.

It was raining harder than ever, but luckily the dairy was not far away and Anne managed to collect a pint of milk and also to buy a loaf of bread from the shop next door in case Marigold had forgotten that too.

They had divided the shopping needs when the electric stove had been put in. They were by no means equal; Sally had taken the lion's share upon herself by promising to find the main dishes both for supper and for breakfast.

This was by no means easy although Sally made friends with the butcher and the fishmonger so that usually they kept her something even if it was under the counter.

Marigold was responsible for the milk and the bread, while Anne brought in the salads, butter, sugar and other groceries.

Plodding back now across the slippery pavements Anne thought without resentment that Marigold seldom, if ever, remembered her part of the housekeeping.

Somebody nearly always had to run out at the last moment for the milk and bread, and more than once, when they had been too tired or it had been after closing hours, they had to borrow from Mrs. Jarvis.

"As Marigold is out so often," Anne thought, "I had better offer to do her share of the shopping. It would be much simpler."

Back in the house again she put her umbrella carefully in the stand so that it would not drip on to the polished linoleum and then realised that her shoes, now soaked through, were making a mess wherever she walked.

She slipped them off and went upstairs in her stockings. Marigold was half dressed as she entered the room.

"Did you get the milk?" she asked. "Thanks awfully, I am sorry I forgot."

"That's all right," Anne answered.

She suddenly felt so utterly weary that she could hardly speak. She was shivering, but her cheeks felt unbearably hot. She put the milk and bread down on the table.

"Is there any chance of a bath?" she asked. "I'm so terribly wet!"

Marigold looked guilty.

"I am afraid I have just had one and the water is quite cold. I am so sorry, sweet, I wish I had known."

"It doesn't matter," Anne answered. "I'll just get out of my wet clothes."

"Why not boil some water and put your feet in it?" Marigold suggested.

"Yes, I could do that," Anne replied.

She thought that if it had been Sally she would have done it for her, but Marigold was busy dressing for the evening. Slowly she started to take off her wet things. She wished she did not feel so tired.

She was afraid it was too late to prevent herself having a cold and she hoped the Duchess wouldn't be annoyed.

"Is there any aspirin?" she asked.

Marigold, who was arranging her hair in front of the mirror, turned round.

"Aspirin?" she repeated. "There was some. I took some last week when I had a headache . . . but I believe I finished the bottle. Look in the drawer."

Anne crossed over and pulled open the drawer of the dressing-table. Sure enough there was the bottle, but it was empty!

"Why didn't you say you had finished them?" she asked.

"I didn't think of it," Marigold answered cheerfully. "I don't believe they do the slightest good anyway. Have you got a headache?"

"No, I think I have a cold starting. Isn't it annoying?"

"Maddening! And a summer cold lasts for ages besides being particularly unbecoming. Don't give it to me."

"Perhaps it is only my imagination," Anne said soothingly.

She sat down wearily on the end of her bed. Somehow it was an awful effort to take off her wet clothes. At that moment Sally came rushing up the stairs.

"Did you think I was lost?" she asked. "I am late, aren't I? Mr. Dunstan sent me home in the car. Wasn't it marvellous of him? I had to wait because the chauffeur had a letter to deliver at the House of Commons. He seemed to take ages, but at least I am dry."

She looked at Anne.

"Oh, Anne darling, you are wet! Are these your shoes?"

She picked them up from the floor, saw the soles and exclaimed:

"You must be soaked to the skin! Why don't you have a hot bath?"

"There's no hot water," Anne said limply.

Sally looked at her. The others always said she had

eyes like a hawk where their health was concerned. She came over and held the back of her hand, first to Anne's cheek and then to her forehead.

"You look feverish, darling."

"I think I've caught cold."

"You had better jump into bed then. I will fill your hot-water bottle. Let me help you off with your things; I will ask Mrs. Jarvis if I may put them in her airing-cupboard."

Like a child Anne let Sally undress her and help her into her nightgown. She had the absurd feeling that nothing mattered now Sally was home. She crept into bed unable to prevent herself shivering as her feet touched the cool sheets.

"I won't be a minute with your hot bottle, darling," Sally said.

She had seen Anne shiver, but she was wise enough not to comment on it. She hurried from the room. Marigold crossed to Anne's side and looked down at her with a worried expression on her face.

"I'm sorry if you feel rotten, Anne. I didn't realise you were ill. I oughtn't to have sent you for the milk. Don't tell Sally, she will think it so mean of me."

"Of course not. I am all right. I'm just tired, that's all."

"Tired? Are we ever anything else?"

"Why don't you stay in at night for a change? I couldn't dance until the early hours and then work all day."

"It is better than sitting at home and looking at the wallpaper!" Marigold said fiercely.

"Is it?" Anne asked.

"I think so!"

Anne was too tired to argue. She was conscious only that her teeth were beginning to chatter and that little shivers of cold were running down her spine. Sally came back with the hot-water bottle and some hot milk.

"I have got you a sole for supper," she said cheerfully. "Isn't that lucky?"

"I don't think I could eat anything," Anne said.

She wondered why the hot-water bottle cuddled tightly in her arms did not warm her.

"You will when it is ready," Sally assured her.

"Listen!" Marigold interrupted. "Yes, I can hear the bell. I'm going now. I hope you will be better by the morning, Anne. Good night, Sally."

She blew them a kiss and disappeared down the stairs. Sally went to the door and listened.

"Yes, someone has called for her," she said after a moment. "I wonder who it is. Did she tell you?"

Anne shook her head.

"I expect it is Mr. Barlow," Sally sighed, "but Marigold never tells us anything these days."

She took the bread and the other parcels which had been left on the table out on to the landing. When she came back she was about to speak to Anne when she saw that her eyes were closed.

"If she has a sleep," she thought to herself, "that will be better than anything."

She tidied the room. Marigold invariably left everything in a muddle—shoes separated—coat-hangers on the floor—the dressing-table a mass of spilt powder, cotton wool and emery boards.

Sally put everything away and was just moving through the curtains into the sitting-room when Anne opened her eyes.

"I say, Sally, I do feel rotten!"

"Do you, darling?"

"I feel as if I can't breathe; could I have another pillow?"

"Of course!"

Sally took one from her own bed. As she arranged it she wondered desperately what they would do if Anne was really ill.

Twelve

Marigold dragged herself wearily up the long, narrow flights of stairs.

She was tired, but she felt as though it were her brain that was aching rather than her body. It had been a disturbing, perplexing evening. She had gone out to dinner with Ben because he asked her and because in these days she would dine with anyone rather than be alone with her own thoughts.

She felt at times as if she were a squirrel in a cage, twirling round and round in an effort to escape from herself and getting no further, only revolving as it were on her own axis.

Fortunately, or so she believed, she had scores of invitations with which to fill in her free time.

She was becoming a personage in that strange new world which she had tried to describe to Anne and which consisted of people who were called "smart" for reasons which could not exactly be explained in words.

Marigold realised with an almost cynical amusement that she was becoming both smart and the right sort of person.

She was asked to parties by hostesses who entertained because they wanted their hospitality written up in the gossip columns; she was asked to lunch and dinner by young men who liked to be seen with the most beautiful and most talked of young women of the moment.

Besides these engagements there was always Ben— Ben asking her to do this—to do that with him—forcing his attentions on her when she made futile and not very strenuous efforts to avoid him.

She had tabulated Ben in her mind, had put him into

a little pigeon-hole—only to find disconcertingly that he wouldn't stay put.

He would not remain in character, proving, it seemed to a tired Marigold at this moment, that one could never be sure of anything—not even oneself.

Earlier in the day Ben had telephoned to remind her that she had promised to dine with him.

"What shall I wear?" she asked, meaning what type of dress would be suitable for the entertainment he was arranging.

"Anything," he replied.

"Don't be silly, Ben; I mean, are we going to dance, go to a theatre, or what?"

"I am taking you to meet someone who is very important to me," he said in what seemed to Marigold a tone of voice which suggested some secret joke of his own.

"A dinner-frock, then?"

"You look lovely in anything," Ben replied with a surprising ring of sincerity in his voice.

Marigold was never quite certain about Ben's compliments. They came too easily and glibly to his tongue as if he had been making them for years and they were just a part of his conversation.

But this time she had a feeling that he was speaking the truth, and it suddenly struck her that Ben might be getting really fond of her.

"That would be amusing!" Marigold told herself as she left the telephone and went back to the mannequins' room.

Yes, in a way it would be amusing, for she had learnt quite a lot about Ben during these past weeks.

He was by no means the easy, susceptible young man she had imagined him to be on first acquaintance. Underneath the froth and bubble of Ben's very chequered career he had a hard streak of shrewdness.

He was not deceived by the women who sought him

out because of his bank-balance. If he gave them presents he did so because he liked to be generous and because in some obscure manner it gave him pleasure to pander to their greed.

It was almost as if he stood apart and watched them scrambling as animals might scramble for the crumbs he scattered to them.

Orchids and lipsticks set with diamonds were, Marigold learnt, but chicken-feed to Ben Barlow.

He was rich, astoundingly rich, and to her surprise she found out quite by accident that a large amount of his money was expended in far better and more serious ways.

Ben had not meant her to learn this about him. It was part of the strange complexity of his character that he liked to present himself as a dissipated, thoughtless young man-about-town.

He gloried in his reputation, so much so that Marigold began to guess that it was merely reaction from the hard-working, respectable ancestors from whom he had sprung.

She had gone to Ben's flat one evening as he had invited her to a cocktail party. When she arrived, she found to her surprise that there was not the usual chatter of voices and the sound of the radiogram.

Instead there were only three men's hats in the hall and everything was very quiet. The manservant who opened the door looked surprised to see her.

"I think Mr. Barlow is expecting me," Marigold said.

"Are you sure, miss?" the man asked. "Mr. Barlow has got a meeting of his trustees."

Marigold looked at the clock. It was nearly twenty past six.

"I am sure the party was this evening," she said.

At that moment the door of the sitting-room opened and an elderly man with white hair came out.

"Good-bye, Ben, my boy." he called through the

open door. "I am delighted with what we have just decided. That Trust of yours is going to be one of the finest encouragements there has ever been for the young engineers of the future."

"I agree with you, Chester," said a voice from within the room, and then Marigold heard Ben say:

"For heaven's sake keep it under your hat. I would ruin my reputation for spontaneous gaiety if people got to hear about it."

There was a roar of laughter. Marigold looked at the manservant.

"I think I had better go," she said quietly. "I am afraid there has been some mistake. Will you tell Mr. Barlow I called?"

She went through the flat door out on to the landing and rang for the lift. While she was waiting the grey-haired man they had called Chester came out of the front door. He was followed by Ben.

"I'll come with you," Ben was saying. "I'm late as it is." Then he saw Marigold. "Good heavens, Marigold, didn't you get my message?"

"What message?" Marigold asked.

"Damn it all," he exclaimed, "that secretary of mine is the most incompetent woman on earth. I shall have to get rid of her. I told her to telephone everyone and say that the party was at the Savoy, not here."

"I am sorry," Marigold said, "but she must have forgotten to tell me."

"Well, there's no harm done, we'll go along together," Ben suggested. "By the way, I don't think you have met Sir Chester Johnson—Miss Granville."

"No, I don't think we have met before," Sir Chester said, taking off his hat and shaking Marigold by the hand.

The lift came up and they all got in together.

"Why don't you come along to my party, Chester?" Ben asked.

"Heaven forbid!" Sir Chester replied. "Your parties are much too young for my grey hairs. Besides, my wife is waiting for me. Miss Granville will doubtless disagree with me when I say that the sort of party you give, Ben, is either for the very young or the unhappily married."

"Of course she will disagree with you!" Ben retorted. Marigold smiled.

"I think Sir Chester is right, Ben. Unfortunately, one does not have to be married to be unhappy."

There was a little note of bitterness in her voice which Sir Chester noticed even though it escaped Ben. When they reached the street he shook hands with Marigold again.

"Good-bye, Miss Granville. May I, as an old man who still appreciates a very pretty girl, hope you will find happiness?"

There was a warm sincerity in his voice as he said the last word, and as Marigold got into the car beside Ben she thought how strange it was that Ben should have such a man as Sir Chester as a friend and a trustee.

Suddenly the full import of what she had heard came revealingly to her mind.

She looked at Ben out of the corners of her eyes as he drove her swiftly through the traffic chattering nonchalantly about this and that as if a few moments before he had not been making serious and worth-while decisions.

"How quick we are to judge other people!" Marigold thought.

She felt ashamed of herself because so often, in her thoughts at any rate, she had been ashamed of Ben.

When they reached the Savoy and she saw the motley collection of friends waiting for him, she wondered if she was not dreaming and if Ben was not in reality just as shallow and frivolous as she had believed him to be.

The little episode had, however, almost faded from her mind during the course of the party.

Keeping Ben at arm's length, laughing at his flirtatious tendencies, finding him with all his faults an amusing companion with whom to while away an idle hour, she had been too busy to recall a chance conversation. But this evening had brought it all back.

Ben called for her as usual in his big car and took her not towards the glittering lights of the West End but across the Park, then up the long, empty side streets which lead to St. John's Wood.

"Where are we going?" Marigold asked curiously.

"To dine with my mother," Ben replied; "I want you to meet her."

"Your mother?" Marigold repeated the words in astonishment. She had not expected this.

"Yes, my mother! She doesn't often come up to London but she is here for a few days and so we are dining with her tonight. Do you mind?"

"Of course I don't mind, I am delighted," Marigold replied, and she spoke truthfully.

She was in reality intensely curious. She had heard so many references to Ben's mother and the fact that she had been a barmaid. It seemed that it was one of the things always repeated about him whenever his name was mentioned. Ben's father, old Mr. Barlow, commanded a certain respect. People spoke of him as "a grand old man of industry," but the legend of Ben's mother had become a joke.

She had heard several cheap references to her one way and another, even from the women whom Ben considered his more intimate friends. Now at last she was to meet Mrs. Barlow.

She realised that it might in some way be a revealing guide to Ben's true character.

Years ago Marigold remembered her father saying: "People are seldom as simple as they appear."

It was a remark that she thought might have been made about Ben.

He was by no means as simple as he appeared. He was certainly not the degenerate, brainless playboy which he liked to pretend to be, but what else was he?

Now she would meet his mother. What would she be like—this barmaid who had married a clever, ambitious mechanic and produced Ben?

The car drew up at a small house in a tree-shaded street. There was a neat little garden in front with a rose tree and tidy flower-beds bordered with lobelia. Ben led the way up the steps and rang the front-door bell.

The door, Marigold noticed, was protected from the sun by a striped holland curtain.

They waited a few moments and then the door was opened by an aged parlourmaid wearing an old-fashioned, starched cap and apron.

"Good evening, Ellen," Ben said cheerfully.

"Good evening, Mr. Ben."

"Is my mother down?"

"Yes, sir, she is sitting in the garden and said you were to join her there."

"Very good! Come on, Marigold, I'll show you the way."

He led Marigold down a passage and into a large, neatly-furnished room the front windows of which opened into the garden.

Marigold just had time for an impression of soft, pastel-shaded walls, of comfortable armchairs set before a polished brass fender, then Ben led her through the window into the garden.

It was only a long strip of garden but there were roses everywhere and the flower-beds were a blaze of colour. There was a paved terrace in front of the window and seated in a padded chair was a little old lady.

Marigold had a feeling of shock.

Somehow she had expected somebody large, rather full-blown, perhaps with dyed hair, an older edition of Laura and the synthetic blondes who so often graced Ben's hospitable dinner-tables.

Instead she saw a very small, very thin old woman with sparse white hair dragged severely back from her forehead, her face wrinkled with age, and with glasses on the end of a thin, pointed nose.

"Hello, Mother!"

"Oh, here you are, my boy!"

The old lady looked up from the book she was reading and smiled. There was something in her smile which told Marigold that once she had been attractive.

She raised her face and Ben bent to kiss his mother; then she turned to Marigold.

"This is Marigold, Mother, whom I told you about."

"How do you do, my dear?"

Mrs. Barlow held out her hand, the thin, bony hand of an old woman, but there was strength and decision in the grip of her fingers.

"Won't you sit down?"

She indicated a chair beside her, which Marigold took.

"I'm glad to meet you."

There was something warm and homely in her tone. Her voice was not educated and there was more than a suspicion of a North Country accent.

"It is very kind of you to have me," Marigold said, almost too astonished to remember her good manners.

"My Ben's talked a lot about you," the old lady said. "He has told me how pretty you are and how you and your sisters have come to London to earn your own living. How do you like London?"

"Very much," Marigold answered, "and I have been lucky enough to get a job."

"So Ben tells me. Is that one of the dresses you model? It is a very attractive one."

Marigold looked down at her dinner-frock so simply made that it was obviously expensive.

"Yes," she answered, "we get the opportunity of buying the models cheap. It is a great help."

"It must be," Mrs. Barlow said. "I often wonder how the young girls manage to look so smart these days. Things are not so cheap as they were when I was young and you want so many more of them."

She gave Marigold an appraising look as if she were taking in every detail of her appearance, then she turned to her son.

"What have you been doing today, Sonny? Not wasting your money on those horrible horses, I hope."

"Yes, Mother, I've been racing, if that's what you mean."

"Oh dear, when will you learn sense, I wonder? Father used to say that no one who was not a fool or a knave would waste their time on a race-course."

She looked at Ben severely for a moment, then she laughed, a deep, chuckling laugh which was somehow unexpected.

"However, you must have your fun!"

She turned to Marigold.

"I cannot help wanting the boy to enjoy himself— his father worked hard, too hard, and so did I until we had money—then we were too old to enjoy it. It is when you are young you want things, isn't that a fact?"

"It certainly is!" Marigold answered.

She felt herself liking Mrs. Barlow enormously.

She was so genuine, so unpretentious, and it was strange to see the redoubtable Ben being in her presence just a little boy again, listening to and taking notice of an adoring parent.

They had a simple, homely dinner, waited on by Ellen.

There was a chicken and a fresh salad Mrs. Barlow
194

had brought up from the country, fruit from her garden, and a cream cheese she told them she had made herself.

"Ben always like my cream cheeses," she explained to Marigold, "and somehow the girls don't seem to get them to his taste."

"This is perfect!" Ben said.

"I am so glad you are pleased, Sonny. I wish you would come down for a week and let me fatten you up. You look thinner every time I see you."

Ben laughed.

"If I stayed with you for long, Mother, I should be so fat I would have to have all my clothes altered, and that would be a terrible expense."

"Ben always has a back answer," Mrs. Barlow said to Marigold. "The truth is he likes gadding about London! I only have a little place in the country but I am ever so fond of it. It gives me such an interest. My cows are looking wonderful now and I had two heifers last week, but there, I don't suppose it would interest you."

"I don't suppose she knows what a heifer is," Ben teased.

"Of course I do," Marigold told him. "We had two cows of our own when we were children. My mother was very fussy about the milk we drank. We gave them up not only because they died of old age, but also because my father had a theory that we were depriving the milkman of his rightful dues."

"Well, if you have kept cows," Mrs Barlow said complacently, "you will realise how fond one gets of them. I often say to Ben that my cows are my best friends. I really think that they understand half I say to them."

Ben smiled at his mother.

"I only hope they listen to you and do exactly what you tell them—it would make up for me."

When they left Mrs. Barlow, Ben insisted on going

on to a dance at Ciro's. There he met a lot of old friends and they joined up with a big supper-party and had what Ben described as a "rollicking time."

Marigold found herself continually thinking of the little old woman who was Ben's mother and the atmosphere of the quiet little house in St. John's Wood.

The conversation about the cows and the cream cheese remained in her mind when Ben exchanged wisecracks and witticisms with young women wearing orchids who undoubtedly thought that milk was planned by nature to arrive in a bottle.

"You are quiet, sweetie; anything the matter?" Ben asked Marigold more than once.

She could not tell him that she was puzzling over him, trying to make up her mind which was the real Ben and which the superficial one.

What had started as a quiet evening ended very gaily and noisily, and it was two o'clock before Marigold finally persuaded Ben to drive her home to Chelsea.

"I'm tired," she thought as she slowly climbed the stairs in the Saracen's Head.

To her surprise, as she reached the top landing she heard voices. She opened the door. The lights were on and she was astonished to see that David was there.

"Hello, David, what on earth are you doing?" she exclaimed.

Sally came through the curtains as she spoke.

"Anne's ill," she said quietly. "I sent for David because I was so worried."

"Ill?" Marigold exclaimed. "What is the matter with her?"

"I hope it is nothing worse than a touch of pleurisy," David answered, "but I shall come again in the morning. Try to get some sleep, Sally."

He put his hands on Sally's shoulders and looked down at her kindly. He then turned to Marigold.

"Have you had a nice evening?"

There was something hard in his voice, something harder still in his eyes. Marigold felt as though he had slapped her.

"Very nice, thank you," she replied, and added, as though in self-defence, "I had no idea Anne was ill when I went out."

"No, of course you hadn't," Sally said quickly. "She tells us now that she felt rotten all day, but you know what Anne is, she never talks about herself."

"No, she wouldn't," David said.

He turned to the table and started to pack some things into a leather bag. Marigold stood for a moment looking at him, then she pulled her coat from her shoulders and threw it over a chair.

"You haven't been to see us lately, David."

"I have been busy!"

His reply was sharp.

"So many sick people?"

"No, I am working with Sir Hubert in his laboratory; didn't Sally tell you?"

"Oh yes, of course, I remember her telling me. Are you discovering a cure for all our evils?"

"Not all of them, unfortunately."

David shut his bag with a snap and turned to Sally.

"You understand exactly what do do, don't you, Sally? If you are worried, telephone me at once, but anyway I will be here about eleven o'clock."

"That's wonderful, David, thank you so very, very much for coming."

"Don't be silly!" David brushed her thanks aside. "Good night, Sally. Good night, Marigold, although there is not much of the night left."

"Good night, David," Marigold replied. "It is amusing to see you being 'professional'."

"I am glad I amuse you!"

Their eyes met across the room and it was Marigold who turned half petulantly away.

197

"Don't come down," David said to Sally. "Good-night, my dear."

He was gone and Sally shut the door behind him and came back into the room. Marigold turned an anguished face towards her.

"Sally, tell me the truth," she said in a whisper, "is Anne really ill?"

"I was frightfully worried about her," Sally replied. "She was breathing so strangely. That is why I sent for David. He has given her something to make her sleep. We must be as quiet as we can."

Marigold looked at Anne through the curtains, then she came back into the sitting-room.

"Sally, I have got to tell you," she said. "A lot of it is my fault. I forgot the milk. I asked her to go out and get it. She went back into the rain . . . I never thought. It was horrid and selfish of me."

Sally put out her arms.

"Oh, darling, don't worry. She must have been wet through anyway. She ought to have had her shoes mended days ago."

"If she is really ill, I will never forgive myself," Marigold said. "Anne hates illness so much."

"Let us pray that she will be all right," Sally answered.

She drew Marigold a little further away from the curtains and then in the far corner of the room whispered so that Anne could not possibly hear what she said.

"David says she may also have appendicitis. She complained of a pain but it has subsided now. We don't want to say anything about it but he is going to examine her properly tomorrow."

"Oh, Sally!" Marigold clung to her sister and suddenly there were tears in her eyes. "I have been so beastly to both of you just lately. I have not meant it, Sally, you are all I have got, you are all that matters, but . . . but . . . I have been so unhappy."

"I know, darling."

Sally put her arms round Marigold and held her close.

"I am sorry, desperately sorry," Marigold whispered.

"It's all right."

Marigold said no more and Sally would not force her confidence. After a moment the sisters drew apart and Marigold began to undress.

Anne appeared to be asleep and finally they crept into bed. Sally, worn out, fell into the natural easy slumber of a child, but Marigold lay awake staring into the darkness.

Her thoughts went back over the evening. She thought of Ben and his mother, the chatter of voices and the chink of glasses at Ciro's and the bands to which they had danced. Ben's arm had held her close as they moved rhythmically together in unison.

Then she saw David's face, heard the reproach in the tone of his voice, saw it in the expression of his eyes. There had been no admiration in the way he had looked at her.

"What does it matter?" she asked herself; but it did matter.

David, Anne and Sally—they were her world, the real world which mattered.

It was solid and firm beneath her feet while everything else was elusive and unsatisfactory as the music and champagne which Ben and his friends considered essential to amusement.

David, Anne and Sally!

"And who else?" her heart asked her. "Yes, tell me, who else?"

Thirteen

David's suspicions were confirmed and his diagnosis upheld when he arrived the following morning with Mr. Drayson, head surgeon at St. Anthony's Hospital.

Frederick Drayson was a small, white-haired man with a disarming smile and the clever, sensitive hands of a successful surgeon. He examined Anne with such charm and tact that she had no idea how thoroughly she was being overhauled.

Afterwards he led Sally downstairs on to the landing where they could talk without being overheard.

"I want to take your sister into hospital at once," he said, and added as Sally gave a little gasp: "Don't be frightened—it is not because she is in any great danger but because I want to have her under observation. There are X-rays to be done and she will also have the benefit of expert nursing."

"How bad is she?" Sally asked.

"Do you want me to be frank?" Frederick Drayson asked.

"Of course," Sally replied.

"Well, I am a little worried about one of her lungs," he said. "It may be nothing but the effect of her present feverish condition, but I want X-rays and I want every possible test before I can pass her fit, besides which she has what the layman calls a 'grumbling appendix' and the sooner it is out the better."

Sally put her hand to her forehead.

"Oh dear," she said, "I can't really take it in. You see, Anne has always seemed so fit and healthy. I cannot remember when she was last ill. She hates illness!"

"We all do," Frederick Drayson said quietly. "But your sister seems to me a sensible girl who will bear what she has got to bear with courage and good humour."

He took out a small note-book, asked Sally for various particulars and patted her in a fatherly manner on the shoulder.

"Don't worry," he said, "we will look after your sister. All three of you have got a staunch and loyal supporter in David. I have heard quite a lot about the beautiful Granvilles."

Sally smiled.

"You should not believe all David says—he is prejudiced!"

Mr. Drayson looked at his watch.

"I must be off," he said; "tell David I am not going back to the hospital, I have a call to make. I will see him about two o'clock. I will send an ambulance for your sister in about an hour's time."

"In an hour's time?" Sally repeated to herself, aghast.

But she did not say it out loud for fear Mr. Drayson would think she was complaining.

She ran up the stairs to David and gave him the surgeon's message about their meeting. She did not tell him in front of Anne what else Mr. Drayson had said.

"I must go, too," David said. "I have a consultation at noon." He turned to Anne. "Good-bye, Anne. Keep cheerful. We will have you well in no time."

"Thank you, David," Anne said weakly, and tried to force a smile to her lips."

Sally followed David down the first flight of stairs to the half-landing where she had talked with Mr. Drayson. As she reached him he turned to look at her and saw the fear in her eyes.

"I'm sorry, Sally," he said involuntarily.

"Oh, David!" Sally cried; "Mr. Drayson is sending an ambulance for Anne in an hour's time and he thinks that one of her lungs may be affected. What are we to do?"

There was a note of desperate appeal in Sally's voice, and instinctively David put his arm protectively round her shoulders.

"Poor little Sally," he sympathised; "I am afraid it is a bit of a shock. But don't be too worried, Drayson is always a little on the cautious side when he is making a diagnosis. What is more important is that he is a brilliant surgeon and I would rather he operated on Anne than anyone else."

"She is so afraid of being ill," Sally faltered.

"I know," David murmured, "and it is hard on you, too."

"If I could only nurse her myself I would feel happier," Sally went on. "We have never parted before."

There was a break in her voice and David's arm tightened round her shoulders.

"I know, Sally dear," he said comfortingly, "I know. But it is not like you to give way, you are always the brave one who keeps us all going."

"Couldn't she stay here?" Sally asked, and even as she said the words she knew they were spoken out of a vain hope.

David shook his head.

"You don't really want me to answer that question, do you? You don't think I want to take her away? It is going to be a dickens of a job to get her a bed as it is. You would like her to have a private room, wouldn't you?"

"Oh, yes—yes, of course. Anne would hate sleeping with other sick people."

"I must get back now," David said. "And you must just trust me to do the very best I can for Anne . . . and, Sally, you know it will always be my very best."

"I know that," Sally answered a little unsteadily,

"and I will try to be all the things you want me to be, David. But look after Anne, won't you? I love her so!"

Sally's eyes were full of tears. David turned away quickly as if he could not bear any more and taking up his bag said "good-bye" in an unusually grave voice.

He ran down the stairs. Sally watched him go, turning a moment later with obvious effort to go back to Anne.

Anne was lying with her eyes closed. She opened them as Sally came into the room. She felt calm and detached, the result of the tablets which David had left the night before with instructions that they were to be taken four-hourly.

Sally approached the bed.

"Mr. Drayson says there is nothing to worry about, darling, but he wants to take you to hospital—David's hospital—so that they can give you proper nursing and also take some X-rays."

"Go to hospital?" Anne echoed apprehensively. "I would much rather stay here!"

"Yes, darling, I know, and we would much rather have you; but Mr. Drayson is insistent and so is David."

"Oh, well," Anne sighed, "I suppose it will only be for a day or so."

Sally was thankful that there was no more vigorous protest from Anne and she busied herself getting together clean nightgowns and bed-jackets.

She chose the best of what belonged to all three of them and she also included among Anne's luggage a photograph of their father and a little china ornament of the Christ child which had stood on the mantelpiece of their bedroom at the Vicarage ever since they could remember.

As she packed it she felt superstitiously but with a profound conviction that it would help Anne when she was alone in the hospital.

The ambulance arrived almost before Sally was ready. There was a nice nurse in charge and while the men were lifting Anne on to the stretcher and wrapping her round with warm blankets Sally put on her own hat and coat.

Marigold had gone to work as usual as Sally had said there was no point in both of them staying at home, and first thing that morning before David had come Sally had thought there might be a possibility of their having to take it in turns to nurse Anne.

"I would like to stay if there is anything I can do," Marigold said—an unusually humble Marigold who was reproaching herself bitterly for her part in Anne's illness.

"I really think it would be better for you to go this morning," Sally had answered. "You will telephone to the Duchess and the flat, won't you? Ask to speak to Mr. Dunstan or Nanny and explain about Anne. Say I will telephone later today after the doctor has been,"

"I will do all that," Marigold promised.

Before she left Marigold went to Anne's bedside and bending down kissed her affectionately.

"Get well quickly, Anne," she whispered. "I feel so awful about you—as if it were all my fault."

"Don't be silly," Anne answered. "It is nobody's fault but my own for catching this ridiculous cold."

In answer Marigold kissed her again. When she got outside the door on to the landing where Sally was warming some milk on their new stove, she said:

"Poor darling Anne! I could kick myself! Oh, Sally, why am I so awful when you are both so splendid?"

"You are not awful," Sally answered.

"Yes, I am," Marigold retorted; "I'm selfish and a beast and I hate myself!"

She ran downstairs without waiting for an answer and Sally wondered a little at the violence of her expression.

Now as she saw Anne being lifted into the ambulance her heart turned over with sudden fear. There was something terrifying in seeing someone one loved being carried away weak and helpless.

It was with an effort that Sally made herself talk quietly to the nurse during the journey to the hospital. Nurse spoke warmly of David.

"We like Dr. Carey so much!" she said. "He has not been with us long, of course, but he is very popular with the patients and with some of the nurses, too!"

She looked at Sally and her eyes twinkled.

"He is good-looking, isn't he?"

"We have always thought so," Sally answered, "but then, we have known him since we were children."

Nurse looked startled.

"But isn't he a relative?" she asked.

"Oh no," Sally replied, "only a friend."

"Oh, then I must apologise," Nurse said. "I should not have said what I did. I thought at first Dr. Carey was your brother and then when I realised the name was different I thought he must be a first cousin. You must forgive me, Miss Granville, but he really spoke as though you were all one family."

"So we are," Sally smiled, "and please don't apologise. David has always been a very popular person and I agree with you that he is very good-looking."

Nurse laughed in a rather embarrassed way.

"You must have thought it awful of me, but in hospital one gets into the way of talking carelessly. You wouldn't believe some of the things which get discussed. But I expect Dr. Carey has told you what we are like."

"I know he loves being at St. Anthony's."

"I am not surprised, it is the nicest hospital in London."

Sally had very little experience of hospitals, but she

205

had not seen much of St. Anthony's before she began to think Nurse was right.

As soon as the ambulance arrived they were greeted by the matron, a good-looking, grey-haired woman who radiated a calm confidence that reacted immediately on the most hysterical patient.

It was part of her charm that she made everybody entering St. Anthony's think she was taking a special and personal interest in their particular case.

Sally loved the way she seemed without being a bit professional to make Anne feel that everyone was eager to look after and help her speedy recovery.

They were taken up in the lift to the fifth floor, where there was a tiny, delightful little room overlooking the roof-tops.

"This room faces south," Matron said, "so your sister will get the sun. Dr. Carey tells me you are from his part of the world. I'm afraid we can't provide you with Cornish air, but this is the best we can manage."

"It is very nice, thank you," Sally said gratefully.

Soon Anne was comfortably in bed, while Sally sat beside her in the golden sunlight which flooded the room.

"If you feel all right now and won't miss me," Sally suggested, "I will go out and get you some flowers and also get myself something to eat. I expect the doctors will be along early this afternoon and I would like to be here when they come."

"You will come back, won't you?" Anne asked in a low voice.

Sally knew that her sister was frightened not so much of being alone but of what was going to happen to her.

"Of course I will come back," Sally replied, "but if you would rather, I will stay here for a little longer; but I think they would like you to go to sleep."

"I'll be all right so long as you come back."

"You know I will."

Sally turned back from the doorway to have a last look at Anne lying in the sunlight which was lighting up her hair. Anne made an effort to smile, but there was the dark shadow of fear in her eyes and Sally saw that her fingers were plucking nervously at the edge of the sheet.

"O God," she prayed, "make her well soon—please, please, God!"

At the end of the corridor there was a lovely little statue of St. Anthony holding the child Jesus in his arms. Sally looked up into the sculptured face. It held an expression of perfect trust and faith.

"I, too, must have faith," Sally thought; but her thoughts were thrown together in frightening inconsequency.

For the first time in their lives they were being separated and yet she realised that Anne's physical condition was no worse than the barrier which had separated them from Marigold these past weeks.

Somehow, Marigold had been apart from both her sisters, not in body but in everything else.

Sally thought of the pain and bitterness which tinged her voice so often and wondered if now at last, drawn closer by their common anxiety, Marigold would reveal what had been worrying her.

How much there was to worry about—for all of them!

Sally came out of the hospital into one of the long, grey streets which seemed characteristic of that part of London. She managed to get some flowers for Anne and then went to a café, where she bought two sandwiches which, however, proved quite uneatable.

She also ordered some coffee, but it was badly made and she left half of it in her cup. Feeling a sudden urge to be back with Anne, she paid the bill and hurriedly retraced her steps to the hospital.

The lift took her up to the fifth floor and then, as she

was passing the sister's room, someone called out to her.

"Is that you, Miss Granville? I was hoping I would catch you."

The nurse who spoke to her was small, Irish and apple-cheeked. She was not the nurse who was in charge of Anne, but Sally remembered seeing her on arrival.

"Dr. Carey has seen your sister. He would like to have a word with you about her. He asked me to let him know when you returned."

"Oh, thank you," Sally said, and went into the office while the nurse telephoned to David.

"Miss Granville is here, sir," the nurse said after being connected. "Would you like to speak to her? . . . Very good, sir."

She handed the receiver to Sally.

"Hullo, David."

"Have you had anything to eat?"

"Yes, I bought some sandwiches."

"I was going to suggest your coming out with me. We could go to that place where we lunched before."

"But, David, I think I ought to be with Anne."

"On the contrary—I want her left alone. Nurse has given her something to send her to sleep."

"Oh, in that case," Sally said, ". . . but I promised her I would come back."

"You can just pop in and look at her, then I will expect you at the main entrance in three minutes. Don't keep me waiting!"

Sally smiled. She could remember hearing that tone of voice from David years ago when he was an impatient schoolboy ordering the youngest Granville sister around.

"I will try not to be late . . . sir," Sally answered mockingly.

She heard David chuckle at the other end as she replaced the receiver.

She had forgotten until she heard the nurse speak to him that he would be formally addressed as "sir" when on duty. There was something amusing about it.

She could remember how often they had pulled each others hair and bawled at each other in childish tantrums.

Nurse was waiting outside in the passage and Sally, thanking her for the message, hurried along to Anne's room. She turned the handle of the door furtively and peeped in.

The curtains were drawn across the window, but they were unlined and in the dim light she could see Anne quite clearly. She was asleep. Her head was turned a little on the pillow and her lips parted.

She looked very lovely and at peace.

Very quietly Sally closed the door and tiptoed away. She found Anne's nurse.

"My sister is asleep," she said. "When do you think she will wake?"

"Not before three o'clock at least," Nurse assured her, "if then. Don't hurry back if you are going for a walk, Miss Granville."

Sally went down in the lift to meet David.

"Was she asleep?" he asked.

"Yes."

"I thought she would be. Now stop being a fussy old hen and relax."

Sally was forced to laugh.

"Is that the way you talk to your patients?"

"No, only to very special ones. I charge extra for affectionate familiarity."

They walked into the street. The sunshine was full in Sally's face and after a moment David said accusingly:

"You look worn out."

"I am only a little tired," Sally replied: "I didn't sleep last night."

"We mustn't have you ill, Sally."

"I won't be ill, but I'm worried about Anne."

"She will be all right, you are not to worry about her."

"Don't be so pompous and authoritative."

David looked down at her and grinned.

"It is with the greatest difficulty that I'm able to remember you are grown up and that I can't spank you for that!"

"Well, you can't," Sally said demurely. "And you mustn't get smug although, as one of the nurses has told me, half the nurses of the hospital are madly in love with you."

To Sally's surprise David changed colour.

"There is too much chatter among the nurses, and of course it's nonsense."

"I believe it's the truth," Sally laughed. "You are looking terribly guilty!"

"You don't know what nurses are like," David retorted. "Some of them are angels, but some are awful and think only of gossiping about the doctors. The trouble is, of course, that they don't have enough to think about."

"So they have to think about you," Sally teased.

"If I hear any more," David threatened, "I shall bar you from coming into hospital."

"You would need an armoured division to keep me out," Sally replied.

When they reached the little restaurant where they had dined once before, David, ignoring Sally's protest, ordered a large meal for her.

"This is treatment for shock, Sally."

"All right," Sally said, capitulating, "I'll try to eat. It is easier to do what you want than to argue with you."

They talked of many things over luncheon. David had a lot to tell Sally about himself and his work with Sir Hubert.

"He wanted me to give up the hospital altogether,

but Drayson and the others would not hear of it. We are terribly short of staff at the moment and they told Sir Hubert they could not spare me. So now I am on duty every morning and two afternoons a week.

"The rest of the time, including the evenings and most of the night, I spend in the laboratory. It is frightfully interesting, and, what is more, Sally, I believe we are getting results."

"Tell me about it," Sally begged.

David went into long and intricate explanations which meant little or nothing to her, but she knew by the brightness of his face and the enthusiasm in his voice just how important it was to him.

They finished luncheon and Sally realised with surprise that she had eaten a good meal, and what was more, she had enjoyed it.

"I must get back," David said, looking at his watch. "Are you feeling better?"

"Much better, and thank you, David."

She spoke solemnly and he knew that she was thanking him for far more than the luncheon.

It was only when they reached the hospital that Sally remembered that she wanted to telephone to the flat and speak to Elaine. She told David about this and asked if she could telephone in the building.

"I have a tiny sitting-room," he said. "You can telephone from there. Anne will not be awake for some time, so you can sit in there if you like. I have a consultation, so we must hurry."

He led Sally along various corridors until she felt quite lost; then he opened the door which was marked with his name.

"We are very up-to-date in St. Anthony's," David explained. "Doctors who live in have tiny flats of their own."

It was certainly tiny but not unattractive. There was

211

a little hall, a small single bedroom with the bathroom opening out from it and a minute sitting-room.

Sally noticed at once that David had furnished his flat with things from his own home.

She recognised the velvet curtains of a rather ugly shade of blue, the armchair with its dark patch in the centre of the back where David had rested his head for many years, an embroidered tablecloth which David's mother had worked for him when he first went to the University.

It was certainly not an expensive-looking sitting-room, nor was it very tidy, but it was homelike.

There were books, masses of them, crammed into a big bookcase and overflowing on to the floor; there were silver cups on the mantelpiece, most of them in need of a good clean, which David had won at his University for running and swimming; there were photographs, mostly stiff groups of football and cricket teams.

Over the mantelpiece there was a big, gilt-framed oil-painting—it was by no means a masterpiece but it held Sally's attention although she had often seen it before. It was a picture of the bay at St. Chytas and it had been painted by David's father.

It was rough and amateurish, and yet for those who knew and loved Cornwall it was a vivid reproduction of the golden sands, the rugged rocks and tumbled, broken sea. Sally stood very still.

"If only we could be there!"

She spoke the words hardly above a whisper, but David heard them.

"You miss it so much?"

"So much! I hate London!"

"I can understand that. You always belonged there. Dad ought to have put you in the picture running down to the sea."

"Don't, David!" Sally made a little gesture of protest.

"I feel so homesick. I feel if I were there now I would swim out to sea and never come back!"

"Poor little Cornish fairy torn from her Cornish soil."

David was teasing her, but there was something warm and understanding beneath the lightness of his words. Suddenly Sally felt as if she must cry.

To hide her face from him she walked quickly across the room and stared at the books in his bookcase.

"What a pedant you are! I don't believe there is a detective story or a novel amongst them."

"Of course there isn't," David replied; "don't you know I'm a worker?"

The clock on the mantelpiece chimed the quarter to two.

"I must go," David said, "I shall be late and my reputation will be ruined. Use the telephone, Sally, and then sit down and rest."

He waved his hand to her and rushed from the room. A second later the door of the flat slammed behind him. Sally was alone.

She stood looking round her as though she were only playing for time before her eyes came to rest once again on the picture over the mantelpiece.

At last she allowed herself to look at it—to look and look as though she could never have enough of the beauty, the wildness and the wide expanse of sea.

For a long time she stood still, and then at last she sat down in David's armchair and let her head rest against its arm.

How long she sat there she had no idea before with a little start she realised that she had not made her intended telephone call. She took up the receiver, gave the number and waited while the hospital operator got the number for her.

At last she was through. She had expected the butler

213

to answer, but to her surprise it was Robert Dunstan himself and he recognised her voice.

"Is that you, Miss Granville? I am so sorry to hear about your sister. Is it anything serious?"

Sally told him what was wrong with Anne and added that she was speaking from the hospital.

"So you have taken her to St. Anthony's?" Robert Dunstan said. "What is the number of her room?"

"No. 563—the fifth floor."

"I would like to send your sister some flowers."

"That is very kind of you."

"Not at all. May we expect you tomorrow?"

"I think so," Sally replied. "You won't mind my coming away at lunchtime to see Anne?"

"I think it would be better," Robert Dunstan suggested, "if you went to see your sister before luncheon or after, otherwise you might miss your meal."

The surprise she experienced at the consideration shown by his remark made it difficult for Sally to answer for the moment. Then she found her voice.

"Thank you, but I was thinking about Elaine's lessons."

"You don't suppose Elaine will worry about those? Nor will I."

"Oh, thank you," Sally said, "thank you very much indeed."

She rang off and stood for a moment thinking how much easier in every way Robert Dunstan was since they had come to an understanding over Elaine.

The child was happier, too, and already Sally believed that she was getting Mr. Dunstan round to her way of thinking with regard to sending Elaine to a boarding school.

They had not discussed this fully as yet, but often indirect references had been made to it and it seemed obvious to Sally that Mr. Dunstan was more or less taking it for granted that sooner or later Elaine would need the companionship of other girls.

"He's a strange man," Sally thought, "but I like him."

She looked up at the picture over the mantelpiece again. It made her think of her father.

It was her father who had helped her—her father who had learned so much about human nature from nature itself. How well he had understood the need for friendship and affection, the craving in everyone, however hard they seemed externally, for that inner warmth which only love could bring!

Quite suddenly Sally thought: "How lucky I am! I have so many people to love, so many people who love me."

She thought of her sisters, of all the people who had helped them since they came to London, of Mr. Dunstan, the Duchess and the Jarvises who had given them a home. What could they have done without such kindness?

And now in a moment of crisis they had David beside them, David loving and understanding, David who was, as she had told the indiscreet nurse, "one of the family."

"I am lucky," she thought.

She rested her cheek confidingly against the shabby arm of David's old armchair.

Fourteen

Anne lay in bed and looked at the flowers which scented her small room.

They were so lovely that every now and then she found herself asking if they could really be for her.

She had no idea that people could be so kind, yet here was a tangible proof not only of their kindness but of their interest.

There was a great vase of carnations which the Duchess had had sent to her from Cheyn; there was the spiked beauty of gladioli which had come in a large, expensive box with Ben Barlow's card attached to it; there were small bunches of anemones from Mrs. Jarvis and of marigolds from the servants at Berkeley Square.

Anne had been particularly touched by the latter, for she had no idea they even so much as noticed her existence.

By her bedside there were two or three gardenias which Sally had given her knowing that she would love the soft, symmetrical purity of their petals and their strange, haunting perfume.

Marigold had brought her grapes, which Anne guessed had cost her more than she could afford; but most surprising of all was the enormous basket of spotted orchids, which had come from Elaine and her father.

Orchids! Somehow Anne had never expected to be the recipient of anything so exotic or so expensive, and yet there they stood—symbolic of a luxurious world of which she knew so little.

"How kind everybody is—how terribly, terribly kind!"Anne repeated to herself.

She felt that being ill was almost worth while if it made one realise the affection and generosity even of strangers.

She was so much better in herself. David was pleased with her and so was Mr. Drayson, but they had at last told her the truth—that her recovery was only temporary and that she would have to be operated on for appendicitis.

For a moment the news filled her with panic and fear but she had managed to keep control of herself and after a few seconds of dark terror she managed to say in a voice that quivered a little:

"If you really think it is necessary."

"I am afraid it is," Mr. Drayson said, and his disarming smile was somehow infinitely comforting. "But we'll look after you, won't we, David?"

David had nodded.

"Anne knows we will do that."

"You have been awfully kind," Anne said.

But when Mr. Drayson had gone she turned to David urgently.

"What about the expense, David? We cannot possibly afford it."

"I am afraid you will have to, Anne. It is one of those things that can't be economised on. But don't worry, Sally says she will manage."

"Yes, Sally will manage," Anne said, "but that means she and Marigold will give up everything for me. It isn't fair on them, David."

"Well, it's not going to be as expensive as all that," David answered. "I have explained the circumstances to Drayson and he is an awfully decent chap."

Anne was still for a moment, then in a very small voice she asked:

"How much does this room cost?"

David looked at her as if he would avoid the truth, but something in Anne's honest gaze demanded frankness.

"Eight guineas a week," he replied; "it is a uniform fee, you know, for private rooms."

Anne took a deep breath.

"I want to be moved into a public ward."

David sat down opposite her and took her hand in his.

"Listen, Anne, I understand what you are feeling, but honestly we will manage it somehow, and when I say 'we' I mean Sally and I."

"You are going to do nothing of the sort," Anne said firmly. "I want to be moved into a public ward now and at once!"

"Don't be difficult, Anne."

"I am not being difficult. I know what I want and I mean to have it. It is sweet of you, David, and don't think that I don't appreciate that you are trying to help us, but I know only too well how hard up your family is."

"They would give their last penny to help you," David replied, "you know that. And so would I."

"Apart from the fact that I wouldn't take your money you haven't got many pennies to give me; you aren't earning as much as you anticipated because you are working with Sir Hubert. That is true, isn't it?"

David smiled rather ruefully.

"Damn it, Anne, you know as much about me as I do myself."

"And your father is an old darling, but half Cornwall owes him money which is never likely to be paid."

David nodded.

"We are all rather in the same boat," Anne went on. " 'Impoverished', is the word, I believe. So, David, stop trying to wrap me up in cotton wool. I won't mind a public ward, I won't really!"

"You have never been in one," David protested.

"Then it's about time I started, and you are not to tell Sally. You know perfectly well Sally would say I was to stay here."

"I wouldn't dare to move you without asking her," David confessed.

"I am the eldest," Anne said with unexpected dignity. "It is about time I stopped taking orders from Sally; after all she is only the baby."

"Sally a baby?" David expostulated. "At times I feel as though she were my great-grandmother."

His ejaculation was so spontaneous that suddenly he

and Anne were both laughing and giggling together as if they were schoolchildren being impertinent about their teacher. But David looked worrried as he got to his feet.

"I don't know what to do about you, Anne, I don't really."

"Well, do as I tell you, or else I will make a general nuisance of myself."

"I will see Matron," David said at last, defeated by the calm determination in Anne's tones. "But I shouldn't think there is a chance of a bed for a few days. We are full to bursting!"

"I will take the first one that becomes available."

"Very well"

David stood looking down at her for a moment and then he said:

"I suppose there are three other girls in the world as nice as the three Granville sisters but I don't suppose I would be lucky enough to come across them."

"Don't flatter us, David," Anne smiled, "we are not always as nice as we seem!"

In answer David pressed her hand.

"Bless you, Anne," he said, "you are a brick!"

Then he was gone.

Lying alone, Anne tried to realise what the decision she had just taken would mean to her. She felt that every nerve in her body shrank from the contact with other sick people and yet something stern and resolute within herself told her that she was doing not only what was right but what was the only thing possible in the circumstances.

She must not penalise the others. They would be hard put as it was to find the money for the operation and all the many little extras which are inevitable when someone is ill.

There was, too, her share of the rent at the Saracen's Head and her share of the electric cooker to be paid.

"Why, oh why did I have to be ill now?" Anne

asked herself, and then looking at her flowers found comfort from them.

How could one despair or even be miserable when there was so much kindness in the world?

"I am lucky," Anne thought, "terribly lucky!"

She closed her eyes for a moment and then opened them again as there came a little knock on the door. Nurse came in.

"Feeling well enough for a visitor?" she asked.

"Of course I am," Anne replied. "Who is it?"

"A gentleman," the nurse answered, and going to the door spoke to someone outside.

There was a moment's pause while Anne waited expectantly, wondering who the "gentleman" could be; then to her surprise the door was opened wide to admit Robert Dunstan.

His entrance was so unexpected that for a moment Anne could only stare at him, but as he advanced towards the bed a sudden thought struck her. Something had happened to Sally!

Before she could speak he had reached her side.

"I was passing the hospital, Miss Granville, and thought I would come to see how you were for myself. Your sister has given us good news of your progress but Elaine is unceasingly curious about you."

With a throb of relief Anne realised that her imagination had led her astray and with an effort she held out her hand and forced a smile to her lips.

"That's very kind of you, Mr. Dunstan; won't you sit down?"

Apparently quite at his ease, Robert Dunstan pulled forward a comfortable chair and seated himself to his own satisfaction.

"I must thank you," Anne said, feeling somehow extremely shy, "for the lovely flowers you and Elaine sent me."

"I am glad you like them."

"They are the first orchids I have ever received."

He smiled.

"I am glad we were able to offer you something unique but we were obviously not the only 'givers of gifts'."

"No, everybody has been so very kind. It makes me feel rather ashamed of myself to be lying here in such comfort while everyone else is working so hard."

"Your sister certainly works. I don't know what we should have done without her," Robert Dunstan said appreciatively. "She and Elaine have gone to see the Duchess this afternoon. 'Anne's Duchess' as Elaine calls her."

"She will be delighted to see them. I have been worrying about her; I left so many things unfinished."

"I can assure you, Miss Granville, all your interests are being looked after while you are away from us."

There was something about his tone which was rather strange, yet Anne knew he meant to be kind and she found her shyness passing from her.

"He is not so very formidable," she thought.

She remembered the last time she had seen him in their tiny sitting-room at the Saracen's Head; then she had hated him and thought him cruel.

Now, for the first time, she realised he was a comparatively young man and that there was something nice about his serious, clean-cut face.

She tried to think of something to say that would interest him and realised that his eyes were resting on her father's photograph.

Robert Dunstan sat forward in his seat.

"Surely," he said, "I know that face?"

"It is my father."

"But wasn't he A.C. Granville?"

"Yes, Arthur Christopher."

"But how absurd! I knew him. I never thought of

221

course to connect the name with that very brilliant writer of Cornish history."

"My father published several books on Cornwall. Where did you meet him?"

"He came up to London to lecture," Robert Dunstan replied, "and I was fortunate enough to be asked to dinner especially to meet him. We had a most interesting discussion at the time. A year or so later I found a reference in one of your father's books to a Spanish play I was particularly anxious to read.

"It was out of print and I wrote and asked your father if he had a copy and whether he would lend it to me. I wrote to him care of his publishers and the letter was forwarded to a place beginning with St. . ."

"St. Chytas," Anne supplied.

"Yes, that's right. He sent me the book and also a commentary on the play which was a great help to me."

"I think I remember the book you must have been writing about," Anne said slowly. "Hadn't it rather amusing illustrations by a Spanish artist called de Perez?"

"Yes, but don't tell me you have read it!"

"Not in the original edition," Anne replied, "my Spanish is not good enough for that, but my father made a rough translation of it. I think he intended publishing it one day, but like many other things he did he never had time to finish it off. I remember the book well and how much I enjoyed it."

"This is extraordinarily interesting!" Robert Dunstan exclaimed. He went on to talk of Arthur Granville's work and of many other books and literature with which Anne was well acquainted.

It was with something like a sense of surprise that she realised he had been with her for over half an hour when he rose to his feet.

"I must not tire you, Miss Granville, but please may I come again?"

"I hope you will," Anne said eagerly, and then she remembered. Her expression changed and for a moment she hesitated.

"Have you changed your mind?" Robert Dunstan asked.

"Oh no, it isn't that, it's just that I will not be in this room. Tomorrow or the day after I may be moved."

"But I understood from your sister that . . ."

"I have asked Dr. Carey, who is looking after me, if he will put me in the public ward."

"Why have you done that?"

"It's quite simple," Anne said. "You see, I can't afford to stay here."

"But that is absurd!"

"Not really. Let us be frank and admit that my father's books, clever as they were, only sold to a few connoisseurs like yourself. When he died he left a wealth of affection and respect behind him but very little money."

"In that case," Robert Dunstan began, "as an admirer of your father may I. . ."

Before he said anything further Anne knew his intention from the expression on his face. Swiftly she made a little gesture with her hands which checked him.

"Please, Mr. Dunstan, don't say it. I would not have told you only I thought it might be embarrassing if you came again."

"But won't you let me . . ." he began.

"Do you think we are likely to?" Anne asked. "You know Sally well enough for that. We may be poor but we are proud and Cornish!"

"You are cutting the ground from under my feet before I can begin," Robert Dunstan protested.

"It has been so nice talking to you, I don't want to have to argue."

"I am much too afraid to do that."

"I am glad—it would tire me so much," Anne smiled. "And now may I ask you a favour?"

223

"Of course."

"I want you to promise me something," Anne said, speaking easily and not realising fully to what a friendly basis their acquaintanceship had progressed.

"Very well," said Robert Dunstan, "I promise."

"Don't tell Sally that I am changing my room," Anne begged. "She is going to be angry with me, but I am hoping that I shall have been moved before she knows anything about it and then it will be too late for anything to be done."

Unexpectedly Robert Dunstan laughed. It was the laugh of a man who is not used to being amused.

"I have never met people like you," he exclaimed. "Do the Miss Granvilles always get their own way?"

Anne nodded and a smile curved her lips.

"Usually."

"I will keep my promise," Robert Dunstan said, "and I will come and see you again if I may—wherever you may be."

He held her hand for a moment and then he picked up his hat and his umbrella from the chair on which he had laid them and went from the room with a quiet dignity.

Anne lay looking at the door after it had closed behind him. What an unexpected visitor and a very unexpected conversation! She went over it slowly and methodically in her mind. In the end she spoke her thoughts aloud:

"He is nice. We were mistaken in him."

She looked at the big basket of orchids and added:

"How strange it must be to be as rich as that and yet so alone!"

Sally was sorry for Elaine but Anne knew she was also sorry for Elaine's father.

She thought of all that Sally had told her about the flat—the servants who were attentive only when their employer was there and who were slack and indifferent when he was not, the gloomy, unhomelike atmosphere, the lack of friendliness and happiness.

Somehow quite clearly Anne could see Robert Dunstan sitting alone in his library night after night with no one to talk to, no one to tell of his triumphs and big business deals, or to sympathise with him over his doubts, difficulties, worries and apprehensions.

"He must be lonely . . . terribly lonely!" Anne whispered.

She thought of the three little divan beds where she, Sally, and Marigold slept close together.

There was something warm and comforting about the arrangement and it occurred to her that being in a public ward might not be so bad after all. At least it would not be a bitter, sterile loneliness with only one's own thoughts for company.

Strangely enough, at that very moment Sally was also understanding and sympathising with another's loneliness.

The Duchess, sitting up in bed wearing an ermine wrap round her shoulders, looked, as Elaine put it later, rather like a witch. She was complaining bitterly:

"How long is your sister going to be ill? Tiresome girl! Here am I, lost without her—nobody to look after me, nobody to do anything except the servants who seem half-witted and a nurse who whenever I make the simplest requests tells me it is her time off!"

"Anne is awfully worried about you," Sally said sympathetically.

"And so she ought to be!" the Duchess retorted. "It isn't fair for young people to be ill. It is quite enough bother with the old ones like myself going down with Anno Domini without chits of Anne's age indulging in the luxury of being laid up."

"Anne said we were to try and look after you," Elaine piped in. Until now she had said nothing except "How do you do?" but had stared at the Duchess

225

wide-eyed, obviously taking in every detail of her strange appearance.

"She told you to do that, did she?" the Duchess questioned with a faint smile. "Well, what are you going to do about it?"

"What would you like me to do?" Elaine asked. "I could read to you. I'm not terribly good at the long words though. Or perhaps I could arrange your flowers. Miss Granville says I am very good at that and Anne did yours for you, didn't she?"

"She did," the Duchess answered, "and now the housemaid does them. Just look at them, jammed together like a Sunday School competition. I tell you I am missing my companion."

"We are missing her, too," Sally agreed quietly.

There was a note of sincerity in her voice which arrested the Duchess's attention.

"You are good girls," she said unexpectedly. "You are fond of each other and loyal. Your other sister came to see me the evening before last. The one with the fancy name."

"Marigold," Sally supplied.

"Yes, that's right—Marigold! And yesterday she went to fetch me a library book in her lunch-hour. Very kind I thought it was of her. She is extremely pretty!"

"We think so, too."

"You're not the only ones I'll be bound. I am sure there are plenty of young men thinking the same thing." She looked at Sally. "You are not as pretty as your sisters, child."

Sally smiled.

"No, I am the ugly duckling."

"I wouldn't say that," the Duchess replied, "and according to your sister you are the wise one of the family, so perhaps you will come off best in the end."

"It depends surely on what you mean by 'the end'?"

226

The Duchess was silent for a moment while she considered the question, then she said:

"Well, you three came to London to seek your fortunes, or was it to find husbands? I suppose it will be the end of one period in your lives when you all achieve your hearts' desire."

"I doubt if we shall be lucky enough to do that," Sally answered.

Then quickly, as if the Duchess had probed too deeply into something essentially intimate, she got to her feet.

"Isn't there something Elaine and I can do for you, Duchess? We are longing to make ourselves useful."

"I wonder if this sudden energy is due to the fact that you consider my conversation indiscreet in front of the child," the Duchess said with a shrewdness which Anne would have known was characteristic of her.

It did not, however, disconcert Sally.

"There is always that point of view to be considered," she answered quietly.

The Duchess gave a little chuckle as if she were amused.

Later, walking back to the flat from Berkeley Square, Elaine chattered gaily of the Duchess and all that she had seen and heard.

"She is terribly, terribly old, isn't she, Miss Granville? Is she a hundred?"

"No, not yet," Sally replied. "Very few people live to be a hundred."

"Would you like to?" Elaine asked.

"No, I would like to die while I could still be of use to people, not when I was a nuisance and everyone had to look after me."

"I expect people would love looking after you," Elaine said. "I would!"

"Thank you, darling, but I don't think we need worry

227

about it yet. It will be a great many years before I am anywhere near a hundred."

"The Duchess is very lonely without Anne, isn't she?" Elaine went on.

"I am afraid people are always lonely when they get very old," Sally replied. "You see, their own friends are either dead or very old too, so there is no one for them to talk to except younger people who are taken up with their own interests and their own families."

Elaine considered this for some time and then she said:

"But you don't have to be old to be lonely, do you, Miss Granville?"

It was one of those shrewd, disconcerting remarks which Elaine often made unexpectedly. Sally, wondering where her thoughts were leading her, answered simply:

"No, of course not!"

"I was lonely until you came to look after me, and I think Daddy's lonely, too."

Sally said nothing for a moment, not quite certain as to what form her answer should take; then, before she could answer, Elaine went on:

"There were always lots of people in our flat, of course, but that didn't make me un-lonely. I think if you are lonely you want someone very special with you, someone you can love."

It was with difficulty that Sally prevented herself from applauding Elaine's remark.

She knew that this process of reasoning was the result of the developing of Elaine's brain, of making her try to understand her own reaction to things rather than just expressing them by temper and sulkiness.

Now, as she held the child's hand waiting to cross South Audley Street at the traffic lights, she said:

"You are quite right, darling, and when you think

228

people are lonely you must just try and love them. Then they feel better."

They got back to the flat to find tea laid for them in the schoolroom and a special treat for Elaine in the shape of a small iced cake with her name on it.

Tired of the dull, unimaginative meals which the cook considered quite good enough for the schoolroom, Sally had asked Robert Dunstan if she could order what she considered suitable things for Elaine.

"Don't you do it already?" he asked in surprise.

"No, of course not," Sally replied. "It is usually more than a governess's place is worth to interfere in the kitchen."

"But you, being an unusual governess, feel you can attempt it?"

"I will try if I have your authority behind me."

His eyes had twinkled at her.

"I don't suppose you really need my authority, Miss Granville, but of course it is yours."

Sally had therefore approached the cook and managed with consummate tact and a great deal of flattery to put her on her mettle with regard to tempting Elaine's appetite.

The result had been a considerable change in the menus and Elaine's delight at this afternoon's effort with an iced cake was gratifying.

"Isn't it lovely, Miss Granville?" she exclaimed over and over again.

"You will have to tell Mrs. Marlow how pleased you are," Sally suggested.

"I will ask her to have a slice and taste it for herself."

"That's a good idea, but wash your hands before we start tea."

They were just finishing the meal when the footman came to tell Sally she was wanted on the telephone. Instinctively she felt it must be something about Anne. Perhaps something was wrong, perhaps she had taken a turn for the worse.

She ran across the hall to the morning-room and a moment later there was a little click as the line was switched through from the pantry.

"Hello," Sally said. "Hello!"

There was a moment's pause, then a man's voice replied:

"Is that you, Sally?"

"Yes, who is it?"

"Have you forgotten me so quickly?"

"Peter! We haven't heard from you for so long!"

"Yes, I know, that is why I have rung you up at Robert Dunstan's. Can you talk?"

"Yes, of course. I am alone, if that's what you mean."

"I want to know how Marigold is."

"Peter, what is all this?" Sally asked. "Where have you been all this time? Why did you disappear without a word? We have so often wondered about you. Marigold has told us nothing."

"She couldn't tell you what she didn't know. Look, Sally, I don't want you to say anything to Marigold. Will you promise not to tell her I have telephoned you?"

Sally hesitated.

"Will you promise?" Peter insisted.

"I don't know that I will," Sally replied. "Marigold has not been at all happy lately, Peter. I didn't know what was wrong with her. Now I am wondering if it has had anything to do with you."

"I hope it has!"

"Peter, I want to help you. Can't you explain?"

"No, Sally, not yet, but I just had to know how she is. Marigold has got to grow up. I want you to trust me and believe I am doing the right thing."

"How can I believe it, when I don't know what you are doing?"

"Dear Sally, always so practical. Well, if it is any consolation, I am working hard for Marigold."

"At your painting.

"No, that is a thing of the past. I am working for the future, my future and also for Marigold's. Now tell me how she is.

"She is well, but I don't think she is happy."

"Good! That's the best bit of news I have had for years! But Sally, there isn't anyone else?"

Sally didn't answer.

"Tell me," Peter insisted. "I would rather know the truth."

"I don't know what the truth is," Sally answered. "Marigold is very gay but I know she is not happy. That is all I can tell you, Peter, and I am not certain whether I am being loyal to Marigold in telling you as much as that."

"Yes, you are, Sally; don't worry your head. You have told me all I want to know. Bless you and take care of her for me."

"But Peter, where are you speaking from?"

Sally called out the question, but even as she spoke she realised she was speaking to a dead line.

Slowly she put down the receiver. It was all very mysterious and yet why hadn't she guessed at some of it before? Peter and Marigold! It was after Peter had disappeared that Marigold became so strange.

What was the explanation of it all?

Sally's face wore a worried expression as she went back to eat iced cake with Elaine.

Fifteen

Robert Dunstan, who was writing at his desk, looked up as the door opened.

"Are you busy, Mr. Dunstan? Could I speak to you for a moment?" Sally asked.

He got to his feet.

"Of course, Miss Granville. Come and sit down."

He pulled forward a chair at the side of the desk and waited while Sally crossed the room.

"You are sure you are not busy?" she asked.

Robert Dunstan smiled at her.

"Even if I am, I want to hear what you have to say."

"It is not so urgent as all that," Sally said, smiling back.

It was extraordinary how her relationship with her employer had altered during the past month. Now she was utterly at ease with him. They could talk and even laugh together.

"Well, what is it?" Robert Dunstan said. "Has Elaine been getting into mischief again?"

"No, she has been terribly good lately," Sally answered. "I am really very proud of her."

"She ought to be proud of you."

"I never thought I would hear you say that to me," Sally challenged, then added: "But I must not waste your time, I have come to ask you a great favour."

"What is it? If it is in my power I promise to do it."

Encouraged, Sally took a deep breath and began:

"As you know, Anne's operation has been very successful, also the doctors are satisfied with her condition as a whole. We had one awful moment when they thought her lung was affected, but with care Mr. Drayson believes that everything will clear up and be completely normal.

"The only thing is, he insists on her having a holiday. He wants her to go away from London to the country for at least a month."

"Where do you suggest sending her?" Robert Dunstan asked.

"Of course, I would like to send her to Switzerland or the South of France, but as those places are out of the question, I am taking her back home."

"Home?"

"St. Chytas. Of course, she cannot go to the Vicarage but I know various cottages in the village where she could stay. The only thing is that she really isn't well enough to be alone for the first week or ten days and I wondered if it would be asking too much, Mr. Dunstan, if I might go with her and take Elaine. It is lovely down there and Elaine would love the sands and the sea."

It would be difficult for anyone to resist Sally when she was pleading for something, and she had been so certain in her own mind that Robert Dunstan—the new, changed, easy-to-get-on-with Robert Dunstan—would agree to her plan that she was surprised when he hesitated.

There was a long pause before he spoke while Sally waited apprehensively and willed him to agree. At last he said:

"I suppose you will not allow me to send your sister to Switzerland?"

"Oh!" It was an ejaculation of sheer surprise which came from Sally's parted lips.

"Wouldn't it be possible," Robert Dunstan went on, "for me to suggest that she accompanies Elaine and you of course? Can't we contrive a plan, you and I, which your sister will accept without question?"

Sally smiled.

"It is terribly kind of you," she said, "but honestly it

wouldn't work. I don't think Anne would like it and I know I wouldn't. I was only teasing, of course, when I spoke about Switzerland and the South of France. It sounds now as though I were asking you to help us."

Robert Dunstan looked at her solemnly.

"You know I would not think that of you, Miss Granville."

"Thank you," Sally replied, "and thank you, too, for your very kind thought."

"Why can't you accept it?" Robert Dunstan asked. "It is ridiculous not to. Your sister's health is at stake . . ."

"But it isn't," Sally interrupted, "not to that extent. It isn't really a question of pride, either, it is just . . . well . . ."

She hesitated for words.

"There are certain things we are brought up not to do."

"Such as taking presents from strange men. You make it sound as though I were a casual acquaintance in the train."

"No, it isn't that." Sally knitted her brows together. "I wish I could explain. It is because it is so easy for you—because you are rich and because it would not have occurred to you if I were not here looking after Elaine. It is all those things which make it impossible for us to take such a generous present from you."

"I don't understand," Robert Dunstan said. "I wish I did."

He got up suddenly and walked across the room and back again as though he were turning something over in his mind.

Suddenly Sally saw that he was worried, and because it was so much part of her training she forgot her own troubles in an effort to reach him.

"Could I help you, Mr. Dunstan?"

Her voice was soft and inviting. He stopped walking

234

about and stood opposite her, towering over her so that she looked very small and defenceless as she looked up at him.

"I wonder if I dare tell you the truth."

"But of course!"

"You may not like it when you hear it."

"I should risk that," Sally advised him solemnly.

"Very well then. I will tell you. I am very much in love with your sister Anne."

"With Anne?"

Sally was too astonished to do more than ejaculate. Somehow this was the last thing she had expected—from Robert Dunstan of all people.

It seemed as though her surprise was what Mr. Dunstan had expected, for he looked down at her, saying no more, only watching the expression on her face.

At last Sally found her voice.

"But you don't know her. You have not met her more than once, as far as I know."

"Several times more than that," Robert Dunstan replied. "I went to see her twice in the hospital when she was in a private room and twice since she was moved to the public ward."

"She never told me."

"No? And I did not tell you either. It wasn't a conspiracy, it was just, I think, a natural reticence on my part because it mattered so tremendously."

"But Anne! Oh dear, I must think about this."

Sally put her hands up to her cheeks, then she said:

"Please sit down. You make me feel so nervous when you stand over me."

With a smile Robert Dunstan did as he was told.

"I am sorry, I had forgotten what a little bit of a thing you are physically, you are so very formidable in every other way."

He smiled at Sally and suddenly the smile was rather tremulous and embarrassed—there was even the hint of the schoolboy Robert Dunstan must once have been behind the solemnity of his eyes.

"Won't you help me, Sally?" he asked, and she realised with a start that he had used her Christian name.

"I can't make Anne love you," she replied, "if that's what you mean."

"No, but you could put me in a good light. You could help me to show her how much I love her."

"Do you?" Sally asked.

"I do."

There was something in the nature of an oath in the words. Then Robert Dunstan was fidgeting again with the top of the silver inkpot.

"I want to tell you something about myself, if I may," he said after a moment. "A few things which will perhaps make it easier for you to understand why I am as I am."

He pushed the big leather-bound blotter aside and put his elbows on the table.

"I know quite well," he went on, "that I must appear to you hard, inhuman and at times aggressive. I have taught myself to be like that, Sally. When I was young I was absurdly and ridiculously over-sensitive. It seems strange now to think of the agonies I went through in my teens.

"I was a clever boy at school. I won prizes and scholarships with the greatest of ease. I was useless at games, chiefly I think because my father, who was fanatically ambitious, never allowed me to play any.

"I think I can honestly and truthfully say that when I went to my preparatory school was the first time I ever held a ball in my hands. It was little wonder that I was looked on as a swot by the other boys.

"They found me a bore and I was not surprised. It was not only that I had not learned to play games, it was that I had had little or no contact with other children and therefore I talked in a pompous, rather

236

grown-up fashion which was obviously calculated to make me a laughing-stock to boys of my own age.

"Because their taunts and teasing hurt me I tried to despise them. I rose quickly to the top of the school but I knew in my heart of herats that my place there was a barren one. I had the affection and respect of neither the boys nor the masters.

"I went on to a famous public school and much the same thing happened there. Already I had begun to segregate myself from my fellows, to concentrate on my work, telling myself I was content with the praise my father gave me.

"After I left school I went to the University. There I made a few friends—I would have made more if, at the end of my first year, my father had not sent me abroad, first to a German counting-house, then into a French bank.

"He made a special arrangement that I should work hard; in fact. I think it must have been harder than anyone had ever worked before. I only know that at times I was utterly exhausted with all that was required of me; I had not even time to think, but I achieved what he desired.

"By the time I was twenty-four I was already spoken of as a coming man in the world of finance. I came back to England to work with my father. It was only then that I realised why he had been so impatient. He was a dying man.

"Still he kept on until the end and he kept me working beside him. When he died I was so involved, so burdened with the work he had heaped upon me, that I did not realise that at last I was my own master and could relax if I wished.

"At the same time, I suppose in a desire to escape, I got married the year my father died."

Robert Dunstan paused for a moment. He looked at

Sally, then away from her across the big, gloomy, expensively furnished room.

"It is difficult for any man to speak of his wife," he said after a moment, "but as I am trying to be frank with you, Sally, I must tell you the truth. I made a terrible mistake in my marriage. I think, looking back on my own life now and trying to be dispassionate about it, what I craved was tenderness.

"My mother had died, you see, soon after I was born. I had no memory of being loved or comforted or made a fuss of. That was what I wanted although I did not realise it at the time. I married because my wife had appeared to my father and to many of my friends as someone eminently suitable for me.

"Her father was a distinguished banker, she had been brought up in the world of finance and understood it almost as well as I did. She was extremely intelligent and was as much at home on the Continent as in England.

"She was also outstandingly clever. There were several men who wanted to marry her and I was thrilled when I realised that she was interested in me. It was not difficult in my inexperience to imagine myself in love with her.

"We got married and it was only then that I discovered that I had discarded the yoke my father had put upon me for one which was even more exhausting. My wife was insatiably ambitious. She craved power, money and importance as another woman might crave beautiful jewels.

"They were the only things which satisfied her. I found myself working, if possible, even harder than I had worked before. But you must remember that I had only a dim glimmer of what was happening to me; I had not yet reached the stage of introspection when I could examine myself and realise what was wrong.

When Elaine was born I thought that a baby might alter my wife's attitude, might make her softer, more kindly both to me and to the child. But she was furiously angry that Elaine was not a boy.

"She wanted a son so that he could carry her ambitions one step further. It was then I began to be afraid, afraid for myself and afraid for Elaine.

"My wife had already got everything mapped out as to what the future would hold for both of us. Elaine was to be educated in the most elaborate and comprehensive fashion. Almost before she could lisp her first words my wife insisted on engaging a French governess so that she could take up her first foreign language.

"I began to protest—small, ineffectual protestations, I admit; they were swept on one side imperiously and I realised I was up against something almost hideously formidable."

Robert Dunstan pulled out a handkerchief from his pocket and wiped his forehead. Sally knew it was a tremendous effort for him to tell her this; she knew, too, that it was the first time he had ever spoken to anybody of such intimate matters.

"Go on," she said quietly.

"When one looks back," Robert Dunstan continued, "it is always difficult to know when and at what moment one began to wake up to the truth. I only know that suddenly it was there—the knowledge of what a fool I must be.

"My chains were heavily upon me, I could see no way of breaking loose from them, of escaping. It was not myself with whom I was so much concerned as Elaine.

"My wife was talking of schools and tutors and special courses abroad, and, ultimately, a university, while I knew only too well what the result of such intensive teaching would be. I thought of the years when my youth had been wasted, thought of the times when I had wanted to play but had been forced to work.

"When I looked back I could hear the high, happy

voice of the boys playing in the sunshine while I sat at my desk. I tried to argue with my wife but she laughed at me.

'Don't be ridiculous, Robert; look what you have achieved! Hasn't it been worth it?'

'No, it hasn't!' I said to her, and was forced to apologise because she did not understand."

Robert Dunstan got to his feet as if it were intolerable to stay still any longer.

"Can you understand?" he asked. "When she died I was glad—yes, glad—because I believed that by her dying Elaine was saved."

The pain in his voice broke against the silence of the room.

"I am sorry, so terribly sorry for you," Sally whispered, and there were tears of sympathy in her eyes.

Robert Dunstan stood with his back to her looking out of the window. Sally knew that he was not seeing the sunshine outside but, instead, the grey misery of his past.

At last he turned round.

"Can you understand a little," he asked, "why I was so insistent about Elaine? Why I wanted her to remain a little girl playing with her dolls, enjoying herself?"

"Of course I understand," Sally said, and her voice was unsteady. "But don't you see, you forgot that she would want people to play with, not things. What you have missed all your life is companionship, someone to do things with."

"I suppose that is true," Robert Dunstan said. "It wasn't the ball I wanted but the boy to throw it to. I am afraid, Sally, I am not a success at anything except at making money, and when I have made it, what use is it?" He made a gesture and added, "Even you will not let me spend it on anything I want."

Sally looked up at him.

"It is all going to come right. Now you know where things went wrong, they will begin to right themselves."

"You think so?"

"I am sure of it. My father always used to say that it was no use building on a bad foundation, we had got to go back to the beginning and get the foundations right, then we could build something worth while."

"I am rather old to start again," Robert Dunstan said ruefully.

"Are you?" Sally asked. "But I thought that was just what you wanted?"

"You mean I might begin again with Anne?"

"Yes, if that is what you want."

"I do want her, Sally. I want her to marry me—I want her to give me a chance to start again, to build up the sort of life I have always wanted—a house in the country, a home, a garden and perhaps one day other children."

"And Anne would like all those things, but you must make it quite clear to her that that is what you want. She doesn't like what we call modern civilisation, she doesn't like smart people and so-called gaiety, she wants a quiet life—one that is leisurely, calm and dignified."

"One has only got to look at her to know those things," Robert Dunstan said; "but, Sally, she frightens me—you all frighten me. You are so different from anyone I have ever known before."

"Have you said anything to Anne to make her think that you like her?" Sally asked.

"I wouldn't dare," Robert Dunstan confessed. "It seems silly to say this but I am nervous, more nervous and afraid than I have ever been of anything. You see, Sally, nothing has ever mattered so much as this before."

There was no doubting the sincerity in his voice.

Quite suddenly Sally smiled, the radiant and happy

241

smile which was hers when she was confident and assured.

"If you really love Anne as much as that," she said, "and I believe you do, I feel sure she will grow to love you; but don't be in a hurry, Anne hates being hurried. What I think would be the best thing, if you will agree to it . . ."

"I will agree to anything," Robert Dunstan interposed quickly.

". . . is," Sally went on, "that you should come down to St. Chytas when we are there. There are lots of hotels in St. Ives where you could stay. You could motor over to see us and you would get a chance to be alone with Anne where it is quiet and there is no telephone to interrupt you or call you away. I think if she saw you there it would be very different from seeing you here, in this flat."

"What is wrong with the flat?" Robert Dunstan asked with a twist of humour in his voice.

"Oh, it is all right," Sally said quickly, "but it isn't any of the things Anne likes."

"What does she like?"

"I don't think I had better tell you that—that is for you to find out from her. I will only say that she likes security and all that is beautiful and traditional in life rather than just expensive luxury."

"I understand. That bears out some of the things we have talked about when we have been together. Very well, Sally, go to St. Chytas and take Elaine with you. Make any arrangements you like and please don't be too proud to charge some of the expenses to me."

"Thank you," Sally said simply.

"And thank you for trusting me as you have. May I take it that you approve of me as a future brother-in-law and will give me your blessing?"

Robert Dunstan's question was a serious one.

"It is the last question I ever expected to be asked in

242

the whole world," Sally said, "but I can answer it absolutely truthfully in one word—Yes. I am glad!"

Robert Dunstan held out his hand and Sally put hers into it.

"It is half the battle if I have your friendship, Sally."

"Of course you have got it," Sally answered. "Although once I thought you were my worst enemy."

"That ought to be a lesson to you not to judge people too hastily," Robert Dunstan said, and she saw that he was teasing her.

"Perhaps I ought not to change my mind so quickly."

She liked the twinkle in his eyes as he answered:

"It is no use, Sally, you never let me have the last word."

"It would be a mistake to forget that I am a woman," Sally laughed.

"Very few men would be likely to forget that," Robert Dunstan said gallantly.

When Sally had finished with Elaine that evening she hurried to St. Anthony's Hospital.

On the way there she turned over in her mind the amazing events of the afternoon. Somehow she would not have believed it possible that this could happen.

Robert Dunstan was the last person in the world she would ever have thought of as a possible husband for any of them, yet now she realised she must have been blind.

Almost every day she had noticed beside Anne's bed great baskets of flowers which she had been told had come from Robert Dunstan. Even allowing for Elaine's interest in her governess's sister, they were overwhelmingly extravagant for a girl lying in the public ward of the hospital.

It seemed to Sally, too, that Anne had taken an unusual interest in what had been happening at the flat.

She had asked about Elaine and invariably Sally had told her not only about Elaine but about Elaine's father. Now she wondered if she had presented him in a pleasant enough light.

Had she over-emphasised the difficulties in the flat? It was true that the servants were still inattentive at times and there was room for improvement.

There was no need for Anne to be put off by these details which could only affect someone in the position of another employee.

"I must be careful, very careful, what I say," Sally warned herself.

She entered the ward to find Anne chatting happily with the occupant of the next bed.

Only Sally had guessed what an effort those first days in the public ward had been for Anne. She had been astounded when she had learned from David that Anne had insisted on giving up the private room.

When she had gone in to see her lying pale and exhausted at the end of a row of other sick people, she had felt that such sacrifice was unnecessary and slightly hysterical.

She had pleaded with Anne and even argued quite fiercely with her in her efforts to persuade her to enjoy the luxury of a private room. But Anne had been adamant and at last Sally had begun to realise that there was more in the gesture than just unselfishness as far as she and Marigold were concerned.

This was Anne's penance, this was her retribution to herself for having shrunk from and disliked sick people; and in forcing herself to be amongst them while she herself was ill was forcing herself to accept life as it was and not as she wished it to be.

Only Sally realised that every nerve in Anne's body was tense, that every instinct within herself screamed out to be taken away, to be allowed to be alone; and yet she stayed there, stayed until gradually the horror passed, until the panic within herself was conquered and assuaged.

She fought a hard battle and came through it victorious!

Only Sally understood why the first two days after her operation she did not react as well as could be expected. Sally knew that it was not physical pain which made Anne quiver but a reaction within her own mind, a revulsion which had to be conquered and subdued.

Once she understood, Sally ceased to make things worse for Anne by arguing with her.

Instinctively she set out to make things easier for her, getting to know with her usual friendliness the occupants of the other beds, making Anne see them as real people, relating stories of their lives, making them at times amusing, at other times pathetic.

At last Anne relaxed, at last she found out that illness was not a thing to be run away from but to be faced with all that was finest and best within oneself, and Sally seeing her now smiling easily at the woman in the next bed, knew that Anne would emerge from this ordeal a finer and better person both physically and spiritually.

"Hello, darling," Sally said to Anne, and then to the woman in the next bed, "How are you this evening, Mrs. Hull?"

"Mustn't grumble, dearie," was the reply.

Sally, sitting down beside Anne a moment later, thought the reply might apply to her own sister.

Anne was looking lovely. She was still a little thin and slightly transparent-looking after what she had been through, but her eyes were clear and very large in her face and her hair shone like gleaming gold.

"What have you been doing?" Anne asked. "You look as if something exciting has happened."

"It has," Sally answered. "I have been making plans, and I am sure you will approve of them."

"What are they?" Anne asked.

"We are going down to St. Chytas on Monday."

"We?" Anne queried. "Does that mean you and I?"

"You and I and Elaine. You don't mind her coming, do you, Anne? I didn't want to leave the child in London."

"Of course I don't mind," Anne replied; "she is a darling and she will have lots of fun on the beach."

"I have already wired Mrs. Barkus to ask her to put us up," Sally said.

"Supposing she is full up with lodgers?" Anne questioned apprehensively.

"I am sure she won't be." Sally answered. "She only took people during the war when her boy was away, but now he is at home she told me she was not going to have anyone else but that if we wanted to go down he could go to his uncle."

"Could we all manage in one room?"

"Well, as a matter of fact," Sally said, "I think you should have a divan in the front room. You could always make it look nice if you wanted to sit there in the daytime, but if the weather is fine we shall be out most of the time on the beach. That leaves the upstairs bedroom for Elaine and me."

"You seem to have got it all planned," Anne said. "What did Mr. Dunstan say?"

"He was awfully pleased for Elaine to go with us," Sally replied, "and he said he might possibly come down and stay for a night or two at St. Ives and motor over to see her."

Was it her fancy, she wondered, or did Anne's cheeks deepen slightly in colour?

"Elaine will like that," Anne murmured, but she did not look at Sally.

Sally wondered whether she should tell Anne about Robert Dunstan. The story was burning at the back of her mind.

She longed to clear up so many misapprehensions that Anne must have about him and yet she thought perhaps it was too soon. It would be a mistake to rush things.

It would be easy for Anne to take fright, to shrink away from him even as she had shrunk away from other things in her life.

"I will leave it," Sally thought.

Aloud she said:

"Mr. Dunstan has been awfully kind about everything; in fact, he offered to help us in any way I thought fit. I think he must like you."

She spoke casually enough, but this time there was no mistaking the crimson flood of colour which crept into Anne's pale cheeks.

Sixteen

Sally and Elaine went round to Berkeley Square to say good-bye to the Duchess before going down to Cornwall.

Elaine was in a wild state of excitement and her childish joyfulness seemed somehow to percolate into the grey, quiet old house so that even the servants smiled in response to her happiness and seemed somehow younger and less crabbed with age and eternal grumbling.

The Duchess was in her sitting-room, arranged on the sofa by the window with a rug of faded ancient mink covering her.

There was no mistaking her pleasure at seeing Sally and Elaine. She liked the child, and indeed it would have been difficult not to like Elaine in these days.

Her sullen manner had vanished and she was a quick, intelligent little girl with a sunny smile and good manners.

"We have come to say good-bye," she told the Duchess, adding spontaneously, "We are awfully sorry you arc not coming with us."

The Duchess smiled at the tribute and there was something in her expression which told Sally all too clearly that once she had been a very beautiful woman and that however old she grew her gracious charm would never be completely lost.

"Thank you, dear," she said to Elaine, "but I expect you would find me a bit of a nuisance. One invalid on your hands will be quite enough to look after."

"But Anne will not be an invalid for long," Elaine protested. "Miss Granville says she will get well very quickly in the sea air. She got up yesterday and walked about! She was all right but she said her legs felt funny."

"They usually do after you have been in bed for a long time," the Duchess remarked, and turning to Sally asked, "How is your sister?"

"Amazingly well considering everything," Sally answered, "but she is going down to Cornwall by ambulance. The doctor would not hear of her attempting a train journey."

"Quite right," the Duchess approved.

"But we are going in the train," Elaine cried. "We are going to have sleepers—isn't it exciting?" "It sounds very exciting," the Duchess agreed, and glanced at Sally.

"Mr. Dunstan has made all the arrangements," Sally said quietly.

"Why not?" the Duchess queried. "He wants his child to be comfortable of course!"

Her keen old eyes seemed to Sally to be watching her and instinctively she guessed that the Duchess imagined that Robert Dunstan was interested in her.

Sally was almost sorry that she could not reveal the truth—that it was her sister on whom Robert Dunstan had set his heart.

She knew how much the Duchess would enjoy the

romance, but it was far too soon to say anything to anyone, even to Anne herself, so she smiled back at the Duchess, well aware of the speculation that was going on in the inquisitive old lady's mind.

As it happened, Sally was feeling a little nervous this afternoon and not as much at ease as usual, for Anne had given her explicit instructions that she was to try if possible to put in a good word for the Duchess's grandson, Montague.

"I promised the Duke I would try," Anne had said that morning to Sally, "and I hate breaking a promise. I didn't get an opportunity of course but I would have liked to do what he asked before I went away."

"It can't be helped, darling," Sally soother her, "and you will be able to do it when you come back."

"Yes, I know," Anne replied, "but that will be a long time to wait and I know the Duke will be disappointed; besides, the Duchess is very old. . . ."

The sisters were silent, both thinking that was best left unsaid—that the Duchess might die before Anne could return to her as her companion.

"Do what you can, Sally," Anne pleaded suddenly. "You are much more tactful at that sort of thing than I am."

"But it is so difficult for me," Sally protested; "she doesn't know me as well as she knows you— she might think it an impertinence."

"Nothing you could say to anyone would seem an impertinence," Anne answered promptly; "besides, you always get what you want."

"Do I?" Sally queried.

"Well, don't you?"

"Not always. Not when it is things I want very, very much indeed."

"Oh, Sally, what do you mean? Do tell me."

Sally shook her head.

"Secrets," she said, repeating with a smile what had

been a password with them as children. "But I will do what I can about your Duchess and her grandson if I get the slightest chance."

"That is sweet of you. It would make me so much happier if you could manage to say something."

"Well, don't rely on it," Sally warned her.

Now, looking at the Duchess, Sally wondered how she could possibly begin such an intimate conversation.

Elaine was moving restlessly amongst the tables of knick-knacks, fingering little silver and china ornaments, snuff-boxes, cut-glass scent-bottles and ivory card-cases.

"What is this, Duchess?" she asked.

She held up a tiny silver sword which, beautifully made, could be drawn from its sheath.

"I think it was meant to be a paper-knife," the Duchess answered. "My children gave it to me one Christmas many, many years ago; in fact, Stebby was only twelve at the time. I think he chose it when coming back through London for the holidays."

"It is perfectly sweet," Elaine enthused.

"Have you any photographs of your family when they were children?" Sally asked, feeling this was an auspicious opening.

The Duchess chuckled.

"Photographs? Hundreds of them! I used to make my companions stick them into albums. It kept them busy and I did not have to listen to so much of their inane conversation. You will find them in that book-case behind the piano if you want to look at them."

"I would love to," Sally answered.

She went to the bookcase and found there were piles of heavy photograph albums all covered in bright blue leather and embossed with the ducal coronet in gold.

She chose one at random and carried it back to the window. Elaine watched her wistfully before she said:

"While you are looking at those, Miss Granville, could I go down to see Dalton?"

"Of course you can," the Duchess answered before Sally could reply, "and I know exactly why you want to see him. Chunky coffee sugar, isn't it? We used to have it even when I was a child. Go along with you, then, but don't eat too much or Miss Granville will be annoyed with me for encouraging your greed!"

"I won't," Elaine promised.

She sped from the room like a small streak of lightning.

"It is funny how all children are the same," the Duchess remarked as Elaine shut the door behind her. "We used to have that heavy brown coffee sugar when I was a little girl—then later my children were always sneaking away to the pantry to beg lumps of it. Dalton had a big store when the war started and I believe my grandchildren have never called here without a visit to the pantry! It is a profound truth, my dear, that while customs and fashions change, children remain unalterably the same."

"Which is a blessing"—Sally smiled—"both for us and for them. Thank goodness they don't have to start being worried about atomic bombs and jet engines until they have got past the sugar-eating stage."

"Do they ever get past it?" the Duchess asked. "Aren't we all looking for sugar one way or another, whatever age we reach?"

"I suppose we are," Sally admitted.

"Sometimes we find it and sometimes we don't. I have been lucky."

The Duchess gave a little sigh.

Sally opened the big album and looked at the first page of photographs.

"I think you were very lucky to have such a lovely family. Look—here's a photograph of you all. How beautiful you look, and the children are sweet!"

"Bring it here!"

Sally carried the book across to her side.

"I remember that photograph being taken," the Duchess said. "The photographer came all the way down to Cheyn from London and of course, because we all wanted to look our best, there were many mishaps and disagreements. Stebby's nose bled—nothing we could do would stop it.

"Then the girls started to quarrel and one of them pulled the other's hair, and Catherine—yes, I think it was Catherine—was reduced to tears! I remember my husband being very angry with them. We all went into the drawing-room looking solemn and rather sullen.

"It would have been a terrible photograph if Adrian —that was my second son—had not made us laugh. He was a happy little boy and an awfully good mimic and just as the photographer had got us arranged and we were looking a pompous and miserable group, Adrian said in a voice exactly like the Vicar's,

'Let us pray!'

"It made us all laugh and after that the photograph was a good one. That is Adrian," the Duchess said, pointing with her finger to a small boy with a large grin standing at his father's side.

"He was the one who was killed in a motor accident, wasn't he?" Sally asked quietly.

The Duchess nodded.

"Sometimes I wonder if it wasn't all for the best. If he had not been killed then, he would certainly have been killed during the war. He would have wanted to fly or do something equally crazy; but in reality he would have been too old for this last war and it would have broken his heart. He always wanted to do everything faster and better than other people. Dear Adrian, he was much more my son than one of the Cheyns."

"He had a son, too, didn't he?" Sally asked, and was conscious that the Duchess stiffened.

"Yes," she answered after a short pause.

"Is he like his father—wanting to do things faster and better than other people?"

"I don't know," the Duchess answered. "I don't see him."

"How sad for you," Sally replied, and seeing an ominous darkness in the Duchess's expression she went on quickly: "I always think it is sad when families get out of touch with each other. We have so few relatives ourselves that I always envy big families who can get together and be a clan all on their own.

"My father had the idea that families were incomplete one without another. He once told me of a very extraordinary thing which happened to him in that connection. Would you like to hear it?"

Sally was speaking almost breathlessly because she was so afraid that the Duchess might interrupt and change the conversation.

The Duchess was frowning and Sally knew that even the mere reference to her grandson had perturbed her.

"Yes, go on," she said after a moment, somewhat ungraciously, "let us hear your story."

"It happened a long time ago when my father first went to St. Chytas," Sally began. "There was a woman there who had a family of five sons. She sent for him one night and told him she was going to die. He saw no reason to disbelieve her because she was very old and had been ill for a long time.

"Then she told him that she was going to entrust him with all her savings and that on her death he was to divide them amongst her family.

"The woman's husband, who had been dead for some years, had been a fisherman, but she had inherited some money and they had been frugal all their lives and to my father's amazement she produced a box containing nearly eight hundred pounds, some of it in gold, some in silver and some in coppers.

"She had hoarded this fortune, keeping it secret from everyone and hidden in a box beneath her bed. Very few of the fisher-folk in those days trusted the bank. My father asked how she wanted the money divided.

'Equally amongst my four sons,' she answered.

'But surely you have five sons?' he said.

"She shook her head.

'I have four sons!'

"My father was not to be put off by this. He had known the family ever since he was a little boy and he knew that Albert, the youngest, had had a row with his mother and had run away from home.

"All this happened in the winter of 1914 and it was rumoured in the village that Albert had joined the army. However, the old woman was adamant.

'My four sons,' she repeated, 'are to have equal shares.'

"Reluctantly, my father agreed to do what she wanted, and taking the box home with him he put it in a safe place until she died.

"It was nearly three months later that Mrs. Mullin —that was her name—passed away, and the first thing my father knew about it was that he woke in the middle of the night filled with the strange conviction that Mrs. Mullin wanted him.

"He sat up in bed wondering for a moment whether anyone had called him, but everything was still and silent—only the impression remained that Mrs. Mullin needed him.

"Finally, the feeling was so strong that he got up and dressed and walked down the village to the old woman's house. Just as he got there one of her sons came out.

" 'Why, Vicar,' he exclaimed as he saw my father, 'I was just coming to fetch you. My mother died twenty minutes ago.'

"Well, my father comforted the family and made arrangements for the funeral; but for the next few days he could not escape from the thought of Mrs. Mullin. Somehow, whatever he was doing, he felt as if she were there beside him.

"At first he believed it was only his imagination; then he became convinced that it was more than that and he felt in his heart of hearts that the old woman required something of him.

"When the funeral was over there came the moment when he must tell the family of the fortune that awaited them.

"He told me often how he went into the little front parlour of Mrs. Mullin's house where her four sons and their wives were waiting—the men looking clumsy and somehow unnatural in their best suits instead of their fishing clothes, the women in black, their eyes red from weeping.

"My father carried in to them the big box of money just as their mother had given it to him and put it on the table. He started to tell them how much money there was and how it was to be divided, and as he spoke he was utterly and completely convinced that Mrs. Mullin was standing there beside him.

"She seemed so real to him that he was surprised the others could not see her. Finally, having spoken of the dead woman in terms of affection and respect, he said, 'I have here the money she gave me to be divided,' and to his utter surprise his own voice added, '. . . to be divided amongst the five of you.'

"My father said he had not meant to say it, the words were there and even when he spoke he knew that they were the words Mrs. Mullin had wished him to say.

"At that moment it seemed that the whole air was cleared and she was gone, and the sense of her presence, of which he had been conscious ever since she had died, vanished and never came again."

Sally stopped speaking. Somehow she could not look

at the Duchess. She was half afraid that the story had been too pointed. After a moment she spoke again.

"The fifth son came home a year later. He had lost an arm in the war, but he had a splendid record and had been recommended for the V.C.

"He did not get it eventually, only the D.C.M.; but everyone was very proud of him and after a time he married a local girl and with the money he had inherited from his mother he opened a small grocer's shop. They are still there in St. Chytas. I know him quite well."

The Duchess said nothing and because she was embarrassed Sally quickly turned over the pages of the book.

"Ah, here is a photograph of your children when they were older," she said.

Still the Duchess did not answer.

Sally finished the album and rose to get another one.

She tried to move naturally without embarrassment, but she was well aware that the Duchess on the sofa was frowning, her eyes staring blankly across the room as if she were seeing visions of the past.

As Sally came back with another album she spoke:

"I wonder if your father would have been so Christian in his old age as he was in his youth? As we grow older—or rather, should I say, as we grow very old—we get intolerant."

"But surely," Sally said quickly, "you should be old enough by then to know that you are being intolerant and be able to stop and be . . . sensible."

Unexpectedly the Duchess laughed.

"You seem to have an answer to everything," she said, "but I wonder if, when you are my age, you will find it easy to bring up a family and to watch them grow away from you—to do your best for your grandchildren and to know that they think you an old fool."

"I'm sure they don't think that," Sally said. "I expect you frightened them."

"I don't frighten you," the Duchess said sharply.

"No, but I am not your grandson."

The moment Sally had said the words she wished them unsaid. But the Duchess, instead of being angry, merely asked a question.

"Who told you about my grandson?"

"Anne."

"And who told her?"

"I think the Duke did. I believe he and your other children are distressed that there should be any quarrel which might separate the family."

There was silence for a moment, then Sally added softly:

"They, too, loved Lord Adrian."

The Duchess made an impatient movement.

"Love? What do they know of love? He wasn't their son!" Suddenly her voice changed. "Perhaps you are right, child. I think they were all fond of one another."

"Everyone seems to have loved Lord Adrian," Sally said, "and if you all miss him, how terribly his own son must miss him, too!"

"I wonder!" the Duchess snorted, "Montague always seemed to me a very unfeeling young man."

"Perhaps he was bad at expressing his feelings, or maybe he was jealous of you."

"Jealous of me?" The Duchess stared at Sally incredulously.

"Yes," Sally replied. "If two people love one person very much, it often happens that they are jealous of each other. I don't know—it is only an idea of mine, but I can't help feeling that Montague must have loved his father very deeply because he was such a very lovable person. So perhaps he resented you a little bit."

"Upon my word," the Duchess exclaimed, "you do make the most astounding statements. Of course, there may be something in what you say. Adrian was devoted to me. No one ever denied that. I often thought his wife was inclined to be jealous."

Sally wisely said nothing more. Elaine made a welcome return, her lips sticky with coffee sugar, bubbling over with the excitements she had found in Dalton's pantry.

"He has got a little ship in a bottle," she told Sally, "and you just can't imagine how it got in there! Dalton thinks it is magic and so do I!"

Sally looked at the clock.

"We must be getting home," she said. "We have all your packing to finish."

She got to her feet. As she did so the album which was resting on the armchair beside her toppled precariously.

"Look out, Miss Granville!" Elaine said, and caught the book in her arms.

Several loose photographs which had not been stuck in slipped to the floor.

"I am so sorry," Sally said as she retrieved the photographs. "It was careless of me. I do apologise. Were they put in any special places?"

The Duchess held out her hand.

"Give them to me."

Sally did as she was told. The Duchess looked through them and separated one from the others.

"This is Montague in whom you are so interested," she said to Sally.

She handed her the photograph of a young man in the uniform of the Grenadier Guards.

Sally stared at the photograph. For a moment it seemed as if she were about to speak, to say something impulsively, but with an effort she checked herself and handed the photograph back to the Duchess.

"Thank you for letting me see it," she said.

The Duchess put the photograph down beside her.

Sally had the impression that she would look at it again when they had gone.

"Good-bye, Duchess. We will make Anne well and she will come back to you very soon," Elaine said.

"Thank you, my dear, and look after yourself and Miss Granville."

"I will," Elaine promised.

"Good-bye, Duchess," Sally said.

They turned towards the door. As they reached it the Duchess spoke again.

"Tell your sister," she said distinctly, "that her emissary has succeeded in her mission."

Sally paused for a moment wondering exactly what the words meant, then she understood.

"You mean that you will write to your grandson?" she asked.

"I suppose so," the Duchess answered. "It would be such an effort to come back and haunt you all to get things done that I had left undone. When I die, I want a little peace and quiet!"

There was a humorous twist to the tone of her words, but Sally felt she was glad that the decision had been made. Impulsively she went back across the room and stood beside the Duchess.

"I am so glad," she said softly.

Then she bent down and laid her lips for a moment against the old lady's hand with its blue veins and glittering rings.

"I am so very glad!" she repeated.

Then she sped after Elaine, but not before she had seen a smile of warmth and affection alter the Duchess's expression.

Sally followed Elaine down the stairs and out into the street.

The child was chattering excitedly of the train journey which lay before them, but there were two questions repeating themselves over and over again in Sally's mind—

How could she get in touch with Montague, and how, having persuaded his grandmother to hold out an olive branch, could she be sure he would accept it?

Seventeen

Marigold hung the grey sports model up on the rail in the dressing-room and slipped into her own blue-and-white frock.

"I'm hungry," she said to the girl sitting next to her at the dressing-table. "Thank goodness it is lunch time!"

"Is someone taking you out to lunch?"

Marigold nodded.

"Yes, otherwise it would mean one of those nauseating salads at the café round the corner."

"It is all very well for you," the other girl said enviously, "you are naturally slim, but if you knew how hungry I get at times you would be sorry for me."

"I am," Marigold replied. "But it gives you a yearning, spiritual look which men find most attractive."

"I am yearning all right," the girl replied,, "yearning for a good square meal and a suet pudding."

"Well, I will think of you as I eat," Marigold laughed, and having put on her hat at the right angle turned towards the door.

As she ran down the stairs which would lead her not into the front of the building but out into the mews at the back, she thought once again that she was hungry.

The morning had been a hard one—it was always the same, the girls told her, at this time of the year, when the buyers arrived from overseas and the mannequins showed the new winter models from first thing in the morning until the shop shut in the evening.

The sunlight gleamed through one of the windows as Marigold passed and she thought wistfully,

"I would like a holiday."

There was no time to loiter, however.

She had to get her luncheon and be back within the hour, and she was relieved to see as she came out of the door that Ben's big car was waiting for her. He jumped out at the first sight of her and stood bareheaded and smiling as she approached.

"You are late," he said accusingly.

"Nonsense!" Marigold answered. "I downed tools at five minutes to one—or should I say downed clothes? It sounds so immoral!"

Ben laughed and helped her into the car.

"Well, you look clothed, in your right mind and very attractive at the moment."

"Thank you. Where are we lunching?"

"I have got a table at the Ritz Grill. It's quiet there and I want to talk to you."

"We shall not have much time," Marigold warned him. "If I am back even a few minutes late Nadine Sloe is on my track. How that woman dislikes me!"

"I can understand it," Ben said. "You are a potential danger to any other pretty woman."

"Do you call Nadine Sloe pretty?" Marigold asked, and then added honestly: "Yes, I suppose she is in her own way. I am afraid I feel rather catty about her."

Ben drove very swiftly, with his usual skill, up Berkeley Street, into Piccadilly and round to the Arlington Street entrance of the Ritz.

As they entered the lofty, ornate building Marigold felt herself relax; the tension and haste which had been hers all the morning seemed to evaporate and she "sank", as she phrased it to herself, into the atmosphere of luxury and opulence.

They were bowed to their table by an obsequious *maitre d'hotel*.

"I have already ordered what we are going to eat," Ben said. "I knew you would not have much time. It was quicker that way. I have also ordered some wine— it is here on ice."

"It all sounds lovely!" Marigold approved, and taking off her gloves and putting her elbows on the table, she rested her chin on her hands. "You are very kind to me, Ben."

Ben looked at her in a way which struck her as strangely grave and then, as the waiter disappeared, he said:

"That is what I want to be, Marigold . . . kind to you—very kind."

"You have been that already," Marigold replied, "and I don't think I have thanked you half enough for all the lovely things you have sent Anne while she has been in hospital. She adored your flowers—the fruit, too! They gave her a great deal of pleasure. It was nice of you, Ben."

Ben looked almost embarrassed.

"You don't need to thank me. It was the least I could do for any sister of yours."

"Anne asked me to tell you how grateful she was," Marigold went on. "She is going away tomorrow to Cornwall. Sally is going down by train tonight so as to be there when she arrives." Marigold stopped and gave a little sigh. "I wish I was going with them! I think I need a holiday and I shall be lonely when they have gone."

"I will look after you."

"Thank you, but that won't be the same as a holiday."

A waiter appeared and poured them each a glass of golden wine. Ben sipped his and then when they were alone again he said:

"Listen, Marigold, why don't you give up this job? It is silly having to work when you don't want to."

"Silly?" Marigold echoed. "You don't suppose I work for fun, do you? I work because I have to. Do you ever remember that ordinary people like myself need such things as mere pounds, shillings and pence?"

There was a sharp edge to her voice, and Ben, before he answered, started to eat some of the delicious food that had been put in front of them. After a moment he said:

"How you do jump at a fellow, Marigold! I didn't mean to sound flippant; as a matter of fact I meant something quite different."

"Well, you should say what you mean and mean what you say," Marigold retorted.

Then she, too, started to eat, and after a few minutes felt the food and drink were having a mellowing effect. She did not eat enough as a rule, she knew that, and despite all Sally's remonstrances she was burning the candle at both ends.

She never arrived home until the early hours of the morning and she had to be at Michael Sorrell's at nine o' clock.

That meant that she must be up and dressed soon after eight if she was to have her breakfast and catch the bus for the West End.

As she glanced at Ben, Marigold felt a touch of compunction; she was not very nice to him and at times he irritated her, but she had much to thank him for.

Without Ben's hospitality these past weeks would have been intolerable. Impulsively, because she felt sorry for having been disagreeable, Marigold leaned forward and put her hand on his.

"I'm sorry I was cross," she said with a smile which had always, ever since she was a small child, proved irresistible when she apologised.

Ben caught hold of her hand. They were sitting in a

secluded corner of the restaurant and, as it happened, the tables on either side were unoccupied.

"Marigold," Ben said hoarsely, "there is something I want to ask you."

Coolly Marigold detached her hand from his and taking out her flap-jack glanced at herself in the mirror.

"Yes?" she prompted enquiringly.

To her surprise Ben hesitated. He pushed his plate away from him, reached for his cigarette-case and, at variance with his usual good manners, lit one without asking her permission.

Only after taking a deep puff did he say:

"You remember I took you to see my mother?"

"Yes, of course," Marigold replied. "How is she?"

"I took you for a very special reason," Ben went on, ignoring her question. "I wanted you to meet my mother and I wanted her to meet you."

"Surely that was obvious?" Marigold said.

"Not entirely," Ben replied. "I have taken a lot of women along to meet my mother at one time or another and I don't mind telling you frankly, Marigold, that she has disapproved of most of them. You are different. She liked you and she told me quite frankly that she thought you were the girl for me."

Marigold stared at him for a moment before the full meaning of his words came to her. Then she laughed a little uncertainly.

"You mean?"

"I mean that my mother would like me to marry you."

"But, Ben," Marigold expostulated, "I don't understand. Are you proposing to me because your mother wants you to?"

"I want you, too," Ben answered, suddenly extremely serious. "I have liked you and admired you for a long time, Marigold. I dare say I am not exactly the type of husband you have been looking for, but I would do my best to make you happy and I think we would jog along together all right, don't you?"

Marigold put up her hands to her cheeks in a little defenceless gesture.

"But, Ben, this is ridiculous. You are not a bit in love with me, you know you're not."

"I am," Ben retorted, "at least, I think I am. I have not had much of a chance to find out, have I? You keep a fellow at arm's length. You won't even let me kiss you. But if we are not as crazily in love with each other as we might be, we would learn to love each other. I am sure of that."

"Oh, Ben, Ben!" Marigold was smiling and suddenly there were tears in her eyes.

She was realising how simple Ben Barlow was underneath all his air of sophistication. He was only a little boy at heart playing at being grown-up and yet when it came down to fundamental things doing exactly what his mother told him to do.

Marigold pulled off her smart hat, put it down on the chair and ran her fingers through her hair; then, as if she felt free and untrammelled, she bent forward.

"Listen, Ben," she said. "I understand what you are trying to say to me and I appreciate it; but at the same time you make me feel very old, much older than you are and much wiser in many ways.

"When you marry, Ben, you have to be really in love with someone. I don't believe it is easy to be married and I don't believe it is easy for two people to make a big success of being together for the whole of their lives, but at least you have to have a sure foundation to build on and that has got to be love—real love, Ben, with no pretence about it."

Marigold spoke intensely with a depth of inner emotion welling into her voice.

"But I am in love with you!" Ben expostulated.

Marigold shook her head.

"Not properly."

"But I would be if you would let me."

Marigold sighed.

"It is not a question of 'letting', Ben. Love is a thing which happens or doesn't happen. You don't just say to yourself, 'I am in love with this person because he or she is the right person.' When you love someone, you just love them whatever they are like, whatever they do!"

"You are the right person for me and I want to marry you," Ben said stubbornly.

"Because your mother told you you ought to!"

"Not only because of that, but it is important. Let us face it. Mother is far wiser about these things than I am. She has got me out of a good many scrapes one way and another, and if she says a woman is the right person for me I am prepared to back her opinion against mine."

Again Marigold smiled softly and gently.

Dear Ben, his faith in his mother was a very beautiful thing and she would not do anything to destroy or hurt it. Instead, she could only look away and murmur:

"I am sorry, Ben . . . let my answer be that I don't love you."

"I'll teach you to love me," Ben said eagerly; "Look, Marigold, we can have a wonderful time together, you and I—we could travel, buy a house in London and one in the country, have horses, cars, aeroplanes, anything you wanted. I want to give you things—clothes, jewelry, furs—in fact, all the lovely things a girl like you ought to have."

It was only as Ben spoke of what he could give her that Marigold realised what she had done.

She who had always wanted the rich things in life had just refused to marry a millionaire! Weren't these the very things she had wanted so passionately? Wasn't this what she had come to London to seek?

She heard the questions in her own mind and she knew the answers.

The waiter put their coffee on the table. She sipped from her cup looking at Ben speculatively. He was waiting for an answer, waiting with an expression of anxiety on his face which Marigold had never seen there before.

She put down her coffee-cup and looked at him straight between the eyes.

"Listen, Ben," she said, "you have bribed a good many women in your life one way and another; do you think you can bribe me?"

"Dammit, Marigold, everything I say you seem to twist round to make it mean something else. I don't want to bribe you, but I do want you. I want you to marry me."

Marigold looked at him and was sorry. She knew she had hurt him and she had not meant to do that.

"Why don't you give your brain a chance, Ben?"

"You mean you would like me better if I worked?"

"Everyone would like you better if you gave up the type of life you lead," Marigold anwered. "It is all right for a short while but what will be the end of it? Find yourself some real friends—get yourself some real interests."

"And if I do, will you marry me?"

Marigold shook her head.

"Not unless I fall in love with you, and somehow I don't think I shall; but one day, Ben, one day you will fall in love really and properly with someone a thousand times nicer than I am and then you will be happy —really happy!"

"I don't want to fall in love with anyone but you."

Marigold collected her hat and bag.

"I'm sorry, Ben, but I have got to go. If I lose my job I shall have to marry you just for your money."

"I don't care why you marry me as long as you do!"

"That's not true," Marigold said as she got up from the table. "You want the best out of life . . . so do we all."

She led the way from the restaurant, got into the car and they drove back to Michael Sorrell's. Only as they reached the door which led into the buildings from the news did Ben turn to look at her.

"I like you, Marigold," he said. "You are quite different from any other woman I have known. You are straight and awfully decent—that is why I like you so much as well as loving you."

"Thank you, Ben. That is one of the nicest compliments you have ever paid me."

Ben leaned forward.

"Think it over, Marigold. I am not going to take 'no' for an answer. I shall go on badgering you for years and years until you do what I want."

"You will soon get tired of that," Marigold replied. She jumped out of the car. "Good-bye, Ben, and thank you."

"I will telephone you tomorrow morning," he called.

She waved her hand to him in reply as she ran up the steps.

Despite her haste she was late, and when she reached the dressing-room the other girls were already waiting for the beginning of the afternoon show.

Marigold had no time to think as she slipped into the black afternoon dress which was the first item she was to model. It was only as the afternoon dragged on and the crowd of buyers in the big grey salons gradually thinned out that she began to think over what had happened at luncheon.

How extraordinary it was! She had thought that Ben was getting fond of her, but she had never imagined that his proposal would take such a strange form.

Poor Ben! She could almost feel maternal towards him. He was such a child in many ways.

She had taken off what she thought was the last dress she had to show that afternoon when the dresser came hurrying along the room.

"Marigold! Miss Sloe wants 'Tiger Lily' again."

"Oh, bother!"

Marigold, who had been sitting down, got up irritable. "Tiger Lily" was a complicated evening dress which Michael Sorrell had specially designed for her. The golden tints of the silk exactly matched the fire in her hair.

There was special jewelry to go with it and she carried a bunch of tiger lilies in her arms. It was a lovely dress and ordinarily Marigold loved wearing it, but now she was tired and she longed above all else for a cup of tea and to be able to put her feet up.

"I am sure Nadine Sloe has asked for this on purpose," she grumbled as she got into the dress. "I don't believe there is anyone left to see it."

"There were only three women when I came out," one girl remarked.

"She is doing it to spite me," Marigold said. "Oh, well, this is the last or I go on strike!"

'She picked up the lilies, gave a last pat to her hair and sailed through the grey velvet curtains which divided the dressing-rooms from the salons.

As she entered she saw there were three women sitting at the far end of the room, and beside them Nadine Sloe with a long list in her hand.

Marigold paraded down the room, turned with a swish of her skirts and walked up to the top again.

She knew she looked lovely and she heard expressions of admiration behind her. They were said in a foreign tongue but there was no mistaking the meaning of the words.

She turned again and then as she came slowly down the centre of the room she was vaguely aware that a man had come slowly up the stairs to stand looking at her.

For a second she paid little attention to him, then something familiar about him struck her and she looked directly at him. Her heart stood still. Only her feet carried her automatically forward.

She had a sudden fear that she was going to cry out, to run towards him, and only an almost mechanical self-control kept her going.

The man turned and walked across the rooom to where Nadine Sloe was sitting. Marigold saw him reach Nadine and heard her surprised exclamation—"Peter!"

She almost touched them as she turned, but neither of them was looking at her.

With the greatest difficulty Marigold walked slowly up the room and pushed her way through the grey velvet curtains. In the dressing-room she leaned against the wall, her hands to her burning cheeks.

She was trembling.

So he had come back! After all these weeks when he had not written, when she had never heard from him!

The girls were chattering at the far end of the room but she did not hear them. She was conscious only of the blood pounding in her ears and of the quick, insistent thump in her heart.

Peter! Peter!

The curtains opened suddenly and Nadine Sloe stood there, very straight and dark.

"Mr. Aird wishes to see you, Marigold."

"Now?"

Marigold had no idea how she managed to force the word from between her lips.

"No; as it is nearly closing-time I have given him permission to wait for you downstairs while you are changing."

"Thank you."

Marigold achieved some sort of self-control as she moved to the other end of the room.

She undressed and re-dressed in almost feverish haste and when she was ready she glanced at her reflection in the mirror and saw that, although she felt cold, there was a bright patch of colour on her cheeks. She snatched up her handbag.

"You are lucky to be getting off early," one of the girls exclaimed.

"Yes, aren't I?" Marigold replied.

She ran from the room and went down to the ground floor in the lift. She had wanted to avoid the salon. She had a feeling that Nadine Sloe might be lurking there.

With a feeling of almost overwhelming dismay she found that the front hall was empty. She stood looking round her, feeling suddenly lost and afraid. The girl who was usually on duty at the desk reappeared.

"The gentleman who is waiting for you, Marigold, is outside."

"Oh, thank you."

Marigold passed through the front door and out into the street. Peter was standing on the pavement. His back was towards her and he seemed to be watching the traffic, one hand in his pocket.

She waited for a moment—a moment of apprehension and anticipation, a moment of sudden surging delight—then she went forward.

"Hullo, Peter."

"Hullo, Marigold."

He turned and looked at her and there was something in his eyes which held her breathless.

"Where have you been all this long time?"

Marigold's voice was unsteady. She was so happy to see him that she was afraid he would hear the singing in her heart.

"That is what I have come to tell you," Peter said gravely.

He walked across the pavement and opened the door of his car. It was very small and insignificant after Ben's huge Mercedes, but to Marigold at that moment it was the loveliest car in the world.

As she sat down in the low seat she wondered if Peter remembered the last time she had been in it, and the kisses he had given her.

They drove off in silence, threading their way through the traffic, and after a few moments Marigold glanced at Peter. He looked very grave and it seemed to her as though he had grown older and more responsible.

They turned into the Park and Peter drew up the car in a quiet, unfrequented spot beneath the trees. Marigold clenched her hands together tightly.

She was afraid, desperately afraid, of her own happiness. Slowly Peter turned round in the driver's seat.

"I have come back."

"So I see."

"Do you want to know why?"

"Of course I do! If it isn't a secret."

"There is no secret about it. I have come back to marry you!"

For a moment Marigold prevented herself from looking at him, the world swam before her eyes—a world golden and radiant beyond belief.

Then her eyes met his . . . the words she had been about to say died on her lips. She could only look at Peter and know he was there. Everything else ceased to matter.

They were alone—alone in a world uninhabited by anyone else. For a long, long moment they looked at each other.

Both were aware of a flame mounting within them, consuming them both, drawing them nearer and nearer until at last human nature could no longer stand the strain.

Peter moved. He put out his arms and she was in them, her mouth seeking his as her lips murmured his name.

"Oh, Peter! Oh, Peter!"

Tears were pouring down Marigold's cheeks, but she was not aware of them.

She only knew that she was happier than she had ever been in her whole life, that the misery and loneliness of the past weeks were over—that at last she belonged to Peter and he to her.

It was a long time before they drew apart.

They had no consciousness of people passing, of the children playing on the grass or the distant roar of traffic; they only knew that they were together, man and woman, in a universe of their own.

It was Peter who spoke first. He looked down at Marigold's head against his shoulder, at the tumbled, golden-red hair, the whiteness of her skin, the tears glistening on her cheeks.

"So you have missed me, my darling."

She opened her eyes and looked at him and he saw in them the answer to his question.

"Why did you go away?"

Her voice was hardly above a whisper.

"Because I loved you."

"I thought I had lost you."

"You could never do that!"

"But you didn't write—you didn't let me know where you were."

Her eyes brimmed over with tears. Very gently Peter bent to kiss the trembling red mouth.

"It is a long story, my sweet. I have got a lot to tell you. I had better take you home."

They drove to Chelsea. Marigold leaning unashamedly against Peter, her cheek against his shoulder. As they went she thought to herself,

"Nothing matters except that he is back!"

She wanted to hear what he had to tell her, but it was of secondary importance—all that really mattered was that they were together again and that he loved her.

Now she knew the full desperateness of her misery these past weeks—now she knew why at times she had felt that life was too intolerable to be borne.

She had sought escape from her own thoughts, her own feelings, and she had failed! What did parties or amusements matter? She knew how shallow they were, there was nothing in them to soothe or assuage an aching heart.

She knew now why she had refused Ben's offer of marriage without one thought of what it might mean to her materially.

Not for one moment could she contemplate marrying without love now that she knew what love was.

"Oh, Peter!"

She whispered his name and he looked down at her.

"If you look at me like that, my darling," he said unsteadily, "I shall run into something. Let me get you safely home."

Marigold laughed, a laugh of pure, unsullied happiness.

"Oh, Peter, I ought to be so angry with you."

"I won't let you be angry with me, he said authoritatively.

They drew up at the Saracen's Head.

"We are early," Marigold said. "I don't expect Sally will be back yet."

She ran up the stairs in front of Peter to find that her supposition was correct. There was no one in the little sitting-room, which looked cosy and inviting with a bunch of rambler roses on the table in the centre of the room.

Marigold threw her things down on a chair and turned to face Peter, and throwing back her head opened her arms to him.

He stood for a second looking at her before he went towards her to take her in his arms.

"That's how I wanted you to greet me," he said. "Has my absence really made your heart grow fonder?"

"Don't laugh at me, Peter."

"I am not, I promise you I am not. I, too, have been afraid, terribly afraid, of losing you."

She reached up then and put her arm round his neck, drawing his head down to hers.

"I was a fool," she whispered, "a fool—but I did not understand that I loved you like this."

"Oh, my darling!"

He held her then so closely that she could hardly breathe; he kissed her until the room swam round her and she could only cling to him, returning his kisses with a passion which almost equalled his own.

"Oh, my darling, my beautiful!" she heard him say.

Then, even as she felt she might faint with the intensity of her own feelings, she heard someone coming up the stairs.

They drew apart slowly and reluctantly as Sally came into the room. She saw Marigold first and smiled at her and then, even as she was about to speak, she saw Peter.

For a moment an expression of astonishment crossed her face, then she gave a cry of delight.

"Peter, when did you get back?"

"This afternoon."

Sally looked from Peter to Marigold again. There was no disguising the expression of radiance on her face. She had never looked more lovely.

"Oh, Sally!"

Impulsively Marigold went to her sister and kissed her. Sally understood.

"This means . . .?" she questioned.

"That Marigold is going to marry me!" Peter replied.

"Give us your blessing, Sally; we can't get on without it."

"Oh, darlings, I am so glad . . . so terribly, terribly glad!"

"I am so ridiculously happy!" Marigold whispered.

"And that is all that matters," Sally answered. "But you, Peter, are the one person I wanted to see at this moment."

"Why particularly?" Peter asked, raising his eyebrows.

"Because," Sally answered quietly, "I have discovered who you are!"

Eighteen

"So you've turned detective, have you?" Peter said with a smile. "I rather expected that Anne would catch me out, but I did not anticipate it would be you."

"What is all this about?" Marigold asked, staring from one to the other in bewilderment.

Sally looked at Peter.

"Are you going to tell her or shall I?"

"Wait a minute," Marigold said quickly; "before you tell me anything there is something I want to say. If Sally has found out something horrid about you, Peter, whatever it is, however bad, I don't care. I love you. I have always loved you, only I was such a little fool I would not say so."

"Are you quite sure of that?" Peter asked, and his voice was deep and moved.

"Quite sure?" Marigold questioned. "I'm absolutely certain! Oh, my darling, if the whole world were against you I wouldn't care."

"Even if I had deceived you?" Peter asked.

"I don't care about that either," Marigold said. "I

don't care about anything so long as you love me . . . so long as you will always love me."

Peter's hands went out to clasp hers.

"You know I love you."

He drew her to him and put his arm round her shoulders.

"Now, Sally," he said, "do your worst!"

Sally laughed, then she ran forward and kissed them both, first Marigold and then Peter.

"Oh, if you only knew," she exclaimed, "what it means to hear Marigold speak like that! I have been so worried about her—so upset—but now she is happy again! Peter, you will take care of her, won't you?"

"I will," Peter answered simply. "Now I suppose we had better tell Marigold our deep and dastardly secret."

"You tell her," Sally said.

"Very well," Peter answered. "Marigold, my sweet, are you prepared for a shock?"

"Yes, I am ready for it!"

Despite Sally's laughter and Peter's mocking Marigold was really apprehensive; and her eyes sought his to be reassured.

"Well then," Peter said, "my real name is Montague Peterfield Sebastian Fenwick. It was pretty hard on a man, wasn't it?"

"Fenwick?" Marigold repeated; then realisation came to her. "But surely that is the family name of the Cheyns?"

"Got it in one," Peter exclaimed. "She is clever, isn't she?" he asked Sally.

"But, Peter . . ." Marigold went on in a puzzled voice. "Then you are really . . ."

"The old Duchess' grandson," Peter said. "I wondered how long it would be before Anne found me out. How did you discover it, Sally?"

"I saw your photograph today for the first time," Sally answered. "In one of the Duchess' albums."

"Good heavens, she has kept it, has she?" Peter exclaimed. "I thought it would have been torn up by now, and cast into the flames!"

"On the contrary, you are to be reinstated," Sally said; "that was why as I came home this evening I was longing to see you. The Duchess is writing to you."

"Writing to me?" Peter echoed. "What have I done now?"

"It isn't what you have done," Sally answered, "it is what she has left undone. She is sorry and she wants to be friends with you."

"Who has been interfering?" Peter asked. "Sally, is this your doing?"

"Perhaps I have had a little to do with it," Sally admitted; "but, Peter, I want you to be kind to her."

"I don't want to be kind to anyone except Marigold," Peter answered. "My grandmother is an interfering old autocrat and if everyone else is prepared to kow-tow to her, I am not!"

Sally said nothing for a moment. She did not miss the note of defiance in Peter's voice. Marigold, still within the circle of his arm, looked up at him.

"You must explain everything to me, Peter," she said, "I am bewildered by all this. Isn't your name Peter Aird at all?"

"Well, I was christened Peterfield," Peter replied, "and all the rest of those ridiculous names. I shall never forget how they used to rag me at school. Between ourselves, I was delighted that I had the opportunity of dropping them."

"And Aird?"

"Aird was my mother's name and so I felt I was entitled to it, especially after I had shaken the dust of the Cheyn family off my feet."

"Tell me all about it," Marigold begged.

"Well, you will have to listen to it sooner or later,"

Peter admitted, "so you may as well hear it now. Let me light a cigarette first."

He released Marigold and she sat down on a chair while Sally took another one. Peter lit a cigarette and then, standing in front of the fireplace, started his story.

"When my father and mother were killed," he began, "I had just gone into the Brigade of Guards. I suppose really, looking back at things now I am older and wiser, their death was an overwhelming shock.

"I was devoted to both of them, and I was their only child you can imagine they were pretty fond of me. When they were gone, I felt numb with misery, yet at the same time restless and unsettled. I went to my grandmother and told her I intended to leave the Army and take up ship-building.

"My grandfather, Douglas Aird, had a family business on the Clyde and I fancied that I would like to tackle something hard—something which would occupy my mind.

"As I say, looking back at it now, I think a lot of it was the natural reaction from the shock of my parents' tragic death, but my grandmother made no allowance for that. She was furious.

'There has always been a member of the family in the Brigade!' she told me.

"I replied that, as the world was changing and progressing, it was about time there were some changes in the family, too! We argued. You both know what my grandmother is like.

"She would not give in, neither would I. Finally we had a first-class row. I think I was rather impertinent and she was very overbearing and tyrannical, with the result that I told her that I was going to lead my own life and she could do what she liked about it.

"I went to see my maternal grandfather and told him what had happened. In his own way he was rather amused.

279

"He is a dour, hard-headed Scot and I dare say he thought it would not do me any harm to do some real hard work for a change. He let me go into the shipyard, but I had to start from the bottom; and because I was so angry with my grandmother, I persuaded him—and myself—that it would be best for me to change my name, so I called myself Peter Aird and started to work in earnest.

"I had been North about a year when the war started. I was on the Brigade Reserve and was called up immediately. I went back to my old regiment, went out to France, came back safely from Dunkirk and was sent out East. I had the most extraordinary luck in the years that followed.

"Time and time again I ought to have been killed and wasn't. It was just bad luck that when we were at last on the road to victory and advancing in Italy I got hit by a stray piece of shrapnel."

"You were wounded?" Marigold exclaimed. "You never told me."

"It wasn't really very bad," Peter answered. "It paralysed the muscles of my left leg for some time, but after a certain amount of treatment I was discharged, much to my own fury. I would have been still more angry if, only a few months after I was discharged, the war had not come to an end.

"It was then I began to feel exhausted and tired. I suppose really I had had a pretty strenuous six years of it. Anyway, I needed a rest and that was the one thing my grandfather did not want me to have.

"They were shorthanded at the shipyard and he wanted me to go back at once, but I could not bring myself to do it. The years I had spent in the Army had altered my ideas about nearly everything. I wanted time to readjust myself—to think things over—to learn a little about myself and to find out exactly what I did want from life.

"When I was young I wanted to work blindly and without figuring out my reasons for doing so; now I was older I wanted to know why I should work and for what. I had made great friendships in the Army. I had lost those friendships when the men I loved had been killed beside me.

"I had seen death and destruction; I had seen, too, the amazing courage and fortitude of ordinary men in adverse circumstances. I felt at that time that I was not prepared to go tamely to any job with a rich future just for my own personal advantage. I wanted to work for something—an ideal perhaps—even as I had fought for one.

"Grandfather Aird got rather annoyed with me. He is not unlike the Duchess, fond of having his own way and extremely impatient with people who do not give it him. He more or less commanded me to come North and I replied that I would come when I was ready and perhaps not at all.

"His answer was very much the same as my grandmother's had been—he would cut off financial supplies. That didn't worry me. I had my gratuity and a small sum of money in the bank.

"I had always been good at drawing and I thought I would see if I could make my living for the time being on my own without any influence or the background of rich relations. I am quite prepared to admit that I was not very successful, but at least I didn't starve.

"I took a studio in Chelsea and did illustrations for anyone who was prepared to pay for them. I was not exactly happy, but it gave me a chance to think, to find for myself a sense of proportion and of direction. Then I met Marigold!"

Peter stubbed out his cigarette in the ashtray and walked to Marigold's side and put out his hand. She slipped hers into it.

"I knew then," he said quietly, "exactly what I

wanted. I also knew what I had been waiting for all these years. Someone to work for, someone for whom I could build a future."

"Oh, Peter," Marigold asked breathlessly, "did you love me as soon as you saw me?"

"From the very first moment," Peter answered. "You were all that I ever dreamed of as being ideal in a woman."

He took a deep breath and then remembered that Sally was there and continued his story.

"When I left here, I went North and ate humble pie. It took a bit of time getting my grandfather to forgive me. He did not want to give in too easily.

"Finally I persuaded him that I was not only sorry for what I had done in the past but ambitious for the future. He has taken me back, but I do not want Marigold to run away with the idea that it is all going to be plain sailing. I have a lot of hard work to do and I have lost seven years' priority.

"I have got to work extremely hard, but it is interesting work and worthwhile, too. Ships are going to be wanted. Those ships are going to bring prosperity to England. They are also going to make us prosperous one day, darling," he added, looking down at Marigold; "that is, if you will help me now through the lean times.

"I am not afraid of poverty any more," Marigold said humbly, "not when I am with you. I have talked such a lot of nonsense, Peter, about wanting money, luxury and beautiful things, but I have come to my senses and I realise the only thing I want is you. I'll work for you and I'll work hard. I shall not mind anything as long as we are together."

"We will always be that," Peter answered gently; then he looked across the room at Sally. "That is the end of my story. Am I forgiven?"

"It is not for me to forgive you," Sally answered,

"but, Peter, I want you to make your peace with the Duchess."

"Why should I?" Peter asked. "We can get on very well without her."

"But she cannot get on without you. You see, Peter, she is getting very old. She may die any time now and she wants to make friends with you first."

"That doesn't sound a bit like my grandmother," Peter said; "from what I remember of her she is a strong-minded old woman who will never die."

"She is much older since you last saw her," Sally answered, "and although she is amazing for her age, she is very frail." She paused for a moment and chose her words with care. "You must remember, Peter, she loved your father very deeply. Love takes people in many different ways. You and Marigold have already found that out and perhaps you will find out other things, too, when you . . . have a son of your own."

Marigold tightened her clasp on Peter's hand.

"Sally is right, Peter. You must make it up with the Duchess."

"If you want me to," Peter answered, "I will."

"Of course I want you to," Marigold said. "Besides, I want to tell her about us."

"We will go and see her together," Peter answered. "I'll say I am sorry and be taken back into the bosom of the family."

"How funny to think that I shall be part of the family, too," Marigold smiled, "but I like them all, especially the Duchess."

"Personally, I am terrified of her," Peter said with a grin, "so I shall look to you to protect me."

"You're a coward," Marigold teased. "And the Duke is a darling."

He will be awfully pleased about this," Sally said. "It was he who was so keen on the Duchess making up the quarrel."

"Oh, Uncle Stebby's a dear," Peter remarked. "I shall never forget how kind he was to me after my father and mother were killed."

Sally gave a little exclamation so that Marigold, who had been staring at Peter with adoring eyes, turned to look at her.

"What is it, Sally?" she asked.

"I have only just thought," Sally replied, "isn't it funny—you will be a duchess one day, but it was Anne who wished to marry a duke!"

"A duchess? What do you mean?" Marigold exclaimed, then she looked at Peter accusingly. "Don't say you are the heir? I couldn't bear it! I should be terrified!"

"Not you," Peter answered fondly, "and you will be the most beautiful of all the beautiful Duchesses of Cheyn."

He bent down and kissed her forehead. She rested her head confidently against him.

"I don't care if I am a duchess or a charwoman," she whispered, "as long as I can marry you."

"That is the one thing you can be quite certain of," Peter answered. "You are going to marry me, and quickly!"

"How quickly?" Sally asked.

"Tomorrow—the day after," Peter replied.

Both girls gave a little scream.

"Oh, not as quickly as that! We must have time."

"Time? For what?" Peter asked.

"Clothes!" Sally answered.

"Nonsense!" Peter answered. "Marigold has got all the clothes she will want."

"Well, she must see the family first," Sally suggested.

"That won't take very long," Peter retorted.

Sally clasped her hands together.

"I have got a wonderful idea. Why don't you both come down to Cornwall? See the Duchess first and the

Duke if he is in London, then come to Cornwall and be married there. I can find you both rooms in the village. Then you and Marigold can be married in our own church, the church where we were all christened and which was Daddy's for so many years."

"I think it is a marvellous idea," Marigold cried, "so long as Peter agrees."

"I think it is perfect!" Peter approved. "I was so frightened you would want a fashionable wedding."

"That's settled then," Sally said with delight in her voice. "But you cannot come down tomorrow. That will be too quick. I have got to get Anne settled in and find somewhere for you both to stay. Besides, you must give your family, Peter, the attention they will expect. They will all want to see Marigold, and you."

"We will come the day after, then," Peter said. "That will give you and the family twenty-four hours. No one could expect more."

"I have got nothing to be married in," Marigold exclaimed.

"Nadine will fit you up," Peter replied.

"Nadine?" Marigold echoed. "I shouldn't think she would do anything for me! What exactly does she mean to you, Peter?"

"I suppose I had better tell you the truth," Peter smiled, "although it is rather a shaming story. Nadine was the daughter of my mother's best friend. We saw a great deal of each other when we were children and I think secretly that our mothers always intended we should marry.

"Anyway, we were thrust together and when we grew up it was a more or less understood thing that I should escort Nadine everywhere. Then quite suddenly her father was involved in a financial crash in the City.

"They lost all their money. Nadine came to London and got a job with Michael Sorrell. I was awfully sorry for her. I saw quite a lot of her and I think, because she was lonely and unhappy, she grew rather fond of me."

"She is in love with you," Marigold said accusingly.

"I would not go as far as to say that," Peter replied slowly. "Nadine is far too clever for me! She always was. She is also a good deal older than I am. But I was devoted to her as if she were a sister—nothing else.

"Anyway, of course she knew all about me and it was quite easy for me to write and ask her to give you a job, but at the same time I had to make her promise not to reveal my secret. It was just an amazing coincidence that Anne should have become companion to the Duchess at the same time.

"Nadine has always done everthing I have asked of her and she kept my identity well and truly hidden, didn't she, Marigold?"

"She did," Marigold replied, "but I don't think she likes me."

"Well, it doesn't matter now, does it?" Peter asked confidently.

"No, I suppose not," Marigold answered. "Nothing does matter, except us."

"Are we being frightfully egotistical, Sally?" Peter enquired.

"You have every right to be," Sally answered. "Now you two must forgive me if I go and pack."

She slipped between the curtains and started to put all the things she knew she would need in Cornwall into a suitcase.

She could hear Marigold and Peter talking in low tones, and although she could not catch what they were saying, there was an undercurrent of joy and happiness which seemed to pervade every sound they uttered.

Sally thought of the nights she had lain awake knowing of Marigold's unhappiness and being unable to help her. How wonderful it all was! And she said a prayer of thankfulness in her heart.

When her luggage was ready, Peter and Marigold drove her to the flat to pick up Elaine.

There she kissed them good-bye and promised to make every possible arrangement for their arrival the day after tomorrow.

"Take care of her, Peter," Sally admonished.

Marigold flung her arms round her neck and whispered:

"I'm going to take care of him! Oh, Sally, I am so madly, crazily happy!"

Elaine was waiting for Sally in the hall when she reached the flat.

"Oh, Miss Granville, I'm so excited—and look, Daddy's given me a little dispatch-case all my own."

She held up one in pink leather with her initials on it.

"It is lovely!" Sally exclaimed. "Have you had something to eat?"

"Not yet," Elaine answered. "There is food for both of us in the dining-room. Daddy said you were to let him know when you arrived."

At that moment Robert Dunstan came out of his study.

"Good evening, Miss Granville," he said formally, "I have got the tickets and I thought I would take you along to the station myself and see that the sleepers were all right."

"That will be very kind of you," Sally said.

They went into the dining-room, where a delicious meal had been prepared for all three of them. While they were eating, Robert Dunstan asked:

"Will it be all right for me to come down the day after tomorrow? I find I can get away from the City by then."

Sally laughed and then explained herself.

"The day after tomorrow is going to be a very busy day."

"Why? What is happening?" Elaine asked.

Sally told them of Marigold's engagement to Peter.

"Oh, and they are going to get married while we are down there?" Elaine cried. "How exciting! Can I be a bridesmaid? Please, Miss Granville, ask your sister if I can be a bridesmaid."

"I don't think it is going to be a big enough wedding for that," Sally answered; then, seeing the child's disappointment, she added: "Well, we will ask them. Anyway, run and tell Nanny to put in your party dress. The white net one with the blue sash. I told her you wouldn't want it, but it would make a lovely bridesmaid's dress."

"I will tell her at once," Elaine said, jumping down from the table and running from the room.

Sally and Robert Dunstan were left alone. For a moment neither of them said anything; then at last in a low voice Robert Dunstan said:

"Do you think there is any chance for me?"

"I wish I could answer that question," Sally said, "but I don't know—I don't, honestly!"

"Will you mind then if I, an outsider, come down to Cornwall while all these other festivities are taking place?"

"Of course not!" Sally said. "We want you to come."

"Really?"

Suddenly he looked young and eager and rather wistful. Sally held out her hand.

"I hope Anne learns to love you," she said, "and I will help you in every way I can."

Robert Dunstan took her hand; and then surprisingly with a gesture that was graceful and not in the least theatrical he raised it to his lips.

"Thank you, Sally," he said quietly. "You are a very wonderful person."

Nineteen

Anne lay in the garden and felt the soft sea breeze fan her cheeks.

She felt utterly at peace. The sky above was blue and the mists which had overhung the sea during the morning had been dispersed by brilliant sunshine which had suddenly come from between the clouds and cleared them away as though by magic.

Behind her stood the ugly but familiar grey house which had been her home all her life.

It was strange, she thought, how things had worked out—always the unexpected happening when one least anticipated it.

She could hardly believe that they were really staying in their own home, and yet here was the green lawn and the rather wild herbaceous borders just as they used to be.

There was the oak tree which they used to climb to the detriment of their clothes and not without risk to their limbs; there were the rhododendrons which had been a perfect ambush for Red Indians and beyond them the old overgrown tennis-court which nobody ever had time to weed. It was all so dear and so familiar.

Home again, and Anne wondered if it were true they had ever been away.

Had they really been to London or was it a dream as unsubstantial and unreal as the wishes they had made for their futures?

How blithe and light-hearted they had been that evening when they had each wished for a husband! Anne could hear her own voice saying now,

"I want to marry a duke!"

Well, Marigold was to marry one and she would make a much more suitable duchess, Anne thought.

She had found that ducal surroundings did not bring that peace and sense of security which she had always believed was theirs by right and tradition. She thought of the Duchess worrying about the accounts, the jewelry which had to be sold, the family conferences which usually ended in disagreements and the interminable difficulties over the estates.

Yes, she had learned that life among the aristocracy bore little relationship to the dreams she had dreamed in a country vicarage.

But she realised now that her journey to London had brought her more than disillusionment; it had taught her something very important.

All her life she had shrunk from illness, suffering and all emotional disturbance.

She had wanted to live in a fairy story, wished to be a creature apart, almost unreal in her desire for a detachment both physical and mental from the ordinary feelings of human beings.

Now at last she thought differently.

She remembered when she had first been carried into the public ward of the hospital, aware that every muscle in her body was tense with both horror and dislike.

She would not look at the occupants of the other beds. Matron had arranged for hers to be at the end of the room near a window.

"I can stare out of the window," Anne thought. "I need not look at the other patients—they are ugly and horrible—I hate them!"

She had lain there with every nerve protesting, finding it difficult not to retract her own decision, not to beg David to have her taken back to a private room.

Then very gradually, so gradually that the change had been almost imperceptible, she began not to hate the people around her but to be interested in them.

The woman in the next bed, whose two sons had been killed in the war, had had a severe abdominal operation, yet she managed to speak cheerily.

"I am alive!" she said to Anne. "That's something, isn't it? I often say to myself, 'Well, old girl, at least you're alive!' "

There was a stubborn transcending courage about her which at times moved Anne almost to tears. The girl in the bed opposite was about her own age.

She had been knocked down by a bus one Saturday evening just when she was hurrying to meet "her boy."

"It was the first time I had worn my new costume," she told Anne. "It would be, wouldn't it? There's a hole in the skirt you could put your hand in . . . and I had saved up for three months for that costume."

It did not seem to occur to her that it was worse to have a badly fractured leg and a broken arm and that the skirt did not matter. It did matter!

Anne found herself planning how when she got out of hospital she would try somehow to get the girl another suit to replace the one which had been ruined.

She found herself listening to the other patients' stories, and whereas at first she had shrunk from hearing of their afflictions, she now felt ashamed because they themselves were so brave.

It was difficult when you were with people for long hours in such intimate circumstances not to feel excited when they got better or anxious and worried if they grew worse. It was like becoming part of one big family, and suddenly Anne woke up to the fact that that was what they were.

She no longer shrank from them. She no longer felt sick or disgusted by the intimate details of their illnesses or even by the sight of their infirmities. She liked them—nay, more . . . at times she loved them.

Lying in her bed one night watching the night-Sister pass silently through the ward, the glimmering light she carried flickered for a moment on the head of the little Christ-child ornament which stood beside Anne's bed.

It seemed to her in that moment there came a special revelation to her soul. At last she understood the meaning of the word "love."

At last she understood what it was to feel that one must help, comfort and succour those who were suffering.

She understood for the first time the ideal to which her father had dedicated his life, the feelings and emotions which made Sally find friends wherever she went.

"It is love," Anne murmured to herself. "Love such as God gives us."

She felt as if her whole being welled up into a great out-pouring of heart and soul.

Always before, she had known that there was some barrier between herself and other people, something which prevented her from either giving freely to them or taking freely in return. Now it was gone.

She wanted to hold out her arms to the whole universe, to pour out love and to know the warmth of love in return.

It had been some time before she slept, and when the night-Sister came round at six o'clock to take her temperature she had found Anne fast asleep, the little model of the Christ child cradled in her arms.

The night-Sister had told the story of her discovery in the Sisters' room and added:

"She looked so beautiful I felt as though she were some sort of saint."

Anne did not know this of course, she only knew in the days that followed everything seemed tinged with an echo of the golden radiance she had felt within herself that night.

Sometimes she had wished she could talk about it to someone, but it was too intimately beautiful to put into words even to Sally.

She only realised that at last she knew the real meaning of the words she had heard her father quote ever since she was a baby:

"Little children, love one another."

Anne looked back at the Vicarage. It seemed to her at this moment to be symbolic of all she was beginning at last to understand.

So ugly and weather-beaten externally, but because of those who lived in it warm and welcoming with love, sympathy and generosity. That was what so many people were like; one only needed to dig beneath the surface to find real beauty.

It was at this point in Anne's reflections that Sally came out of the house carrying a glass of milk.

"I've brought you this, darling," she said.

"Not another glass, surely?" Anne protested. "I shall get terribly fat if you go on like this."

"Matron's last instructions were that I was to fatten you up," Sally said, "so be a good girl and do as you are told!"

"I am much too lazy to argue," Anne smiled. "I was just lying here thinking how lovely it is to be home again!"

Sally's face lit up suddenly as with some inner light.

"That is what I keep thinking. We are home again, all three of us!" She paused a moment; then she added, "So much has happened since we were last here."

"Has it?" Anne asked. "I was just wondering if we had ever been away."

"Do you remember Marigold suggesting that we should go to London?" Sally questioned. "How exciting and glamorous it seemed to us then!"

"We certainly did not realise what hard work it was going to be."

"It has all turned out perfectly for Marigold. I have just had a telegram from Peter. They expect to get here about six-thirty. They are motoring down."

"They must have started very early."

"Peter won't mind that. Marigold can sleep while he drives."

"Won't she be surprised to find us here at the Vicarage?"

Sally laughed.

"I am longing to see her face. As a matter of fact, I have just been writing a letter to the Vicar telling him how grateful we are. It was nice of him to let us have the house." Sally looked round with an expression of affection in her eyes. "Darling old place, they haven't changed it much, thank goodness."

"I decided last night that their furniture is nearly as ugly as ours!"

"Oh, Anne," Sally protested, only half seriously, "I always thought everything we had was quite perfect."

"I really believe you did. You are absurdly sentimental, Sally."

"Is it sentimental to love one's home?" Sally asked. "I only know that when the new Vicar came in yesterday morning to the cottage and asked me if we would like to stay here while he and his wife went on their holiday, it was with the greatest difficulty that I prevented myself from kissing him."

"Oh, Sally, he would have been horrified!"

"I don't believe he would," Sally said. "He knew what I felt about his offer although I stood like a dumb idiot with my mouth open, too stunned and too surprised to speak.

'My wife and I heard that your sister had been ill,' he said, 'and we thought perhaps she would like to lie in the garden, and anyway you know all the advantages and disadvantages of the house, so it will not be like handing it over to someone strange!' "

Sally laughed.

"It took me quite a time to answer him, then at last I stammered, 'Do you really mean it?' "

"I think it is awfully good of them," Anne said. "Are you going to give Marigold her old room?"

"Of course I am, and Peter can have the bachelor room. You remember, Daddy always put his guests in there."

Anne finished the milk and Sally put out her hand to take the empty glass.

"I can't stay here gossiping," she said; "I have got a lot of cooking to do before this evening; Elaine is helping me and, incidentally, having the time of her life. She has never been allowed in the kitchen before."

"Poor little rich girl," Anne smiled. "She will soon learn about one if she stays here long enough."

"I consider it is an essential part of her education. At this moment she is making you something special by herself for tea, so be surprised when you see it."

"I will be delighted with anything so long as it is not too filling. After the enormous lunch you gave me to eat and this milk I feel that I never want to see food again."

"You will be hungry by teatime." Sally turned towards the house, then stopped and retraced her steps. "Oh, by the way, Anne, I don't know whether I mentioned it but Elaine's father is arriving this afternoon."

"Mr. Dunstan?" Anne exclaimed in astonishment. "Good heavens, what is he coming down for?"

"To see Elaine, I suppose. You might be nice to him and keep him amused if I am busy."

"I will do my best," Anne answered. "He is not staying with us, surely?"

"Oh no, I booked a room for him in St. Ives. I don't suppose he will be here long, but I expect he will stay to dinner tonight."

"We shall be quite a house-party. You will let me know when he comes?"

"I will," Sally promised, and hurried away.

Anne closed her eyes. The salty tang in the air mingled with the fragrance of the flowers; the leaves on the trees, rustled by the wind, seemed as though they were singing to her. After a moment or so she slept.

She awakened suddenly with a feeling that someone was near her and she opened her eyes to see Robert Dunstan sitting on the grass beside the couch on which she was lying. For a moment she hardly recognised him, he looked so different.

At first she was not sure where the difference lay until she remembered that she had never seen him before in anything but severe, dark clothes which he wore in London.

Now he was wearing a tweed jacket without a waistcoat and a coloured tie which somehow seemed on him almost rakish. He was not looking at her when she first opened her eyes but was staring away across the garden apparently preoccupied with his own thoughts.

She had a chance to examine him unobserved. He was younger than she had thought. His face, which so often seemed harsh in repose, was gentle now as if his thoughts had softened the very lines of his face.

Suddenly he turned and saw her looking at him.

"I have not woken you up, have I?" he asked, and his voice was low.

"How long have you been here?" Anne parried.

"Some time. Your sister told me I should find you in the garden. I found you, but you were asleep."

"I am sorry."

"Why should you be sorry? I have been very happy here waiting for you to wake up."

"It is nice, isn't it?" Anne said. "Sally has told you that this was our home until we came to London?"

"I don't know how you could bear to leave it."

He spoke quite simply and Anne knew that he was not in the very least comparing the bare simplicity of the Vicarage and its badly kept garden with the loveliness of his own possessions.

She had the idea that he understood that it was not money that made a home but something deeper and far more valuable.

"We were so eager to get away," Anne said in her quiet voice, "and now we are just as eager to come back."

"I can quite understand that," Robert Dunstan said. "I have a house too. I would like you to see it. It was never my home, but one day I want to make a home there."

"Did you buy it?"

"May I tell you about it?"

"Please do!"

"I was motoring one day by myself," he began. "I was unhappy at the time. I felt I must escape from all the difficulties and troubles of my life and be myself. I motored out of London not really thinking where I was going. I just followed my nose, as the children say, far too intent on my thoughts to take stock of my surroundings.

"I must have driven for about one and a half hours before I realised I was in a perfectly lovely bit of country, travelling down a narrow, shady lane with the green branches of the trees almost meeting overhead. It led me uphill and suddenly I came out into woodland.

"There in front of me, where the road branched off, was a pair of iron gates. They were open and beside them there was a faded dilapidated board saying that the house was to be sold.

"I don't know quite what possessed me but I turned down the drive. It was very unkempt as if no one had attended to it for years, and then at the end I saw the house."

Robert Dunstan drew a deep breath. Anne was listening intently.

Somehow she felt this was terribly important. She did

not know why, but she knew she must listen to every word.

"It was an old house," he went on. "Parts of it were, I think, original Tudor. It was in a very bad state of disrepair, but I knew the moment I saw it that it was the house I wanted, the house which one day would bring me happiness.

"I got in through an open window and went all over it. Somehow, strangely enough, it seemed familiar, as if I knew each turn of the staircase, each twist of its funny little corridors and big, low-ceilinged rooms.

"I came away determined that the house should be mine immediately. It was not difficult, for apparently it had been on the market for some years.

There was so much that wanted doing to it that people were not prepared to waste their money in repairs and renovations. Before the week was out Four Gables was mine."

"Is that what it is called?" Anne asked. "What an attractive name!"

"It has been called that for many centuries," Robert Dunstan said. "And for many centuries I feel it has been a happy house—now it stands empty—waiting."

"You have never lived there?"

"The right moment has never come."

"What do you mean—the right moment?"

"That is what I wanted to tell you. I have always known deep in my heart that I could never live in that house alone. It is not a house for anyone who is lonely —it is a house for two people who want to share everything together, who want to build within its walls the foundation of a fuller and wider life."

"It seems sad to think of it waiting for you," Anne said lightly.

But even as she said the words her eyes met Robert Dunstan's and there was something in his expression which stilled the words upon her lips and set her heart beating furiously.

For a moment he said nothing and Anne had a feeling as if she were waiting, even as his house was waiting, for something tremendous, something from which she could not escape. Robert Dunstan got to his feet.

As he stood looking down at her she thought how tall he was, and then he sat down on the end of the couch near her feet. Her hands were lying on top of the rug with which Sally had covered her.

Without realising it, but because of the strange tension which had suddenly arisen within herself, she had twisted her fingers together.

Now, very slowly, Robert Dunstan bent forward and took one of her hands in his.

"Anne," he said in his low, deep voice which suddenly had the power to thrill her, "I am afraid."

"Afraid?" she questioned.

The words were so faint that they hardly seemed to part her lips.

"Yes, afraid. I have passed through so much unhappiness in my life that I had grown to believe that there would never be anything else for me. Now I am like a man who has been in the dark for so long that he dare not open his eyes to the sunlight lest it should be just a figment of his own imagination."

Anne lay very still.

"I am a very dull person, Anne," he went on after a moment, and then as she made a little inarticulate sound of protest he said: "Yes, it is true. I know the truth about myself. There is only one thing I understand and that is how to make money. But money is incredibly boring if you have no one to spend it on—no one with whom to share it."

There was a long silence before Anne felt his fingers tighten on hers and he said in a curiously gruff voice:

"You are so beautiful. I am afraid to say any more to you lest you send me away."

It was then that Anne awoke to a sudden, almost maternal tenderness within herself. At last she understood what it was to want not only to love someone else but to help and comfort them. She knew now why the lesson she had learned in the public ward at St. Anthony's had been so all-important to her.

She knew now that through suffering in herself she had come to a true realisation of what suffering could be to other people.

Something within her longed to hold out her arms to Robert Dunstan, to draw him closer, to wipe the pain of past experiences from his eyes, to comfort him and to give him hope for the future.

But because she was so shy she could do none of these things but only hold on to his hand as if it kept her from drowning in her own hesitancy.

There was a long silence; and yet she was not really afraid of it, she was only striving desperately to find the words and expression so that she could say the right thing. Robert was not looking at her.

He had not looked at her since he had begun to speak of himself; instead he stared down at the whiteness of her hand.

At last he raised his eyes and looking at Anne saw that her eyes were full of tears, her lips trembling.

"Oh, my dear," he cried in consternation, "what have I said—what have I done to hurt you?"

Anne found her voice.

"You have not hurt me," she whispered; "it is just that I am so sorry for you. I want—I want to make you happy."

For a moment Robert stared at her as if he could hardly believe what he had heard, and then with a muffled sound that was half a cry he raised her hand to his lips.

He kissed it gently, afraid his control might break and the tumultuous wave of his emotion sweep away his restraint.

Very gently the tears in Anne's eyes slid down her cheeks. She made no attempt to wipe them away and after a moment Robert laid down her hand and taking a handkerchief from his pocket wiped away her tears.

"This is too much for you when you have been so ill," he said softly. "We will talk of it again later. That is, if you will listen to me."

He spoke humbly, almost pleadingly, and this time Anne slipped her hand confidently into his.

"I want to listen—now," she said.

Twenty

Peter got to his feet, a glass of champagne in his hand.

"I think this moment calls for a toast," he said, looking round the table.

First into Marigold's excited eyes seeking his, then at Anne's lovely flushed face, Robert's grave one and lastly at Sally, seated at the end of the table.

"I give you a toast!" Peter repeated. "To us all. May we find great happiness in the future, and especially Sally, because we love her so much!"

The others, who had been looking at him for the first part of his speech, now turned towards Sally and, raising their glasses, said with one accord:

"To Sally!"

The colour came quickly into Sally's cheeks. There was a hint of tears, too, in her eyes.

"Thank you, darlings," she said, "but you should not be drinking to me tonight of all nights."

"But of course we should," Marigold said impulsively. "If it had not been for you I should never have met Peter."

"We can say the same thing, can't we?" Robert asked in his low, deep voice of Anne.

"Yes, of course we can," Anne replied. "We owe everything to you, Sally. Thank you!"

Sally jumped to her feet.

"You make me want to cry," she said. "Let us clear the table and put all the plates in the kitchen. We need not wash them tonight. That angel Mrs. Barkus says she will come in and do them tomorrow."

"Thank goodness for that!" Marigold exclaimed.

"Don't you like washing up?" Peter asked her in mock dismay.

"No, I hate it!"

"Oh dear," Peter cried dramatically. "I knew I was marrying the wrong girl after all!"

Marigold made a little grimace at him.

"I know perfectly well that you want me to say that I don't mind washing up for you. I am not going to say it. I shall mind it—very much! The sooner you get rich enough to keep a houseful of servants for me, the better!"

"Well, perhaps we shall be able to afford just a teeny-weeny one," Peter conceded.

"Who will do all the washing-up. Oh well, that will be better than nothing."

Sally smiled as she heard their badinage. She had already been told privately by Peter that things were not going to be nearly so difficult for Marigold as she anticipated.

"In actual fact," Peter had said confidentially, "my grandfather is going to give us a very lovely house. It is about twenty miles from Glasgow—right in the country —and overlooks the Clyde. Marigold will be very happy there. There are lots of my friends living round about who will give her a very good time, but after all she has said about being rich it won't hurt her to think that she is going to be very poor until the moment comes for me to show her our home."

Sally had not minded his small deception. She realised that Peter knew how to manage Marigold.

He would always be master in his own house and Marigold would adore him for it. Because of her quick, impulsive nature and her loveliness, which was certain to ensure spoiling wherever she went, she would always need to be managed cleverly, and apparently.

Peter knew the right formula for doing so. There was no doubt at the moment that had he suggested walking bare-foot through Tibet Marigold would have gone with him adoringly obedient.

Their love was very much in contrast with the quiet gravity of Anne and Robert, yet Sally was just as happy about them.

Anne would never have been content with an ordinary man of average intelligence.

She had always wanted something more—something different. She was going to find it in Robert Dunstan and Sally knew that for him the years of loneliness were over.

He would worship Anne with all the pent-up emotion of a man who has been unable to express himself for a very long time and Anne's sweet, gentle shyness would arouse everything that was finest and most protective in his nature.

Yes, she was very happy about her sisters, but there was still one worry left at the back of her mind which must not be forgotten—David!

They all helped her carry the things into the kitchen, where they were stacked into the sink ready to be washed the next morning.

"I feel lazy," Sally said with a smile, "and I wouldn't dare to spoil this dress."

"No, you are to be careful of it," Marigold said. "Remember you have got to wear it at my wedding!"

It was a lovely dress which Marigold had bought some weeks earlier at Michael Sorrell's when the mannequins had been allowed to purchase what they wanted from the summer sale.

Marigold had picked out a dinner frock of pale blue chiffon with tiny puff sleeves and a full buffoon skirt. Only when she had got it home had she realised that it did not really become her.

It was a little short, too, and she was exclaiming impatiently at having wasted her money when Anne had suggested that Sally should try it on.

"It is just the right length for Sally!"

"So it is," Marigold said. "Put it on, Sally! Let us see you in it."

Sally had obeyed and when she turned round to confront her sisters they had both exclaimed.

The colour which had somehow dulled Marigold's radiance was exactly the right frame for Sally's dark, misty beauty. It made her skin look very white—it brought out the soft shadows in her hair.

"You look lovely, Sally," Marigold exclaimed. "Michael Sorrell himself could not have designed a dress which suited you better."

"But when would I wear it?" Sally asked.

"Oh, there will be an occasion soon enough," Marigold answered prophetically; "besides, it is awfully cheap. Somebody scorched the underskirt when they were ironing it so it could not be sold to a customer. It is no loss to the firm; if you knew how many hundreds of times they have copied it in different colours!"

"Very well, I'll have it then," Sally said, "if only to hang in my cupboard so that I shall dream about the ball I am never asked to."

"It will come in for some special occasion," Marigold

repeated, and sure enough they had now arranged that Sally should wear it at Marigold's wedding.

It would make a perfect bridesmaid's dress and Marigold was already planning how she could beg, borrow or steal another model in the same colour for Anne.

"I know my wedding is going to be very quiet and simple but I want it to be perfect. After all, it will be the last time in my life when I can really take the centre of the stage—Peter is certain to grab all the limelight from me after that."

"You can be quite sure I will," said Peter, who was present when she made the remark. "I am going to be a really big ship-builder before I have finished. You will be awfully proud to think you have managed to catch me!"

Marigold had thrown a cushion at his head to stop his teasing, but Sally had gone upstairs to look at her dress and see if it really was suitable for such an auspicious occasion.

She put it on and once again both her sisters had exclaimed how becoming it was.

"Wear it tonight," Marigold said, "and we will dress up, too. I have brought all my dresses down here, so Anne can borrow one. After all it is our engagement party."

"Anne really ought to go to bed early," Sally had said, but Anne had pooh-poohed the idea.

"I feel well already," she said.

And Sally had to admit that she looked a different person, for happiness had brought the colour back to her cheeks and such was the effect of mind over matter that she really did seem stronger in herself.

They had told the men about the party and Peter had gone down to the harbour to see if he could get some lobsters for supper and Robert had insisted on producing some champagne.

"How gay we are!" Sally said as she got the supper ready, having covered her dress with a white apron.

"I'm sure the new Vicar would be surprised if he knew what excitements were taking place in his house," Marigold laughed.

"I think he would be delighted," Sally said. "He must be an understanding person. Look how kind he has been to let us come here. Somehow it makes it quite perfect to be home again."

She paused a moment to put down on the table the pile of plates she was carrying.

"I keep thinking we shall hear Daddy calling us," she said softly, "and I never pass the study door without expecting it to open and hear his voice say,

'Sally, where have I put my spectacles?' You remember how he was always losing them."

"I wish he were here to marry me," Marigold sighed, "but as he can't be, I am thankful the Vicar is away. We should have had to ask him, but now it makes it so easy to invite Daddy's old friend from St. Ives to perform the ceremony."

"Yes," Sally said, "everything seems to have turned out for the best. It is funny how often things do. For instance, if Miss Harris had not been driven nearly crazy by Elaine's naughtiness I should never have got her position, Anne would never have met Robert and . . . oh goodness, I could go on for ever. Life seems to be like that—a series of unimportant incidents leading up to something momentous."

"Like your going out to post a letter and falling over Peter!" Marigold cried. "Oh Sally, suppose you had been a minute late or a minute early and missed him!"

Marigold's voice was so tragic that Sally had to laugh.

"It is all right. I didn't miss him, so don't worry."

She paused for a moment and glanced towards the kitchen door. They were alone. The men were busy in the dining-room laying the table. No one could over-hear.

In a low voice, Sally said:

"Marigold, what about David?"

"What about him?"

There was a little note of defiance in Marigold's voice.

"I am worried about him.

Marigold shrugged her shoulders.

"Poor David. It was always hopeless. He knew that from the beginning."

"You know he is coming here tomorrow?"

"Yes, I wish he wasn't. How has he managed to get a holiday just now?"

"I rang him up before we left London," Sally explained. "I felt I must tell him about you. You and Peter were so happy and excited that I felt certain someone was bound to tell David about it sooner or later, especially if you came down here. So I telephoned him from the station after Elaine and I had found our seats. Before I was able to say anything, however, he said:

'Oh, I'm glad you have telephoned, I have got some news for you, Sally!'

" 'What is it?' I asked.

'Sir Hubert has been invited by the Roosevelt Institute to go to America and he has asked me to go with him and remain on there as the British representative after he returns. Of course it is a great opportunity.'

"I congratulated him, but he said:

'Not so fast I haven't made up my mind yet. Anyway I want to talk to my father about it, so I've got a week's leave. I'll be seeing you, Sally!'

"He rang off and I didn't get a chance to say anything more."

Marigold shrugged her shoulders.

"Oh well," she said, "if David is going to America he won't be worrying about me."

"I should not be too sure about that," Sally interposed.

"Well, I can't help it if he does," Marigold said petulantly. "Sally darling, you will tell him about Peter and me, won't you? I can't bear reproaches and recriminations."

Sally said nothing. Marigold took her silence for consent.

"Thank you, darling," She smiled and left the room.

Sally was thinking of David now as the others, having stacked the plates in the sink, went laughing and chattering away towards the living-room.

Marigold waited for Peter, and Sally saw Peter reach out and slip his arm round her waist, pulling her towards him with a sudden possessive gesture as if deep in his heart he were afraid of losing her.

"Poor David," Sally whispered to herself.

Then she ran up the stairs to say good night to Elaine. She had expected to find the child wide-eyed and awake, for Elaine had protested at going to bed at all even though Sally had guessed that a long day on the beach and a bathe in the sea had tired her; but Elaine was already asleep, the bedclothes thrown back and her breathing gentle and rhythmic.

Tenderly Sally covered her up and then slipped downstairs again. For a moment she thought of joining the others in the sitting-room, but on an impulse she opened the door which led out into the garden.

There was no breeze and everything seemed very still. The moon was rising in the sky and to Sally there was something magical in the air.

She walked across the garden and then inevitably her feet led her down the little cliff path to the beach. She knew she ought to go back, that it was dangerous to risk the chance of catching cold or dirtying her new dress, and yet, inevitably, she went on.

Now, at last, she was in the bay and the sea lay smooth and shining before her.

The waves were hardly lapping the sand and in the soft, translucent tones of the twilight the whole world seemed indescribably lovely, a place of enchantment. Sally raised her bare arms high above her head.

At last she had come home—home to everything she knew and loved. She was one with the dreaming water, with the shadowed rocks in the sweep of the bay—she moved towards them, walking lightly with feet that felt winged.

She reached the rocks, which towered above her, deep and secret, their outline where they touched the sky luminous with light.

How often had she sat here in every sort and type of weather! In the winter when the waves came thundering in, drenching everything with their far-flung spray, in the summer when the sun was hot and one could look deep through the crystal water on to the floor of the sea.

This was the place she loved. This was where she belonged!

She sat down with a little sigh, spreading the full skirts of her dress around her. The rays of the moon were touching the sea, the sky was deepening to sable, soon the bay would be enveloped in silver light. How lovely it was!

Sally felt her heart going out in all its fullness to what was to her the one perfect place on earth. If only her father could be with her!

Yet even as the wish was formulated in her mind she knew he was there beside her as he had been so often in the past. She could almost feel his presence—almost be sure of him.

"Are you glad about the girls, Daddy?" she asked

him wordlessly within her heart, and she knew that he was glad.

Somehow, inevitably it seemed to her, he asked the question:

"And what about you?"

She had known sooner or later that this was a question she must ask herself and she had tried to escape it because she was afraid of the answer.

"What about you, my dear?"

Again she could hear his quiet, beloved voice say the words. But what reply could she give him?

She shrank from thinking of the loneliness which lay ahead, of facing the future without either Marigold or Anne beside her. What would she do? Where could she go?

Quite suddenly panic swept over her.

"Daddy, help me!" she found herself whispering, felt he was gone and looked up to see that someone was approaching her.

For a moment she did not see who it was. She only knew it was a man and she thought it must be Peter or Robert who had come in search of her.

She raised her hand in welcome and even as she received a reply saw to her astonishment that it was David.

"David!" she exclaimed.

He drew nearer and nearer until he was beside her. She smiled up at him, saw his face in the moonlight and found there a strange expression.

He stood looking at her and she thought quickly: "He knows! Someone has told him about Marigold."

"We were expecting you tomorrow," she said aloud.

"Yes, I know," he said, "but a friend of mine offered to fly me down. We left London only a couple of hours ago and I have been saved a long and hot journey in the train."

"How did you know I was here?"

"I went to the cottage and Mrs. Barkus told me that you were all staying at the Vicarage. I rang the front-door bell, but nobody answered, so I went in through the garden as I always used to do and saw the others through the window. You weren't there and I guessed where I should find you."

"You didn't speak to the others?" Sally questioned.

David shook his head. Sally took a deep breath. So it was up to her after all to break the news to David.

Somehow she wished she had not got to do it at this moment when everything was so beautiful. She felt detached—almost apart from the world with all its troubles and difficulties, its divided affairs, its heart-burning and sadness.

But David was different—how different only she knew. With a little gesture of her hand she indicated the rock beside her.

"Come and sit down, David," she said, "I want to talk to you."

For a moment he did not move.

"You look different, Sally," he said. "I hardly felt you were real when I first saw you. You looked like something out of your father's fairy stories."

"That is what I feel like tonight," Sally replied. "All the same we have got to talk, David."

At last David moved and sat down, not beside her but half facing her on a rock a little lower than hers.

From where he sat her head was silhouetted against the sky and the moon's light revealed the sweet seriousness of her eyes and the curved tenderness of her lips.

"I have got something to tell you," Sally began a little hesitantly.

"Yes?"

"It is about Marigold."

"That she is going to marry Peter Aird? I saw them together just now. You can hardly expect me to be surprised, Sally."

"I am afraid it will upset you, David, but she loves him and he loves her. They are going to be married in a few days' time."

"Good! That is splendid news."

Sally looked startled at the sincerity of his tone.

"But, David . . ." she expostulated.

"Yes, I know what you are going to say," David smiled. "My dear, you are frightfully out of date. All that was over a very long time ago. At least, it seems a long time ago. Perhaps it isn't really."

"Then you don't mind?" Sally cried. "Oh, David, I am so glad! I have been so worried about you."

"Have you? Why?"

"Because I didn't want you to be unhappy. I think I have always known that Marigold wasn't the right person for you, but you loved her and for your sake I hoped things would come right."

"Do you ever stop thinking of other people?" David asked unexpectedly.

"Why should I?" Sally challenged. "Especially when they are the people I love."

David made a sudden gesture and reaching forward took Sally's hand in his.

"Listen, Sally, I feel I ought to explain things to you. Ever since we have been children together you have all three of you been a part of my life. I grew up with you and I took you all very much for granted. You were there. You were what mattered most to me and I could not imagine a life of any sort without you.

"Then as we all grew up I imagined I was in love with Marigold. I know now it was because she was the least interested in me. When she began to find the power of her own charms she thought I was a bore.

"I did not pay her such fulsome compliments or make such a fuss of her as did the other young men in the neighbourhood. My affection for her was something deeper than that.

"But Marigold could not understand my clumsy, tongue-tied efforts to explain myself, so she dismissed me as a bore and went out of her way to snub me.

"Being very, very stupid and rather unversed in the ways of women, as soon as I realised that Marigold really thought nothing of me I imagined I must be in love with her. She attracted me, her indifference intrigued me and I believed it to be love."

Sally made a sudden little movement as if she would release herself from his hold, but David kept her hand in his.

"I want to tell you all this, Sally, as I have got to make you understand so many things. It was while I was still thinking myself in love with Marigold that you and I had a talk about her. It was a strange time for me.

"My life was changing in every direction. I was thrilled and excited by my work and my belief in the future, and in that transitory but expensive period I still believed that the strange feelings I was experiencing were because I was in love.

"Quite suddenly, Sally, I began to learn the truth. I found myself thinking not of Marigold but of you. When I had cases which worried me I found myself asking the question:

"How would Sally deal with this person? How would Sally save this child or jolly this man into wanting to live?"

"In all my difficult decisions—at operations, in emergencies, when there was a crisis of any sort—there you were, Sally, standing beside me. It was then I realised that you had always been there—part of my life—part of all the really fundamental things in which I believe.

"It seems a stupid excuse to say I was too young to realise it. But it is the truth. You were such a big thing—such an overwhelming thing—to happen in any man's life that I was too young to appreciate or understand it."

313

Sally turned her head away and looked out to sea. Now he could see her profile, the tiny tip-tilted nose, the lips just parted.

"You will wonder why I have not told you this before," David went on, "but somehow the opportunity has not presented itself. I knew the truth before Anne was taken ill, but I think I realised it most fully that afternoon when I left you standing in my room at the hospital looking up at my father's picture.

"I knew then, Sally, that you were my life—so much so that I cannot imagine living without you. You have always been there, and because human beings are often blind, deaf and dumb to the real things that matter, I had not thought of what would happen if you ever went away from me.

"I am slow and stupid in lots of ways; but when at last the revelation came to me of everything you meant, I think in that moment I grew up and became a man. . . . A man who wants you, Sally, more than he has ever wanted anything in his life before."

Again Sally made a little movement so that her fingers quivered in his, and now she turned her face from the sea and looked at him.

Her eyes seemed to him to be pools of darkness. He could not see their expression. He looked at her for a long moment, then he went on speaking.

"Before you say anything, Sally, there is something else I want to tell you. I told you on the telephone that Sir Hubert had asked me to go to America. I have thought it over and I have decided to refuse."

"To refuse?"

The words were almost whispered from between Sally's lips.

"Yes, Sally. You see, at last I know exactly what I want to do now and in the future. I don't want fame, I don't want even the absorbing interest of research with Sir Hubert. Instead, I want two things—a practice where I can help the ordinary man or woman who is ill to get well again . . . and you.

"Perhaps I should have put you first because without you I could not have the practice nor the career I want. It all depends on you, Sally, because I want you to create for me a home—a home to which I belong and which is yours and mine together.

"My father is getting old; he has as a matter of fact been looking for a partner for some time. He has not suggested my going in with him because he has always had such big ambitions for me, but although he will be disappointed because I will not go to America, deep in his heart he will be glad.

"This is where I belong, Sally. These are the people I know and love, the people who will in the future be prepared to trust me as they have trusted my father. I can take over here from him and I can build up a reputation.

"It will not be a reputation for being from a wordly point of view particularly successful or clever, nor for getting rich, but it will be one of trust and affection, of being a doctor who not only heals his patients' bodies but also helps their minds because they trust him and have confidence in him.

"That is what I want of the future, Sally, and it is only possible with you there beside me, you to guide and help me as you have done in the past, but also giving me so very much more . . . giving me all the things I need most because . . . because you will belong to me."

David's voice throbbed into silence.

It seemed to them both that there was a sudden deep silence over the whole world. Even the lap of the water was no longer audible.

They were alone—alone in a world so glorious that their eyes were dazzled by the beauty of it.

Very slowly David got to his feet and stood beside

Sally, looking down at her. Then he drew her to her feet.

She was so small that to see her face he reached out his hand and cupping it beneath her little chin tipped back her head so that he could look into her eyes; but still he could not understand the expression in them.

"Sally," he said at length.

Now his voice was urgent—appealing.

"Say something to me!"

"Oh, David!"

He could hardly hear the whisper which came from between her lips and then as he bent his head to listen she spoke firmly and bravely—courageous as Sally had always been—courageous with that unquenchable courage which comes from an inner faith.

"Of course I will do anything that you want. I love you, David, I have always loved you."

He stared down at her, but he did not yet put his arms round her. She looked so ethereal and unreal in the moonlight.

"Always?" he questioned unsteadily.

"Always," she answered. "Ever since I was a little girl you have been the one I loved. Nobody knew it but Daddy. He was so fond of you. How glad he will be that we . . . we have found each other!"

For a moment it seemed as though David could hardly comprehend the fullness of her meaning; then his arms were round her. He drew her gently to him.

She was so small, so fragile, it seemed as if he were afraid to touch her; then the warmth of her lips was on his and he knew she was very real—very lovely—his own Sally.

"My darling, my little love, how blind I have been! But I love you—I love you . . . my sweet, my precious. I will make you happy."

"Oh, David, I love you so!"

She murmured the words against his lips and then

316

suddenly he forgot everything but the overwhelming joy and wonder of his own heart.

He crushed her to him, kissed her again and again, widly, passionately, with a fire which seemed to run through his veins like wine. . . .

He raised his head. She was lying in his arms in utter contentment, her eyes were looking up to his, her lips were parted beneath his kisses.

She was smiling contentedly, happily, her eyes were like stars.

"Oh, Sally, Sally, Sally!" David cried, and there were exaltation and triumph in his voice.